Ditched 4 Murder

"The wedding from hell embroils a bookkeeper with a talent for solving puzzles in several murder cases . . . A hoot."
—*Kirkus Reviews*

"Sophie 'Phee' Kimball has a lot on her plate in this captivating whodunit, but this feisty, take-charge heroine is definitely up for the challenge. Fun characters, a touch of humor, and a great mystery—the perfect combination for a cozy."—Lena Gregory, author of the *Bay Island Psychic Mysteries* and the *All-Day Breakfast Café Mysteries*

Booked 4 Murder

"A thoroughly entertaining series debut, with enjoyable, yet realistic characters and enough plot twists—and dead ends—to appeal from beginning to end."—*Booklist*, starred review

"You'll chuckle all the way through this delightful romp through Sun City West, as Phee and her mother unravel the mystery behind the sudden deaths of several book club members. It's so cleverly written, you won't guess the perpetrators until the very end."—Mary Marks, award-winning author of the *Quilting Mystery Series*

"*Booked 4 Murder* is a witty adventure that will leave you laughing out loud. Join Phee as she tussles with her wily mother, a cursed book, and a host of feisty retirees in this entertaining and charming cozy."—Stephanie Blackmoore, author of the *Wedding Planner Mystery Series*

"*Booked 4 Murder*, set in an Arizona retirement community full of feisty seniors, is a fast-paced mystery with a mother/daughter pair of sleuths who will keep you laughing until the last page. It will also make you think twice before choosing your next book club selection. THE END might come sooner than you think . . ."—Kathleen Bridge, author of the *Hamptons Home and Garden Mystery Series*

Books by J.C. Eaton

The Sophie Kimball Mysteries

BOOKED 4 MURDER

DITCHED 4 MURDER

STAGED 4 MURDER

BOTCHED 4 MURDER

And from Lyrical Press:
The Wine Trail Mysteries

A RIESLING TO DIE

CHARDONNAYED TO REST

PINOT RED OR DEAD?
(coming in March 2019)

Published by Kensington Publishing Corporation

Botched 4 Murder

J.C. Eaton

KENSINGTON BOOKS
KENSINGTON PUBLISHING CORP.
www.kensingtonbooks.com

KENSINGTON BOOKS are published by

Kensington Publishing Corp.
119 West 40th Street
New York, NY 10018

All Kensington titles, imprints, and distributed lines are available at special quantity discounts for bulk purchases for sales promotion, premiums, fund-raising, educational, or institutional use.

Special book excerpts or customized printings can also be created to fit specific needs. For details, write or phone the office of the Kensington Sales Manager: Attn.: Sales Department. Kensington Publishing Corp., 119 West 40th Street, New York, NY 10018. Phone: 1-800-221-2647.

Kensington and the K logo Reg. U.S. Pat. & TM Off.

First Printing: January 2019
ISBN-13: 978-1-4967-1988-1
ISBN-10: 1-4967-1988-3

ISBN-13: 978-1-4967-1989-8 (eBook)
ISBN-10: 1-4967-1989-1 (eBook)

10 9 8 7 6 5 4 3 2 1

Printed in the United States of America

*To the Sun City West Bocce Club
and all bocce aficionados, this one's for you!*

*A special shout-out to the bocce-playing lady
with the floral hat who managed to hit everything
except the daily number.
You were our inspiration for this book!*

ACKNOWLEDGMENTS

We've got an amazing flight crew that never lets us down. Thank you Beth Cornell, Larry Finkelstein, Gale Leach, Ellen Lynes, Susan Morrow, Susan Schwartz, and Suzanne Scher. And to the cozy mystery and romance authors at Blue Ridge Literary Agency, thank you so much for supporting us!

Dawn Dowdle, our agent at Blue Ridge Literary Agency, has been incredible in every sense of the word. We were neophyte authors with big dreams, and she has been paramount in helping us reach them. Our editor, Tara Gavin from Kensington Publishing, has been absolutely phenomenal, and we are so fortunate to work with her.

Behind the scenes are the dedicated and tireless copy and line editors at Kensington who have to put up with our pesky mistakes. Thank you so much for ensuring that our books are the best they can be.

This is indeed a team effort, and we thank our lucky stars we've got a winning one!

Chapter 1

It shouldn't have come as any surprise to me that my mother's Saturday morning brunch ritual with her Booked 4 Murder book club ladies at Bagels 'N More would be anything other than agonizing. The lucrative little restaurant across the road from Sun City West featured an endless array of bagels, muffins, and all sorts of sandwiches reasonably priced. The gossip and rumor mongering were free.

The agony was a result of the constant bickering over the food or the endless gossip that came out of nowhere. That was why I tried to avoid it at all costs. *Tried* being the pivotal word. Sometimes, however, I got nagged and cajoled to the point where I acquiesced and joined my mother and her friends. Usually once a month, or every six weeks if I was lucky.

I'm the bookkeeper/accountant for Williams Investigations in Glendale, having moved out west at the bequest of my boss, former Mankato, Minnesota, police detective, Nate Williams, who relocated to Arizona once he retired.

Nate needed someone he could trust, and, having known me for twenty years, it was a no-brainer. Plus, he had leverage—all those years of listening to me complain about snow and ice. Unfortunately, he relocated spitting distance from another misery, my mother's retirement community. I could kick myself.

That particular Saturday in February was unlucky. It wasn't that the ladies were more annoying than usual, it was the men seated at the table across from them. Mom's neighbor, Herb Garrett, was surrounded by his pinochle buddies: Bill, Kevin, Kenny, and Wayne. I'd gotten to know them this past fall when my mother decided she and her book club would take part in the local theater production of Agatha Christie's *The Mouse Trap*. When the men weren't playing cards, they were working on construction and lighting for Sun City West's theatrical troupe. And when they weren't doing either of those things, they were complaining.

The men had their noses buried in newspapers, and all I could see were a bunch of bald heads, with one exception—Wayne's. He was the only one who still had all of his brownish-gray hair. There was less conversation at the men's table but more grunting. That was, until they noticed my mother. It seemed each one of the men suddenly had a beef they thought she should deal with. It started with Bill Sanders, who got up from his seat just as I was about to bite into my toasted poppy seed bagel with cream cheese.

He glanced at the table and then at the entrance. "Psst! Harriet! I need a word with you before Myrna Mittleson walks in."

My mother said "excuse me" to the group and swung her chair around.

It didn't matter. Bill's voice was loud enough to be heard

in Idaho. That was three states away, no matter which route you took from Arizona.

"You've got to do something about Myrna. She's destroying the bocce league. Not to mention the havoc she's wreaking on our team. For criminy sake, Harriet, can't you talk her into quitting? Maybe convince her to take up knitting or something?"

"Knitting? Are you nuts? Myrna's all thumbs. Besides, she loves bocce."

Bill let out a groan that made Cecilia Flanagan flinch and pull her black cardigan tight across her chest. Louise Munson and Lucinda Espinoza furrowed their brows and gave Bill nasty looks before returning to their food.

"Yeah," he said. "She may love bocce, but she can't toss the blasted ball. Lofts it all over the place. Last week it bounced into the miniature golf course next door and took out one of the blades on the windmill. And the week before, it bounced out of the bocce court and wound up on the garden pathway. That's right next to the pool. Luckily it didn't hit someone in the head, or they might have drowned."

"It can't be all that bad. Besides, these things happen," my mother said.

"Not every day! Not every time people play! Look, I hate to be blunt, but Myrna's a menace. She's a regular Amazon. All of us are scared to death when it's her turn. She tromps up to the start line as if she's about to throw a javelin. And no matter how many times we tell her to gently toss the ball, she heaves it like a shotput. I'm begging you, Harriet, please get her to quit. The Sun City West Bocce and Lawn Bowling Tournaments begin in three and a half weeks, and she'll get us disqualified."

"You know I can't do that. Plus—"

"Forget about Myrna and bocce ball," Herb shouted, throwing his newspaper on our table, nearly knocking over glasses of water and cups of coffee. "We've got real problems in Sun City West. Did you read this article? Did any of you read this article?"

Then he motioned to his own table. "Check out Sorrel Harlan's editorial on page fourteen. The one that says TURN THOSE GOLF COURSES INTO ECO-FRIENDLY PARKS. That woman is insane. I always thought she had a screw loose, but it was her own screw. Now that she got appointed to the recreation center board of directors, she'll be turning it on all of us!"

He had a point. My mother and her friends weren't all that thrilled to learn that Sorrel Harlan had been chosen to finish up Edmund Wooster's term when he resigned a few months before due to family issues.

"They always resign due to family issues," my mother had said earlier. "If you want to know the real reason, it's probably because they can't stand working with each other."

Herb continued ranting, pulling up a chair so that he and his buddies could now face our table. "This is unbelievable. She wants Sun City West to close two major golf courses and convert them to neighborhood parks. That's sheer lunacy. It'll destroy our property values."

"Let me see that article." Shirley Johnson reached for the paper. Today her nails were deep mauve and looked stunning against her dark skin. "It can't be as awful as all that."

She picked up the newspaper, held it in bifocal range, and proceeded to scan the article, pausing every few seconds to shake her head. "Lordy! I wouldn't have believed it if I hadn't read it myself. What's gotten into that woman? Tot lots for the grandkids? Sandboxes instead of sand traps? Just listen to this—'with ample solar lighting our community can enjoy evening festivities in the park as well.' Evening festivities? Lordy! It's an invitation for every teenage hooligan to smoke and drink behind clumps of trees. And I'll bet that's not all they'll be doing while granny thinks they're out for a stroll!"

"Who's smoking and drinking? What did I miss? I got stuck on the phone with my sister-in-law. Sorry I'm late." It was Myrna Mittleson, plopping herself into the empty chair between Lucinda Espinoza and Louise Munson. Suddenly the expression, "a rose among thorns," came to mind, and I had to keep myself from laughing. Myrna was all dolled up with her bedazzled tortoiseshell glasses and her tight beehive hairdo, while Lucinda and Louise looked as if they had spent the last hour fighting off a windstorm. Much worse in Lucinda's case, with her wrinkled clothing. At least those gaudy polyester blouses Louise wore were wrinkle-free.

"What you missed," my mother explained, "is the latest editorial from Sorrel Harlan about converting some of our golf courses into parks."

Shirley passed the newspaper to Myrna and motioned for the waitress. "Lord Almighty, I don't even live on a golf course, but this doesn't sound good to me."

"Hells bells!" Myrna shouted as she read the article. "Get a load of this—'we can have lovely dog walk trails, barbeque and picnic areas, small ponds for children to sail homemade boats, and a plethora of pleasing vistas for everyone to enjoy.'"

"Pleasing vistas, my ass!" Herb bellowed. "Pardon me, ladies, but honestly, what vistas? We'll have every Peeping Tom in the neighborhood looking into our windows. And think about all the litter and garbage. The cigarette butts, the dog poop . . ."

"Take it easy, Herb," Kevin said.

"That's fine for you to say. You don't live on the golf

course. I do. And I paid top price for that privilege. Not to wake up to an eco-friendly circus in my backyard. And I've got news for you. Just because some of you don't own golf course homes, it doesn't mean you won't be affected. Where do you think people are going to park in order to enjoy these parks? On our streets! The streets will be over-crowded with cars. And don't let me get started about the sidewalks. They'll be full of gum that the little kiddies drop on their way to enjoy the playground. And while we're pulling the gum out of our shoes, we'll most likely be side-swiped by the teenagers on rollerblades."

"Yep, come to think of it, he's got a point." Louise patted her frizzy hair and looked at everyone. "I live right across from the golf course, and it's bad enough at night when the lights from cars shine into my house. My poor bird can't get any sleep. If they put in solar lighting, it will be like living across the street from a stadium."

I leaned back, sipped my coffee, and listened to every-one complain at once.

Myrna managed to order her meal in between the grousing and grumbling. "So, what do we want to do about this? Write a response to the editor?"

"You can go ahead with that if you like, but it ain't going to get you anywhere." Kenny rubbed the stubble on his chin. "The recreation center board will be holding its monthly meeting Monday night. That's the day after tomorrow. I say we all show up and give that Sorrel Harlan a piece of our minds. What do you all say? Are you in?"

More moaning. More grumbling. Finally, a consensus. The Booked 4 Murder book club and Herb's buddies agreed they would all attend the meeting on Monday night.

I'd started on my second cup of coffee when, out of nowhere, Cecilia turned to me and said, "What about you, Phee? Will you be attending?"

"Um, me? I don't live in Sun City West. I don't think I should—"

"Of course you should! They may be talking about legal matters, and who better than you should be there?" I couldn't believe those words were coming out of my mother's mouth.

"Legal matters? Who better than *me?* Anyone would be better than me. I'm a bookkeeper. Just because I work for a private investigation firm doesn't make me an expert when it comes to the law."

My mother wouldn't give up. "Well, you're dating someone who is. I'll bet Marshall knows all about the law."

"Marshall's a private investigator, not a lawyer. And while he may have a familiarity of the law as it pertains to his business, I seriously doubt I'd call him an expert on legal matters."

"It doesn't matter. At least he knows something. That's more than I can say for those buffoons who'll be shooting their mouths off at Monday's meeting."

"You're not suggesting I ask Marshall to attend that meeting, are you?"

My mother was silent for a moment and cleared her throat. A bad sign. She was going to use emotional blackmail on me. I was trapped. There was no way I was about to sabotage my relationship with Marshall by dragging him into another Sun City West escapade. It was bad enough he had to deal with the book club ladies a few months ago, when one of the actors turned up dead during the fall production. Talk about a real Agatha Christie murder. That investigation had fiasco written all over it. I didn't need to introduce another one.

"Okay, Mom. Okay. You win. I'll sit in on the meeting. But I'm not going to ask Marshall to join me, understood?

I'm sure he'd rather spend the evening watching the sports channel or something."

"Good. Good," Herb said. "Now that we've got that settled, we need to get every homeowner we know to that meeting, especially the ones who live on or near a golf course. I've still got everyone's email from our neighborhood block party last summer. I'll shoot out an email as soon as I get home."

Louise scraped some of the butter from her bagel. "Wanda and Dolores are catty-corner from the golf course. They'll want to come. Last year someone cut through their yard from the golf course, messing up their new landscaping. Now, with this idiotic eco-friendly park idea, we'll have all sorts of ne'er-do-wells traipsing all over the place."

Shirley offered to call everyone she knew from the sewing club. Cecilia was going to send an email to the ladies social committee from her church, and Lucinda agreed to email her bridge club.

"I'll call the rest of the Booked 4 Murder ladies who couldn't be here today," my mother said. "Riva had to get her hair done, Marianne's still getting over a cold, Constance has out-of-town company, and my sister Ina is on some retreat with her husband. What about you men? You need to get off your duffs and make some noise, too."

"Fine. Fine. I'll call the canine companions club," Bill said. "And the men's card club, too."

Kenny agreed, somewhat reluctantly, to let his neighbors and friends know as well. "Good thing the meeting's taking place in the social hall. We know that room can hold a crowd."

Nightmarish thoughts of the last time I was in the social hall came back to me in a flash. It was the summer my mother and the book club ladies were convinced a book curse was killing off their members. I tried not to shudder as I took another bite of my bagel.

Herb leaned across the table, moving his head from left to right. "So, are we all set with this?"

A cacophony of noises ensued as everyone responded at once. Then, as if it wasn't bad enough I'd agreed to attend the meeting, Herb gave me a wink. "Maybe Phee would like to speak at the meeting. She did a good job last time."

If I hadn't already swallowed the piece of my bagel, I would have choked on it. "No! I'm not speaking. The last time was different. It was that ridiculous book curse thing. This time I'm going as a spectator only. A spectator."

I reached for my coffee and tried to ignore the two words my mother whispered to me, "For now."

Chapter 2

"I don't mind going with you," Marshall said when I told him about the plan Herb had hatched for the book club ladies and the pinochle crew, and all the rest of the club members to attend the rec center board meeting. "I've got a good sense of humor, and this might turn out to be more entertaining than anything on TV."

Unlike yesterday's meal, we were having a quiet Sunday lunch at the Lakeside Grill near Lake Pleasant prior to spending an afternoon hiking the trails that overlooked the lake. It was the perfect time of year in Arizona, and we were taking full advantage of it.

"Um, are you really sure? Those meetings can get downright explosive. I know. I've been to one of them."

"Can't be any worse than my uncles arguing over poker and my aunts screaming at each other in the kitchen because none of them can agree on the sauce." He smiled as he threw an arm around me and pulled me close.

I gave his hand a squeeze. "All right. You're on. But don't say I didn't warn you."

We tried not to talk about Sun City West during our hike, but the subject kept coming up, like an indigestible piece of food that never should've been consumed in the first place.

"I never realized senior communities would have so many issues." Marshall kicked a rock off our path. "Up until now, the only thing I knew about them came from advertisements. All those photos of people swimming, playing tennis, and eating. I knew it was too good to be true. Except for the clear blue skies. At least they got that right."

"If they printed the real photos, no one would move here. People sweltering in the heat, people arguing at bridge games, people honking their horns because the driver in front of them is going three miles an hour. Still, it beats snow, ice, and freezing rain. And oddly enough, my mother loves living here. I never thought she and my father, rest his soul, would budge from Mankato, but they made the right move."

"Yeah, and now that little piece of Nirvana is faced with a major change. No one likes change, even though political campaigns are always built around that theme."

"My mother and the book club ladies are really getting antsy about it, but Herb Garrett and his buddies are going to attack that plan like storm troopers. Brace yourself for tomorrow night. That's all I have to say."

Nate Williams, my boss and the owner of Williams Investigations, couldn't keep a straight face the next day when Marshall and I told him about the meeting we were about to attend. Augusta Hatch, the office secretary, tried to keep from laughing, but only wound up making weird snickering noises.

"Sounds like a humdinger to me," she said. "I'd be mighty put off if I spent an arm and a leg on a house for its golf course view and wound up on the other side of a neighborhood park."

"I guess I'd feel the same way, Augusta, but lots of these golf course communities are losing income because the younger generations aren't all that interested in golf. I know I'm not. Anyway, the loss of income means either repurposing the golf courses or raising fees. It's not a terrific scenario. My mother told me that last year the rec center sent scouts to golf communities back east and up north, hoping to lure home buyers into the Sun City West community."

"How'd that go?" she asked.

"Obviously, not too great, or the rec center board wouldn't be talking about eco-friendly parks. Then again, it could just be the opinion of their latest board member. Someone named Sorrel Harlan."

"Sorrel? Who would name a kid Sorrel?" Nate blurted out.

Marshall and I shrugged simultaneously, but Augusta broke out laughing.

"Maybe it was a character in some book the parents read. I have a niece named Bella after that *Twilight* series. If she turns out to be a vampire, I'll let you know."

"Well, my accounts aren't going to balance themselves, so I'm back to my desk," I said.

Nate nodded and gave Marshall a jab in the elbow. "Hey, buddy, we've got a client meeting in a few minutes so we'd better get going."

The office cleared out in record time, and the day flew by. Marshall and I had agreed that he would stop by my place in Vistancia and drive us to the meeting. Afterward, we'd grab a bite to eat at a pizza place we discovered a few months back. It was a perfect plan.

At least it started out that way. But I knew something was wrong as soon as we arrived in Sun City West. Traffic was backed up along the main road and moving slower than the line at the post office during the holidays.

Marshall tapped his fingers on the steering wheel and sighed. "Do you think there's been an accident?"

"Nope. I don't hear sirens, and no one's getting out of their cars to look around. I think these people are all going to that meeting."

"Seriously? The meeting will be over by the time we get there."

"We won't be so lucky. Trust me. They'll start a bit later to accommodate the crowd."

As we got closer to the parking lot, I saw a considerable number of posse volunteers at the entrances. "I don't think Woodstock had as many attendees."

"At least they had great music and drugs. Of course, this crowd probably has drugs, too, but mostly over-the-counter ones for headache, indigestion, insomnia, and incontinence. Oh my God! Would you look at the parking lot? We'll need to park in the next county. Maybe I should drop you off in front and meet you inside."

I reached over and patted his shoulder. "No, drive around to the dog park. There's usually plenty of parking there, and we can cut through the back between the miniature golf and the pool."

"Got it."

I saw a sheriff's deputy car parked by the main entrance to the social hall as Marshall continued around the complex. "I think they're banking on this being an onerous meeting. My guess is at least two deputies are inside."

"Relax, Phee. It's a rec center meeting, not a demonstration."

"Give it time."

Luckily, we nabbed a parking spot by the dog park gate as the driver of a white van with bumper stickers that read

I ♥ MY DACHSHUND and DOG MOMMY pulled out. In the back of my mind, I knew it was only a matter of time before my mother plastered her car with cutesy little dog-lover bumper stickers as well.

Marshall and I walked as quickly as we could and got to the meeting just as it was starting. A large computer screen in the front of the room read SUN CITY WEST RECREATION CENTER, FEBRUARY MEETING AGENDA. The room had probably reached capacity, but no one was counting. In addition to the regular table seating that I imagine was always set up, additional plastic chairs had been placed behind the last section of tables.

My mother and the book club ladies, this time eight of them, were seated at a table off to the right near the restrooms. I noticed Myrna right away, mainly because of her height. And that beehive hairdo must've added a few inches. She gave us a wave and nudged my mother, who stood and motioned for us to join them. Seated directly behind them were Herb and his crew.

"You didn't miss anything," my mother said. "So far all they've done is talk to each other."

No sooner did she finish talking when a tall gentleman with thinning hair took the microphone and introduced himself and the nine-member board—five women, four men.

"That's Harold Stevens, the president," my mother whispered.

"I know. He just said so. Which one is Sorrel? The president read off the names. I don't know who's who."

"Shh. No one does."

What followed was the most boring, mind-numbing experience I could ever imagine. The secretary's report. The treasurer's report. The committee reports. Each one longer than the one before. I thought the process would be over after the last committee report, but I was mistaken. Apparently, representatives from the companies responsible for golf maintenance and food services had to give their reports as well.

"And I thought sitting through *Out of Africa* was bad." Marshall grabbed my wrist.

Finally, the board began with the "old business" part of the meeting. Since Sorrel's plan for eco-friendly parks was the only old business on the agenda, we figured things would move along. They didn't. Sorrel was asked to give a brief explanation and recapitulation of the proposal. Unfortunately, the word *brief* wasn't in her vocabulary.

Sorrel Harlan got up from her seat at the end of the table and moved to the podium on stage left, directly across from us. She appeared to be in her seventies and had an oval face with wavy gray hair that covered her forehead and ears. Reading glasses hung from a chain around her neck. She was wearing a nondescript gray suit that looked as if it was from another decade. It probably was.

"Welcome, ladies and gentlemen," she said. "We appreciate your interest in our vital and vibrant community."

Those were the only words I remembered before she babbled on and on about the founding of Sun City West and the great promise it held for retirees who sought a better way of life. Marshall's eyes glazed over. Behind me, I could hear Bill Sanders's voice. I hadn't noticed him when we walked in, but I sure recognized that sound.

"When the hell is that biddy going to get to the point?"

I don't know if she heard him as well, but she finally addressed her vision for replacing two golf courses. It was everything that was mentioned in the article and more. Nighttime concerts, star gazing with telescopes, and Fourth of July fireworks. She was prepared for a totally new venue to replace the golf courses. What she wasn't prepared for was the response from the audience.

Everyone started shouting at once, and the board president had to step in and demand that people restrain themselves.

"The board will allow for questions and comments from the audience. All comments should be limited to two minutes or less," Harold said.

"I've got a comment," a huge man in an equally loud Hawaiian shirt shouted. "If Sorrel Harlan plans on turning the golf courses into community parks, it'll be over my dead body! No, make that hers!"

The board president immediately responded. "We will not tolerate threats, personal insults, or rude comments. All comments must be limited to the proposal."

"Well, here's a proposal comment for you," another man shouted. "You can take that golf course proposal and run it up the community flagpole, if you catch my drift."

The next three comments dealt with the loss of property values as the speakers explained they'd had to pay at least forty percent more for purchasing golf course homes, as opposed to similar homes off the golf courses.

"Bunch of whiners," someone yelled, but Marshall and I had no idea who it was.

Apparently, that response hit a nerve with Herb, and he all but had a coronary as he made his way to the front of the room.

"Looks like Herb might have lost some weight," Louise said as Herb headed down the aisle.

"He's just holding his gut in," Shirley said. "He'll have to let it out to breathe."

The static from the microphone ended any extraneous conversations.

Herb pulled his shoulders back as if he planned to march into war. "For those of you who don't know me, I'm Herb Garrett, and I happen to own a golf course home. Not only is it my place of residence, but it's my investment as well. That's right—investment. I poured a great deal of money into that property, and I don't want to see it get washed down the drain. And believe me, that's exactly what will happen if we allow any of our golf courses to become recreational parks. Good grief! We already have four rec centers with all sorts of activities. And frankly, this is a senior citizen's community, not a children's playground. Since when do we need 'tot lots'? Use your own backyard. Not mine. And as far as nighttime activities go, let me repeat myself. This is a senior citizen's community. Most of us are asleep before ten. And all I want to hear outside my window are owls and coyotes, not a bunch of late-night partiers whooping it up. And one more thing. If Ms. Harlan knows what's good for her, she'll find an eco-friendly park in another neighborhood and leave the rest of us the hell alone."

A thunderous applause followed Herb's comments. He strolled back to his seat, standing perfectly tall, with his gut pulled in.

Sorrel Harlan took the microphone and cleared her throat. It sounded like little chirps. "If we do not convert some of our golf courses, I'm afraid they will turn into weed palaces. Overgrown and unsightly."

Myrna, who had been fairly quiet, got out of her seat and headed to the front of the room.

"Psst!" Bill poked my mother in the shoulder. "See how Myrna's thundering down there? Imagine her on a bocce court."

"Shh! Enough with bocce."

Sorrel stepped aside as Myrna took the microphone.

"I agree with Herb Garrett. Besides, we have other choices. We can open up our golf courses to other communities, we can host special golfing events, and we can create a competitive fee schedule."

Sorrel jumped back in. "Weed wastelands. That's what we'll have in a few years. My solution is the best one for the community, and I refuse to back down. I'll do everything in my power to see to it the board votes to approve my proposal."

Expletives and shouts from the audience filled the room. Some people stood up, screaming, "No way!" while others simply booed.

Finally, the board president spoke. "I need your attention. Your attention please! Now then, we thank you for your input. The board will consider the proposal on the table and vote on it next month. In the meantime, we must move on to the next item on our agenda—selecting a paint color for the exterior of Palm Ridge Recreation Center. We have four choices: desert beige, whispering beige, beige mist, and stone beige."

No sooner did he utter the last choice, when everyone seemed to stand up and head out of the room. My mother's friends were no exception.

"No sense hanging around here," Cecilia said. "Why don't we go over to the Homey Hut for some coffee and pie?"

Bill gave her a sideways glance. "You ladies can feel free to do that, but I'm on my way to Curley's for a brew. Just one round because we have bocce practice first thing tomorrow morning. So, who's in?"

It was a no-brainer. The men were off to Curley's, and the women were one step closer to apple crisp and French silk pies.

"Would you and Marshall like to join us?" my mother asked.

"Um, well—"

"Actually," Marshall cut in, "Phee and I made plans to grab a pizza in Surprise. Maybe another time."

It was elbow to elbow as we made our way out of the

meeting. The board president had to wait until most of the contingency left the room before he could continue with the paint color selections. People were still grumbling and moaning, many of them quite vocal.

"She doesn't want us to see a weed wasteland. Well, I'll tell you what I'd like to see—Sorrel Harlan face down in one of those weedy swamps by the edge of the golf courses! Nighttime star gazing? Mini boat ponds? Fourth of July fireworks? She's a lunatic!"

It was a man's voice, and he was louder than the Hawaiian shirt guy who'd bellowed his disapproval as soon as the meeting started. I looked around to see who'd spoken, but it was impossible to tell.

Sorrel Harlan might have intended to have glorious fireworks displays, but as we left the social hall, the only fireworks that night were coming from the people in attendance as they made their way to the exits.

Chapter 3

The parking lot looked like a tailgate party gone wrong. Small clusters of people gathered all over the place, making it impossible for anyone to get into a vehicle and drive out of there. I heard shouting, grumbling, and swearing. It was awful. Frankly, I'd seen movies depicting lynch mobs that were less intimidating.

"If we skirt around the blue Chevy, we've got a beeline to the other side of the building," I said. "I don't think the crowd's made it there."

"Good thing you knew about that parking area. Geez, I've never seen anything like this. Talk about hitting a nerve. Do you think that Sorrel woman knew how badly her proposal would be received?"

"From what little I know, I don't think she cares. Worse yet, according to Herb, Sorrel Harlan will do anything in her power to get it passed."

Just then someone shouted, "Vote no confidence! Vote that witch off the board!"

"Can they do that?" I asked. "Vote someone off the board?"

Marshall gave me a quick look as we hurried to the car. "I'm not sure. I have no idea what the bylaws say. I know people can vote no confidence for a board, but usually those things take petitions and at least two-thirds of the signatures from all parties in the association. I read about that recently regarding a homeowners association in Phoenix. But Sun City West isn't an HOA, it's a municipality."

"I can only imagine the conversations tonight at the Homey Hut and Curley's. Not to mention what Bagels 'N More is going to be like during the breakfast hour tomorrow. Glad I'll be at work and miles away from my mother."

"When did they say the board would be voting on the proposal? It was hard to hear with everyone talking under their breath."

"Next month, I believe. You don't suppose it will really pass, do you? My gosh, I can't fathom what that would do to the real estate market around here. Do you think Sorrel Harlan has some sort of ulterior motive in this?"

"Hard to say. Is she in the real estate business?"

I shook my head. "No. My mother told me Sorrel and her husband owned a boutique publishing company back east, but he gave that up when he accepted a position as a university librarian."

"Boutique? I thought that was reserved for clothing and gift shops."

"It's a fancy word for specialized and small. They published poetry books, photography, art, and political perspectives."

"How'd your mother find out all of this? Wait! Wait! I shouldn't ask. For a second I forgot who I was talking about. I should know by now that Harriet Plunkett has more connections than the chairpersons for the Democratic and Republican Committees combined."

"Got that right, but she heard it from Lucinda Espinoza. Sorrel Harlan and Lucinda were in the same chair-yoga class a few years ago. Seems Sorrel gets very passionate about certain things and goes full steam ahead."

"Going full steam ahead with this crowd might not be the best move. Do you hear them? We've almost rounded the corner, and the noise isn't dying down. Come on, the car's only a few yards away."

Marshall was right. Either someone was getting that crowd pumped up, or it only seemed loud because everything else was so quiet around there.

"Take the first driveway on your left," I said. "That way I can see what's going on."

I looked over Marshall's shoulder and into the front parking lot. Judging from the size of the crowd, very few people had stayed in the social hall to listen to the discussion about paint colors. "From what I can see, it doesn't look as if anything volatile is going on. I guess the voices are just loud. I'll tell you one thing, though. I sure wouldn't want to be in Sorrel's shoes."

"She kind of brought that on herself, don't you think?"

"Uh-huh," I mumbled. "Still, all of this is really unnerving. Especially for Sun City West. I mean, I don't usually think of this place as a political hotbed or anything, but that lady literally poked a hornet's nest."

By the time Marshall and I left Sun City West and arrived at the small family pizzeria in Surprise, I was starving.

"This is really embarrassing," I said. "Seems every time we come here, I eat as if I haven't seen food in decades."

"Don't worry about it. I'm pretty damn hungry, too."

We finished a medium mushroom and sausage pie plus a small order of hot wings before calling it a night. With work the next day, I had to settle for a cozy kiss in the car before heading into my house.

Marshall gave me another quick kiss. "Want me to walk you to your door?"

"That's okay, Sir Galahad. It's five steps from the curb. I think I'll be safe. See you in the morning."

I couldn't believe it was after ten when I walked in the door. It felt great to slip into my comfy sweats and watch the late night news before setting the alarm clock and turning in. I reached for my cell phone on the nightstand and checked my email messages so as not to miss anything earthshattering. Two were from retail stores and were promptly deleted. The third was from my daughter, Kalese, who is a teacher in St. Cloud. She'd attached a photo of her fourth grade class during their talent show. The message read: "Remember the one I was in? It took weeks to get the glitter out of my hair. Miss you, Mom. Hugs and kisses."

Yup, I remembered all right. Some of that glitter is still trapped in the floorboards of our old house. I emailed back: "Love and miss you, too. I'll give you a call this week. Nana Harriet is driving me crazy, as usual."

Nana Harriet and the rest of her cronies. I tried not to think about the conversations that were probably still going on at Curley's and the Homey Hut. I was certain that, by now, news of Sorrel Harlan's proposal was spilling out into the greater Phoenix community.

"Good morning, everyone!" I called as I walked into the office the next day.

"It's only me," was Augusta's reply. "I just got in a minute or two ago myself. Haven't even had a chance to add water to the Keurig."

"I'll take care of it. I'm right here."

No sooner did I finish pouring the water into the machine's reservoir when Marshall and Nate walked in.

"Heard you had a fun night at your mother's rec center meeting." Nate winked. "Marshall and I had a real early breakfast to go over a case we're dealing with in North Phoenix."

"It's always a fun time at one of my mother's events." I pushed the ON button to the coffeemaker.

Augusta cleared her throat and muttered something about her definition of fun being wildly different from mine. As Nate and Marshall headed into Nate's office, I waited for the machine to give me the "heads-up" blue light. At the first flash, I proceeded to make myself a cup of one of the leftover holiday flavors we had purchased back in December. That done, I went into my office, booted up the computer, and started to review some spreadsheets. Augusta was fielding phone calls in the front office, and it seemed as if the phone was ringing every few minutes. At a little past ten, the phone rang into my office, and I heard Augusta shouting, "You'd better take this one, Phee."

I picked up the receiver tentatively, only to hear my mother's voice.

"Drop what you're doing and drive over to the bocce courts. They're right next to the dog park. Bring Nate or Marshall. Better yet, bring them both."

"Whoa. Slow down. What's going on?"

"What's going on? What's going on? Myrna just called. Hysterical. She thinks she killed someone."

"What?" I could hardly control the volume of my voice.

"You heard me. She said she thinks she might have killed someone. A runaway bocce ball or something. It was hard to understand her with all that crying and gasping for breath. Look, I'm in the car now. I should be at the bocce courts in a few minutes. Hurry up."

Before I could say a word, my mother ended the call. I got up, said something to Augusta, and knocked on Nate's door. The second he said "come in," I proceeded to tell him and Marshall about the call.

"Want me to reschedule the ten-thirty?" Marshall asked, looking at Nate.

"Nah, I'll take this one." Then he turned to me. "Come on, you can tell me all about it in the car. I've got a light morning, unlike your buddy over here. I'll let Augusta know what's happening on our way out."

"Call me if you need me," Marshall said as Nate and I left the office.

Nate's car was parked on the street a few yards away. We drove to Sun City West in record time.

"It sounds like an accident to me," I said, "especially since all I've heard is how badly Myrna tosses those bocce balls. According to one of the men on her team, she practically lofts them into the air like weapons. Maybe she managed to hit someone in the head."

Nate made some sort of a *tsk* sound. "I doubt it. Not a runaway bocce ball. Even one Myrna lofted into the air. Yeah, sure, they seem heavy, but they would have to be hurled at such a high speed to do real damage. I mean, it's not like slamming a baseball with a bat and watching that thing fly across a stadium. I'll bet anything the cause of death was completely unrelated to Myrna's lack of skill on the bocce court. Anyway, it sounds as if she'll feel better knowing you're there to support her."

"You, too," I said.

"I'm just along for the ride, kiddo."

When Nate pulled into the large recreation center parking lot, it was impossible not to see the emergency response vehicles and a sheriff's deputy car. I was about to say something about an ambulance when I noticed another vehicle. I all but choked on my words.

"Uh-oh. This isn't good. That's the county coroner's van over there. My God, Myrna did kill someone."

"Hold your horses. Someone would have to put a lot of strength into throwing a bocce ball hard enough to kill someone."

"Myrna's pretty strong," I said. "Everyone says so."

We got out of Nate's car and walked toward the emergency vehicles. A fairly large crowd was gathered by the bocce court benches. I immediately spotted my mother and Myrna seated at the far end of one of the benches. My mother must have called Shirley and Lucinda because they were there as well.

Off to the side, speaking with one of the deputies, was Bill Sanders. He waved us over as soon as he saw us.

"I'll go see what's going on over there," Nate said. "You'd better head over to your mother."

I nodded and made a beeline to the benches.

My mother got up and motioned for me to sit next to Myrna. "Phee! You made it! Thank goodness. Where are the men?"

"Nate's talking with Bill, and Marshall had a meeting with a client." I tapped Myrna on the arm and spoke softly. "Can you tell me what happened?"

After blowing her nose and wiping away some tears, Myrna gave me the full account of the incident.

"The bocce team got here at nine for practice. We're in the tournament, you know. We need to practice."

I nodded. "Uh-huh. Go on."

"When it was my first turn, I tossed the ball, and I must have tossed it really hard because it bounced off the edge of the court and rolled into the golf course over there."

Myrna pointed to the Hillcrest Golf Course that bordered the bocce courts. "Bill said not to worry about it, that he'd get the ball later. We had extra ones, blue and red.

My next toss was better, and I got close to the opponent's ball on the court."

If I could have rolled my eyes, I would have. "Keep going, Myrna. You're doing fine."

"Anyway, I wasn't so lucky with my next toss. That time it hit a bench and flew right over into the golf course. The team wasn't happy about it, and someone said if I kept it up we'd be out of balls."

"Okay, then what?"

Myrna blew her nose again. "My next toss was good and everything seemed to be fine. Then, when it came time for me to go again, I don't know what happened. All I remember is the ball hit the pole by the awning over the side benches and went flying into the golf course. By then, everyone was really mad. Bill decided to go over to the golf course and get the balls that wound up there."

I looked at the golf course and saw there was a chain link fence around it. "Um, er, how'd he get in? Don't tell me he climbed the fence?"

"Oh, no. The fence has an opening a few yards away. People go under it all the time when their dogs get off the leashes and they have to retrieve them."

Suddenly my mother blurted out, "That happened to Betsy and her little dog, Howard-Elizabeth. Betsy had to practically crawl under the fence to get him."

"Mom! Please!" I shouted. "Let Myrna continue." I gave Myrna a quick squeeze on the arm and a quick nod.

She took a slow breath. "Anyway, Bill went to the golf course, and, the next thing I knew, he was shouting, 'We got a dead body over here! Face down in the brush. Right next to the blue bocce ball.' And that's when I knew it. I killed someone. Hit them with a bocce ball and killed them. Oh my God!"

I glanced at the emergency vehicles. Nate was talking with one of the sheriff's deputies.

"It looks like they're loading the deceased into the coroner's van," I said.

Lucinda lifted her head up and gave a nod. Her once-blond, now mostly gray hair blew around her face. "I'm surprised they haven't sent someone from the sheriff's department over here to talk to you, Myrna."

"You mean *arrest* me," Myrna replied.

Lucinda answered as if they were talking about the latest movie or book they'd read. "Well, that too."

My mother put her arm around Myrna and tried to console her. "I don't think it would be murder. I mean, it wasn't as if you planned on killing anyone. Isn't that right, Phee?"

"Um, er . . . why don't we wait until someone comes over here?"

"Manslaughter! That's what they'll charge her with. Manslaughter! It's always manslaughter on those TV shows, but I'm not sure if it would be voluntary or involuntary. I get that part confused," Lucinda said.

Shirley handed Myrna a handful of tissues and reached into her pocketbook, pulling out a business card. "Lordy, Myrna. This is tragic. Take this card. It's my lawyer, Colton Rainburn. I don't know if he handles criminal cases. I just used him to draw up my trust."

At the sound of the words "lawyer" and "criminal," Myrna started to hyperventilate and Lucinda darted to another bench and rushed back.

"Here! Breathe into this paper bag from McDonald's. Someone left it on one of the benches. It doesn't look too greasy."

"Throw that disgusting thing out," my mother said. "You don't know where it's been."

Myrna took one look at the bag and miraculously started

breathing normally again. "How many years behind bars do people get for manslaughter?"

"Five to ten is what they give them on those TV dramas," Lucinda said.

"My God. Five to ten years. Bill's always said I was going to wind up killing someone the way I toss those bocce balls. He was right. And he wasn't the only one. Other people on my team have said the same thing."

"They were just exaggerating, that's all," I said.

Lucinda was unable to let it go at that. "My mother's Aunt Philomena was once cleaning the bathroom floor by her toilet and leaned over to squeeze water from her cleaning cloth when all of a sudden the toilet seat came down on her head. Got a concussion and died later that night. Those heavy bocce balls must weigh as much as a toilet seat, I'd venture."

Myrna started sobbing again, and my mother gave Lucinda one of those "cut it out" nudges. Behind us, Nate was still talking with the sheriff's deputy. The coroner's van headed out of the parking lot, followed by the emergency crews.

"Nate should be here any second," I said as Myrna's sobs got louder. I didn't think I could stand another minute waiting with the "doom and gloom" crew. "I'm going to walk over there and see what's going on. And, for goodness' sake, stop jumping to conclusions."

Chapter 4

I all but collided with Bill as he headed to the bench where Myrna and the book club ladies were seated. Nate was still talking with the sheriff's deputy. Only the bocce team remained in that vicinity, standing within earshot of my boss. I figured Bill had heard all he wanted to hear from the team and was on his way to share the latest tidbit with my mother's friends.

"Guess one stiff in the theater wasn't enough last fall," Bill said. "Now we got one face down in the muck by the golf course. And that's not all."

"What do you mean?" I asked. "Myrna's beside herself thinking her ball might have been the cause of death. Is that what you're about to tell me?"

"Nah. Gets better than that. I saw that blue bocce ball of Myrna's next to the body, but that wasn't all I saw. There was an arrow sticking up right in the middle of the person's neck. An arrow, for cryin' out loud. What the heck? This isn't the Wild West anymore."

It took a second for his words to register. "An arrow? Like bow and arrow?"

"Yeah, what other kind is there? Look, all I know is what I saw, and I didn't stick around to get a closer look.

The body was face down, but I'm pretty sure it was a woman. Either that or a guy with lousy taste in clothes."

"Oh, how horrible. How on earth can something like that happen, and, more importantly, Myrna needs to know about it at once. Take a look over there. She's one step away from a breakdown."

No sooner did I finish saying that when Nate approached us. If Myrna was off the hook, she'd need to hear it right away. Before hiring a lawyer, sight unseen.

"Nate," I said, "Myrna's convinced it was her bocce ball that killed someone."

"Hardly. More than likely it rolled onto the golf course after bouncing around. Besides, there was other, more compelling evidence."

"I'll say," Bill said. "Looks like Geronimo's back in town."

"Is that true, Nate? An arrow in the neck?"

My boss glared at Bill and pointed to the sheriff's deputy who had made his way to the bench where the ladies were seated. "I imagine the deputy's going to clarify what he can so that the rumor mill doesn't explode. Of course, you know as well as I do, the call is up to the medical examiner. Still, I don't think Myrna has anything to worry about. Well, not the bocce ball anyway."

"What's that supposed to mean? Should Myrna be worried about something else?" I didn't take my gaze off of Nate.

He groaned and took a breath. "Myrna and half the social hall from that rec center meeting the other night. That includes you, too, Bill."

"Me? What the heck are you talking about?"

Nate lowered his voice, forcing us to move in closer. "Look, from what I've heard from my partner, who attended that meeting, lots of irate folks spoke out against converting the golf courses to eco-friendly parks. And I imagine you might have been one of them. Anyway, some of those comments got real up close and personal, to the point of becoming threats against the board member whose idea it was."

"So what?" Bill asked. "Big deal. What's that got to do with someone who bit the dust with an arrow through the neck?"

Nate's voice was barely a whisper. "Because that someone, according to the ID the sheriff found, was Sorrel Harlan."

I let out a gasp and looked at the spot where the body had been. Sorrel's body, to be exact. "My God, this is a nightmare. I've got to let my mother and her friends know."

I was already running toward the women with Bill at my heels when Nate shouted, "Wait! Both of you!"

He caught up to us quickly. "Listen, I probably shouldn't have offered up that information, but one of the sheriff's deputies shouted her name as soon as they found the ID. I'm sure a few bystanders heard it loud and clear. Still, we shouldn't breathe a word until the next of kin is notified. Okay?"

"Yeah, I'll keep my trap shut, but it'll probably be all over tonight's news anyway," Bill said as the three of us walked over to the benches.

The sheriff's deputy was writing notes on a pad, and I figured he was taking down contact information. "Guess that about sums it up, ladies," he said as we approached. "If we need more information, we'll contact you."

Myrna had stopped crying, but she still looked pretty shaken up. "I'm not getting arrested. Not yet."

I pulled Nate aside and whispered, "Shouldn't we at least tell her about the arrow? She'll be a nervous wreck all night."

As it turned out, we didn't have to, thanks to Bill. "Damn. Looks like the archery club isn't going to be holding any contests any time soon."

He went on to explain that he had seen an arrow in the victim's neck, and, in his opinion, that was what killed the person. At least he didn't mention who it was. Not to the book club ladies anyway. He looked at his watch and shrugged. "Our court time is up. If you can pull yourself together, Myrna, we'll be practicing again tomorrow at nine. But I understand if it's too much for you . . . under the circumstances. We can always find a replacement."

I swore his voice sounded almost too optimistic when he mentioned finding a replacement.

Fortunately, Myrna was oblivious. "I won't let anyone down. I'll be here tomorrow."

Bill muttered something about a midmorning card game and took off.

"So, was that true about the arrow in the neck?" my mother asked Nate. "The only thing that deputy told us was the death was under investigation. A moron could have figured out that much. So? Tell me. Was it an arrow or not?"

I knew Nate didn't want to reveal details of an impending investigation to a group of ladies whose greatest pastime was rumor mongering, but he didn't have much choice. Not after Bill opened the proverbial can of worms.

"Yeah. Bill was telling the truth. The body was found face down with an arrow to the neck. That's all I know, and I shouldn't even be sharing that much. Understand? The only reason I'm doing so is because I don't want Myrna to well, um, you know, go off the deep end, so to speak."

My mother looked at Myrna, who was dabbing her eyes with a rolled-up tissue, and then turned to Nate. "There's more, isn't there? Something you're not telling us. Does the sheriff think a maniac is loose? Do I need to install an alarm system for my house? Streetman can't be expected to do everything. He's only a Chiweenie. What do you think?"

I don't know how my boss managed to remain calm during that kind of confrontation, but he did. He put his hand on my mother's shoulder and talked to her as if he was negotiating with a terrorist to release a hostage.

"It's okay, Harriet. You don't have anything to worry about in that regard. No maniacs. No need to install expensive security unless, of course, that makes you feel safer. Right now, it's an isolated incident, and, once the sheriff's department completes its investigation, I'm sure the community will learn more. Meantime, the best thing you and your friends can do is go back home, or, better yet, go get a cup of coffee someplace and calm down. Phee and I have to head back to the office, but if you need us, call."

At the mere mention of the word "coffee," my mother suddenly switched gears and orchestrated an impromptu brunch at Bagels 'N More. Even Myrna seemed to cheer up.

"I'll call Cecilia and Louise," Lucinda said. "They can give the snowbirds a holler, too. We can all meet there."

I took my mother aside and reiterated that under no circumstances should she mention anything about a dead body with an arrow. "You know how these things get out of hand. Besides, the main thing is Myrna doesn't have to worry."

"So much you know. What if it was Myrna's bocce ball that hit them, and then once the person keeled over, someone got them with an arrow?"

"On the ground? Face down on the ground? Who shoots an arrow at a body that's lying face down on the ground? Stop with the craziness and enjoy your coffee. I'll call you tonight," I said.

"Call me the minute you hear anything. I know those sheriff's deputies talk to Nate. Once he knows something, tell me. You hear?"

"Of course."

I waited until Nate and I were within a few feet of the car before I spoke. Last thing I needed was for my mother to overhear us. "Holy cow! What are they going to do when they find out it was Sorrel Harlan with the arrow in her neck? It'll be a disaster."

"Got that right. I wished I could have told them, but the next of kin have to be notified first. I'm afraid that'll happen sooner than later, and it will be all over the news tonight. You wouldn't happen to know anything about Sorrel, would you?"

"Only Herb's rantings and what I heard firsthand with Marshall at the meeting. But it wouldn't be too hard to pull up info on her. When she was appointed to the rec board to replace Edmund Wooster, they did a write-up about her in the local Sun City West paper. I'll have Augusta dig it up."

"I don't know if I hired a bookkeeper, or another detective."

"Don't even mention the *D* word. I'll give Augusta a call as soon as I get in the car."

"Good. Have her order us some sandwiches from the deli. I don't know about you, but I'm hungry."

I couldn't believe I had been handling the accounts for Williams Investigations for over a year. In spite of being spitting distance from my mother's house, I really relished working for Nate. The real boon came when he convinced another Mankato detective, Marshall Gregory, to partner up with him. For years I'd had a secret crush on Marshall, not realizing he felt the same way about me. We began to date shortly after one of the actors was found dead on a catwalk following a theater rehearsal for a play my mother and her book club ladies were participating in. Who knew a murder investigation could bring us together? I beamed just thinking about Marshall.

By the time Nate and I arrived back at the office, not only did Augusta have two printed copies of the article ready for us, but she had also researched some miscellaneous information that was mentioned in the article. It seemed Sorrel had worked for human services in Middletown, Connecticut, where her husband, Milquist, was a university librarian at Wesleyan. No children and no mention of relatives. Augusta also learned Sorrel was active with all sorts of ecology and environmental causes, while Milquist kept a low profile.

"Her husband sounds as dry as toast." Augusta handed us each the paper. "And she doesn't sound a whole lot better. The only thing I could dredge up about them was their membership in the Sun City West Cribbage Club."

Nate glanced at Augusta's information sheet and shrugged. "Her former membership. Her body was the one that was found near the bocce courts. Honestly, I always pictured retirement communities as insulated safe havens for card playing and golf, but Sun City West is beginning to sound more like Cabot Cove with a murder a week."

"And the worst thing is, my mother's book club seems to be embroiled in all of them," I said. "Maybe this time the sheriff's department will be able to solve it before those ladies have a collective meltdown."

Nate's gaze moved from me to Augusta. "I may be going out on a limb, but I don't think so. I have this nagging feeling our office is going to be asked to consult on the case. Hopefully by the sheriff's department and not Phee's mother. Maricopa County is a huge jurisdiction, and those deputies are spread pretty thin. And as for the posse, well, they're volunteers who handle routine matters, not murder investigations. So, I guess I'll really need to familiarize myself with Sorrel and Milquist Harlan."

Augusta grinned. "Who names a kid Milquist? What kind of name is that?"

I couldn't help but giggle. "One that goes with Sorrel, I guess."

Just then, the delivery boy from the deli around the corner walked in with sandwiches, and Nate paid him. "Don't get out your purses. It's my treat. I'll put one of the ham and cheese in our office fridge in case Marshall didn't get a chance to eat."

The three of us thanked him as we sat around the small table in the workroom. Fortunately, we were done before the phone started ringing. I was back at my desk trying to pick up where I'd left off with the billing, but all I could think about was an arrow to the neck. It seemed a bizarre way to commit murder, and, yet, too out of place for some sort of accident. Especially one on the edge of a golf course and not an archery range.

Marshall was out of the office most of the day, and by the time he ate the sandwich, it was close to five. "I'll call you later tonight." He waved as I headed to the door. "I'm dying to know the details about this morning." Then a sheepish look came over him and he quickly added, "And I just want to hear your voice."

When my phone rang around seven, I hoped it would be Marshall. It wasn't. It was my mother.

"The local news just ended and they still haven't announced whose dead body it was. Come on, Phee. You must know something."

"Look, if they haven't released the information, it's for a good reason. Maybe it will be on the ten o'clock news."

"That means I have to watch the same thing all over again. It's like a never-ending loop of information."

"Then you can wait until tomorrow."

"And miss something? Don't be ridiculous. By the way, I called Myrna and she's doing considerably better. She said she plans to be at bocce practice in the morning."

"That's good, I suppose. Although, I'm not so sure the other people on her team feel the same way. Is that tournament such a big deal?"

"Oh yeah. In fact, we had to change our February book club meeting to the week before since so many people plan on attending that three-day event. Thank goodness we're reading a nice cozy mystery by Mary Marks instead of one of those godforsaken tomes your aunt Ina insists we tackle. And speaking of which, she and Louis are taking a Valentine staycation at some fancy hotel in Fountain Hills."

"That's nice. At least she married someone who pampers her," I said.

"He probably has no choice."

"Um, anyway, I've got a few things to do around here, so I'll talk to you later this week, okay?"

"Call me the minute you hear anything. I mean it."

I muttered something and ended the call before she had a chance to nag. When the phone rang again, I was certain it was Marshall, but instead, it was my friend Lyndy, whose aunt happened to live in Sun City West.

"You must have heard the news," she said. "Someone was found face down on one of the golf courses, shot with an arrow."

When I told her about my involvement with the situation, she didn't seem all that surprised. She probably figured it came with the territory since I worked for a private investigator. What surprised me, though, was how much she knew about the murder.

"My aunt has been going on and on about this all day. She was going to the miniature golf course with some friend of hers when they noticed all the emergency vehicles by the bocce courts and golf course. Naturally, she had to worm her way over there to see what was going on. They were a good distance away but apparently close enough to hear one of the sheriff's deputies shouting 'We got an ID. It's a Sorrel Harlan.' Why does that name sound familiar?"

"Because she was the newest appointee to the rec center board and wanted to convert some golf courses into eco-friendly parks," I said.

"Yeesh. That's probably what got her killed. And now that you mention it, I think I remember reading something about that idea in one of the papers."

"I wish the sheriff's department would make an official announcement already. My mother's been plaguing me to tell her who the victim was."

"Think your office is going to be drawn into the case?"

"Drawn, roped, coerced. Yeah, whatever you call it, I have a feeling I'm going to learn a lot more about bows and arrows than I ever thought possible."

Chapter 5

Thankfully the last call of the evening was Marshall's, and I drifted off to a great night's sleep shortly after. It was the ringing of the phone at six in the morning that ended my restful night.

"Phee!" My mother's voice all but scratched my eardrums. "It's on the news right now. Sorrel Harlan. That's whose body it was. Sorrel Harlan from the rec center board. Good grief. Those sheriff's deputies will have to question the entire community. Everyone had a motive. Do you think they'll be knocking on our doors because we attended the meeting? Attendees had to sign their names on the sign-in sheet. That's practically a confession."

"Whoa. Slow down. No one confessed to anything. And yes, I'm sure lots of people were furious with her for suggesting converting those golf courses, but—"

"But what? Face it, it's plenty motive for murder. Oh my gosh. Myrna spoke up against that golf course plan. Loudly."

"Relax," I said. "So did Herb. And the Hawaiian shirt guy. And a few other people. Besides, Myrna was tossing bocce balls, not shooting a bow and arrow."

I thought I could detect a strange whining sound from my mother's end of the line.

"Can't talk now. Streetman needs to go out. Or maybe he wants a treat. We'll talk later."

My mother had adopted Streetman, a small, long-haired Chiweenie, when his previous owner went into assisted living. The dog, although adorable, came with a laundry list of behavioral issues my mother referred to as "idiosyncrasies."

"Um, well . . ."

"I can't keep Streetman waiting. Bye, honey."

If ever I felt like kissing that little dog, it was at that very moment. Wide awake, I took a quick shower, made myself a cup of coffee, and toasted a frozen bagel. Now that the entire Sun City West community knew who the victim was, it was only a matter of time for full-blown panic to set in. I imagined most people would have the same reaction my mother did—petrified of being accused due to their verbal protests over Sorrel's proposal.

I decided to get into the office a bit earlier than usual in case the worst possible scenario turned out to be true and Nate was asked to consult on the investigation. He'd be picking my brain as well since I had a definite *in* with certain members of the community.

I arrived at Williams Investigations a good hour or so before we opened and immediately set up the Keurig for coffee. Arriving early gave me plenty of time to work on the accounting spreadsheets without interruption.

Marshall arrived at twenty to nine and he, too, was pretty convinced we'd be on the case. "There had to be at least three hundred people at that meeting. And most of them were adamant about not converting the golf courses. I know the sheriff's department is going to take that attendance list and start contacting people, after they speak with

Sorrel's husband and any close family or friends they can contact. The sheer numbers are overwhelming. Bowman and Ranston, the two deputies from that theater murder case, must be going nuts with all those folks."

"What about the golfers on the course at the time? Do you know if they were contacted?"

Marshall pressed the lid down on the coffeemaker. "According to Nate, they sent the golf marshals out to see if the players on the course had noticed anything unusual. If one of those golf bags had an archery bow in it, the marshals would have seen it. They also checked the names on the tee-time lists."

"Couldn't someone from one of the houses have stepped out onto their patio and shot an arrow from there?"

"Highly doubtful, unless they were using a crossbow, and, from what I know, that wasn't the case. In the conversation Nate had with the sheriff's deputy on the scene, the arrow appeared to be a standard archery arrow. If the sheriff's department does call us to confer, they'll provide more info."

No sooner did he finish speaking when Augusta walked in. "Good morning! Guess what I did last night?"

If it was anyone else asking an open-ended question like that, I would have kept my mouth shut. But by now, I knew Augusta well enough to figure she was going to tell us she'd cooked some sort of pioneer dinner or made a shawl out of animal pelts.

"What?" Marshall beat me to it.

"I did a little more digging on the Harlan family. Did you know Milquist is a published author? He wrote two books on indigenous cultures of the Southwest. The second book was coauthored by a Marlene Krone. I was able to pull up the back cover of their book on Amazon and saw their photos. He's at least twice her age."

I tried not to laugh. "You're beginning to sound like my mother. He wrote a book with her. It's not like he's dating her."

"You don't know that," she said. "If I were those deputies, I'd be tracking down Milquist's whereabouts on the day of the murder. And that young coauthor of his. For your information, Milquist Harlan is the grandson of Lionel Harlan. *The* Lionel Harlan from the timber industry. Milquist's late father ran that company until it was sold for beaucoup bucks in the late 1980s. Maybe our Marlene Krone is a little old gold digger who wanted Sorrel out of the way."

"Find out if she knows how to shoot a bow and arrow and get back to me," Marshall said as Nate came in the door.

"Who knows how to shoot a bow and arrow?" my boss asked.

Augusta immediately spouted off her research findings, only this time the response was more than lukewarm. Nate didn't exactly dismiss her theory. Of course, he wasn't wild about it either, but, still, it gave Augusta all the encouragement she needed.

"I'll see what else I can find, Mr. Williams. In case you get a call from the county sheriff's department."

"Hold your hats, ladies. You, too, Marshall. I already got the call. I forgot I had given my cell number to the sheriff's deputy on the scene yesterday. It's official. They're going to contract with us to consult on the investigation. They knew we were familiar with the Sun City West community, and since they're spread so thin, they figure we can expedite this investigation."

"Oh dear God, no. If my mother gets wind of this, she'll be impossible. First, it will be lists of people to see. Then questions to ask. Then crazy theories that always seem to involve a love triangle. She and that book club are practically glued to Telemundo in the afternoons."

"Relax, kiddo," Nate said. "We'll take it one step at a time like we always do. And, by the way, the sheriff's department has already ruled out the husband as a suspect. Turns out he was attending a writers' conference in San Francisco, and his plane didn't arrive back to Phoenix until midmorning yesterday. What a crummy welcome back, huh? And before anyone says anything else, I'll find out if his coauthor was at the conference as well."

Augusta gave me a quick smile and walked to her desk.

"Guess that's my cue to get back to work," I said. "Good luck, guys."

I thought I was home free for the rest of the day and could devote my time to the accounts. I was wrong. At precisely eleven fifty-three, my mother called.

"Gloria Wong's niece works for the Maricopa County Sheriff's Department. You remember Gloria, don't you? She was at the Stardust Theater the night we saw *Showboat*. Anyway, I ran into her this morning at the gas station. She told me your boss was hired to consult on the case. Her niece had to fax over a contract first thing in the morning. Why didn't you tell me?"

"I only found out about it myself. And I can't stop work and call you over every little thing."

"This isn't a little thing. We could either be dealing with a psychopathic maniac out to hunt people down like wild game, a cold, calculated killer, a desperate, revenge-seeking murderer, or a jealous lover."

"My vote is the jealous lover. Let's go there."

"I'm serious, Phee. And if it wasn't one of the above-mentioned individuals, then it has to be someone who wanted Sorrel out of the picture because of her eco-friendly park idea. You heard them at the meeting Monday night. While your boss and his partner follow protocol and all that stuff, you can get ahead of the game and find out who really had it in for Sorrel."

Terrific. Just what I want—lists, names, questions, and nagging.

"For the zillionth time, I'm not the detective around here," I said.

"I'm not asking you to be the detective. I'm asking you to simply stop by the dog park and have a nice chat with Cindy Dolton. She's got more info on the goings-on in Sun City West than a national database. And you won't have to get up too early. It's winter now. She doesn't get there until seven in the morning. That gives you plenty of time to find out what she knows before you have to be at work. You can take that information and unobtrusively slip it into the actual investigation your boss will be conducting. That's simple. I would go myself but Streetman hates to get up early, and, besides, you're the one working for a private investigator."

Unbelievable. That neurotic dog of hers doesn't like to get up early. What about me? And it's not that simple. I have to find a pair of old shoes because I'm bound to step in something gross, and I have to be on my guard that no dogs pee on me.

"Look. I'm not making any promises, but I'll see what I can do."

"Do it tomorrow morning. Don't wait."

Chapter 6

With the exception of the winter grass that appeared thicker and more vibrant, the dog park, adjacent to the tennis courts and across from the main recreation center, looked exactly the same as it did the last time I was there months ago.

At least nine or ten people were huddled on or near the benches under the large yellow awning. A few people were following their dogs around the park as the canines peed on the tall palms and smaller trees. Arctic explorers, dressed for the most strenuous expeditions, didn't have the layering of clothing the people in the park were wearing. I felt out of place with only slacks and a blazer.

Cindy Dolton was standing in her usual spot near the fence. Bundles, her small white dog, was sniffing the ground a few feet away.

Cindy waved as soon as I approached. "Another murder investigation? I'll bet I know who. It's been all over the news. Sorrel Harlan, right?"

I nodded. "Yeah. Were you at the meeting on Monday night? It was impossible to tell. Such a huge turnout."

"I was there all right. I live on a corner with a peekaboo

view of the golf course. Still, I don't want anyone peeking around my house. It's a horrible idea."

"Listen, I was wondering if you might know who the guy in the Hawaiian shirt was. He commented at the start of the meeting," I said.

"Only a nickname—Spuds. But I happen to know his dog's name. It's Dooley. A poodle-Maltese mix. Small, white. The guy usually arrives when I'm about ready to leave. But hey, wait a minute. The canine club directory lists the owner by the dog's name as well as the owner's. I can call your office later today and get you that name, if you'd like."

"That would be wonderful. I'd really appreciate it."

"You know, he wasn't the only one who was ranting. Do you think someone from the community killed her because of that idiotic proposal of hers?"

"Maybe. I don't know."

"I've got news for you. Sorrel wasn't exactly the best-loved person on the community gardens committee either. She wanted the garden club to give small plots of land to the homeless so they could grow their own food. Talk about idealistic. And who, pray tell, was going to bus the homeless to Sun City West and provide them with gardening tools? They all but threw her out of the club. My neighbor's a member and, boy, did she have stories to tell."

"Would you mind giving me your neighbor's name? We may need to speak with her."

"Sure. Claudia Brinson. Lovely lady. Has an amazing green thumb."

I was about to thank Cindy when I heard someone shouting.

"Whose brown terrier is that? Who owns the brown terrier? He's leaving a load by the back fence!"

Another voice shouted even louder. "I'm on it. For cripes sake, the pile hasn't even hit the ground yet!"

Cindy rolled her eyes and laughed. "It's the same every morning. Too bad your mom comes so late in the day. She misses all the fun. Oh, tell her to watch out for the benches. The geese have been pooping all over them. It's that time of year, I guess."

"Ugh. I'll let her know. Anyway, thanks for the info. I appreciate you taking the time to look up Dooley's owner."

"No problem. Have a great day! I'll call your office later."

Even though I had slipped into my worst pair of shoes, I looked down and gingerly took one step at a time. No need to bring any prizes to the office. What I was bringing was prize enough—a whole new set of people who had it in for Sorrel.

Augusta was already at her desk when I walked in. "Coffee machine's warmed up. How's it going?"

"If you mean how do I like sleuthing at the dog park first thing in the morning, then it's going great."

Suddenly I remembered I hadn't changed shoes. "Drat. I left my good shoes in the car. I'll be right back."

I hadn't made it to the door when Nate and Marshall walked in. So much for changing shoes. I figured it could wait until I shared Cindy's choice piece of information with them. "Hi! Don't go rushing into your offices yet. I found out the golf course homeowners aren't the only ones who had an issue with Sorrel. She wanted to bus homeless people into the development to use the community gardens and grow their own food. According to my mom's contact from the dog park, the garden club was ready to toss Sorrel out."

"Got that, Marshall? Put it on the list," Nate said.

Marshall gave me a quick wink, looked at Augusta, and

went straight to the coffeemaker. "Nate and I have news of our own, too. The sheriff's posse did a complete search of the area and found another arrow. It was a few feet away from where Sorrel's body was found. If it wasn't for the fact that someone from the posse noticed a feather that seemed out of place, they never would have found that arrow. It was partially covered by brush and leaves. The fletching, or feather, gave it away. You know what that information means, don't you?"

"Um, no." I motioned for him to hurry up.

"It means whoever managed to hit Sorrel with that arrow took more than one try. At least we're not dealing with some modern-day Robin Hood. Still, whoever it was had pretty good aim."

"That's not all," Nate said. "The arrow that was removed from the body was an outdoor, carbon, thirty-inch, fiberglass one with a draw weight of forty to sixty pounds."

Augusta practically leapt from her seat. "Hells bells! Anyone could shoot one of those things. Even Phee, who probably never held a bow and arrow in her life."

"Gee, thanks." I forgot for a moment that Augusta came from a family of outdoorsmen, and anyone who couldn't shoot a gun, spear a fish, or set a trap was probably a sissy in her book.

Nate continued, "Too bad they couldn't pull any prints. I seriously doubt the killer ran all those yards to wipe them off. Most likely they were wearing the kind of archery gloves that cover all the fingers and not those tactical ones. Anyway, the sheriff's department will be busy concentrating on the golfers who were on the course at the time, as well as the rec center board members who were opposed to Sorrel's proposal. Deputy Bowman, *that's right,* the same Deputy Bowman from the last murder, asked us to look into the archery club. Find out if anyone there might have had a motive to kill Sorrel. Other than the motive we already know about."

The second I heard the words "archery club," I immediately remembered the last time we had to track down a killer. Archery was one of his pastimes, too.

"The archery club? Oh my gosh. You-know-who was in the archery club. And we all know how that turned out. The guy's probably still in the Fourth Avenue Jail. So, who's the lucky person who gets to interview those card-carrying archery club members?"

"That would be me," Nate said. "Seems our office will be doing a tad more than consulting. The sheriff's department is faxing us a list of the folks in attendance at Monday's meeting, and Marshall will be running it against the archery club list and a list of golf course homes. Apparently, all the local realtors have those. I'll be starting with the club and your buddy over there will be contacting homeowners."

I cleared my throat, but I wound up sounding like a frog in distress. "And don't forget the community gardens. Someone might have been really freaked out about homeless people planting vegetable gardens a few feet away from the residents' homes."

"I'm sure, by the time we're done, we'll have talked to enough residents to qualify us as telemarketers," Marshall said. "So, uh, you got this info from your mother's friend? Please don't tell me you had to start the day at the dog park."

I pointed to my shoes and all Marshall could say was "oh."

"I'll have more information, too. Remember the big guy in the Hawaiian shirt who sort of threatened Sorrel with his 'over your dead body' remark? Well, he goes by the nickname of Spuds, and his dog is Dooley. Sometime today Cindy from the dog park will be calling here with the guy's full name. It's a start, isn't it?"

"Yeah, it's a start." Nate turned to Augusta. "As soon as that name comes in, let me know, okay?"

Then he took a step closer to me. "Good work, kiddo. Anytime you want to trade spreadsheets for a magnifying glass, let me know."

"Very funny. And speaking of which, I'll be fast at work on my computer should any of you need me." I wanted to mention Claudia Brinson's name in case anyone from the garden club might have threatened Sorrel, but I figured Nate and Marshall were inundated already and perhaps I could check out that possibility on my own. Stopping by a garden club meeting was bound to be more pleasant than the dog park.

We all headed to our respective offices, with the exception of Augusta, who was already going through some paperwork at her desk. It wasn't until early afternoon when Augusta got Cindy's call. Nate and Marshall had already left the office, presumably to start interviewing contacts, so Augusta took down the name and address of the Hawaiian shirt guy.

Russell "Spuds" Baxter lived on the prestigious "millionaire's row" overlooking Briarwood Golf Course. No wonder the thought of an eco-friendly park caused him to explode the other night. Cindy didn't provide any more information than that, but it was enough.

"Marshall will probably get stuck with that interview," I said as soon as Augusta gave me the guy's name. "I figure Nate will have enough to do with the archery club."

"And what about you? And don't tell me you're going to sit this one out because I know better."

"Fine. Please don't say anything to Nate or Marshall. And I'm not investigating. All I plan on doing is having a nice conversation with a lady who happens to be a good gardener."

"Just be careful. Those gardening tools can double as weapons, you know. A good slam to the head with a shovel, and bam!"

"A sweet lady from the gardening club is not going to heave a shovel at me," I said. Of course, the same could have been said for another darling lady who thought nothing of holding a gun to my head. I tried not to think about it. "I'll be fine. Really."

Not wanting to get my mother any more worked up than she already was about Sorrel's murder, I decided to look up Claudia Brinson myself and see if she would agree to meet with me. As luck turned out, I found her number without any problem and gave her a call. Cindy was right. The woman was delightful. We agreed to meet over coffee at Bagels 'N More on Saturday morning. Early in the morning. Before my mother and her book club ladies arrived for their weekly brunch. I didn't say a word to my boss or to Marshall. I figured if I uncovered anything remotely related to Sorrel's demise, I'd let them know. Augusta kept her word, too. I knew she would.

The remainder of the week was fairly uneventful as far as work was concerned. The sheriff's department informed our office we'd get a copy of Sorrel's toxicology report as soon as it was available. Nate was able to meet with the archery club's president who told him that the club members felt as if targets were being emblazoned on their backs. According to their president, "None of the members had a grudge against Sorrel, and more than half of them had no clue who she was." Still, Nate wasn't convinced.

Marshall's luck wasn't much better. Spuds Baxter kept evoking the Fifth Amendment during their conversation on Friday, even though Marshall kept telling him he wasn't under arrest.

"My God! The guy actually slammed the phone down on me," he said later that night while we were having dinner at the Arrowhead Grill. "Maybe your mother's got the right idea after all."

"What's that? Nag them to death?"

"Nah. Although that's a pretty tried and true practice. I mean snooping around."

A piece of steak all but caught in my throat. Snooping around was exactly what I planned on doing with Claudia tomorrow morning.

"You okay, Phee? You look as if something's wrong," he said.

"What? Um, no. I'm fine. I was thinking about Spuds Baxter, that's all. Somehow he doesn't strike me as the kind of person who would be proficient with a bow and arrow."

Marshall laughed. "No kidding. I'm not sure where he'd put the bow so that his stomach wouldn't get in the way."

"That's awful. Giggling about someone's physique."

"Hey, you were the one who mentioned it in the first place."

"True, but I was politically correct and unassuming."

"That's what I love about you," he said.

"My political correctness?"

"No. Your diplomacy. Listen, I'll be on the case tomorrow, so why don't we plan on getting together Sunday? Maybe a late brunch and a hike?"

"Sounds terrific."

I made up my mind that if I wound up with a significant lead as a result of my appointment with Claudia in the morning, I would let Marshall know. I hated keeping secrets, even if my intentions were good.

Chapter 7

Of all days for that annoying Streetman to get up early, Saturday had to be the day. The change in his schedule prompted a change in my mother's, and she and the book club ladies decided to have an early breakfast at Bagels 'N More, instead of their midmorning one.

Claudia and I barely had a chance to introduce ourselves and order breakfast when I heard that all too familiar voice.

"Phee! What are you doing here? Aren't you working today? Oh, it must be next Saturday. I keep forgetting with the every other Saturdays."

"Mom, I—"

"I know. I know. The dog got me up early. What can I say? The ladies will be here any minute."

She turned to Claudia before I could utter a word. "Harriet Plunkett. Phee's mother. Nice to meet you."

Claudia smiled, shook my mother's hand, and, in that split second, I managed to introduce her.

"Claudia is Cindy Dolton's neighbor. I wanted to talk with her about the gardening club," I said.

"The gardening club? Your house is a virtual death zone

for any living plants. Even the ones that don't require water. Are you going to give it another try?"

"Maybe." I was squirming when who of all people but Bill Sanders raced over to us.

"Harriet! I was going to call you later. Um, hi, Phee. Hi . . ."

"Claudia," I said as he glanced at my table companion.

"Yeah. Good. Hi, Claudia." He turned immediately to my mother, but there was no way Claudia and I could avoid hearing their conversation. We sat intently and took it all in.

"Harriet. Listen carefully. You have *got* to talk to Myrna. She'll ruin us. That bocce tournament is two and a half weeks away, and she's gotten worse. I didn't think it was possible, but she has. Ever since Tuesday, when she thought one of her bocce balls killed that Sorrel lady, she's taken a whole new approach. Hardly tosses the ball at all. Lets it drop slowly in front of her and waits to see if the damn thing can even roll toward the target."

My mother wasn't at all moved. "Well, whose fault is *that?* Granted, she kind of heaved those balls, but it didn't help that all of you kept telling her she'd wind up killing someone. Oh my gosh. Speak of the devil, she's walking in. Shh. Not a word."

"Talk to her, please," Bill said. "And, uh, nice meeting you, Claudia. Bye, Phee."

Bill took off and was out the side door before Myrna made her way toward us.

"Oh no," my mother said. "I'd better grab that middle table before someone else does. Usually they know we're coming and hold it for us. Come on over. I insist."

"Um, our orders are on their way. Maybe when we finish. Okay?"

My mother muttered something to herself and raced to

the middle table, arriving there at the same time as Myrna. I quickly turned to Claudia and gave her the rundown on Myrna's bocce team before I asked her if anyone in the garden club had had it *in* for Sorrel. Fortunately, Claudia couldn't wait to spill the beans.

"That woman had more than a screw loose. Always coming up with bizarre ideas like distributing organic seed packets to shoppers in supermarket parking lots. Just what they needed—propaganda extoling the virtues of home gardening. Then, of course, her plot of land idea for the homeless. It kept getting worse and worse. Finally, we found a solution."

Oh hell. Is she going to tell me they killed her?

"Um, er, uh . . . so, what did you come up with?"

"We pulled some strings and got her appointed to the recreation center's board of directors. We figured if that didn't keep her busy, nothing would. And it worked. It really worked. Until she wound up dead, that is. We feel awful about it."

"Tell me, how did you get her on the board exactly?"

"Oh, real easy. Marlee Madison's husband is friends with someone on the board, and Marlee is in our club. She convinced her husband to have his friend recommend Sorrel for the appointment."

"I see." *That's one way to solve a problem.*

Claudia twisted her bracelet as she spoke. "Probably not exactly 'kosher,' but we were desperate."

"I understand. I won't divulge anything. But I do have one more question. Does anyone, I mean, *did* anyone have a real problem with Sorrel, other than those bleeding-heart ideas of hers?"

"Actually, quite the opposite. One of our members, Frank Landrow, had a thing for her."

"A thing? As in a crush or something?"

Claudia gave me a slow nod just as our waitress delivered our food. "Not exactly a crush, more like one of those kindred spirit things. You know, where two people aren't so much attracted physically as idealistically. Frank always supported Sorrel's ideas, no matter how far-fetched they were."

"Do you know if they ever saw each other outside of the garden club?"

"Offhand, no. Unless you consider both of them volunteering to distribute flyers for our annual plant sale. They worked together on that."

Distribute flyers . . . go out for a long lunch . . .

I wasn't about to jump to conclusions, but it sure was tempting. So tempting that I had to find out more. "Do you have any idea if Frank is married?"

"He's married all right. Wife's name is Eleanor, but that's all I know. I've only seen her one or two times, usually at our holiday parties. Quite the opposite of Sorrel."

"What do you mean?" I asked as Claudia cut into her omelet.

"Sorrel Harlan never got out of the seventies. Wavy gray hair and Birkenstock shoes. God forbid she would wear a pair of heels. Shied away from makeup, too. Eleanor, on the other hand, dresses to the nines. Classy clothes, bright lipstick, eye shadow. You get the picture."

"Yeah, I do."

I tried not to give in to my mother's usual explanation for unsolved murders. It always involved a love triangle gone wrong. Maybe because that seemed to be the plot for so many of the mysteries she and her friends were reading. Still, the Sorrel and Frank connection was rather tempting as a motive for murder. Especially if it was a love affair gone wrong.

Claudia took a bite of her toast and glanced at the middle table, where the Booked 4 Murder book club ladies were seated. "I'm sorry. I know your mother invited us to join them when we finish, but I really have to get going. I've got a million errands to run this morning, not to mention a load of wash that's been staring at me for days. Please give her my apologies."

"No apologies needed. This was so nice of you to agree to meet with me. We all want Sorrel's murder to be solved as soon as possible, and any information at all is a big help."

Claudia and I finished our meals and paid at the counter. She headed out the door, but I wasn't so fortunate.

"Is that you, Phee?" It was a voice that made the little hairs on the back of my neck stand up. My aunt had walked in the front door as I stood near the cash register.

"Aunt Ina! Nice to see you."

"This is an ungodly early hour for the book club to get together. Whatever was your mother thinking?"

"The dog got her up early."

"I know. And thanks to that little ankle biter, all of us have had to rearrange our schedules. Good thing I'm rested from my staycation. Nothing like being pampered at a four- or five-star hotel."

I wouldn't know. My idea of being pampered is getting one of those chair massages at the mall.

"Come on, the table is filling up."

"Um, actually, I ate already, and I was headed—"

She grabbed me by the wrist. "Tell me at the table, Phee. I need a cup of coffee."

Something furry brushed against my face, and I realized it was some sort of faux fur scarf my aunt was wearing. She had given it a toss as she raced to the table. I figured it wouldn't hurt if I joined the ladies for a minute or two before heading out.

The usual crew had arrived—Shirley, Lucinda, Cecilia, Louise, and the new snowbirds, Riva, Marianne, and Constance. Riva was a short, gray-haired woman with wire-rimmed glasses and tiny crystal posts in her ears. Marianne had curly brown hair and freckles that were trying to peek out from under a layer of makeup. She appeared, by far, to be the youngest member of the group. And Constance looked like what I pictured someone who was named Constance to look like, a Pilgrim who had arrived on the Mayflower. Tight, wavy brown hair parted in the middle and pulled into a bun, starched long-sleeved white blouse, and no jewelry. All she was missing was the long apron.

My aunt practically shoved me into a seat and plopped herself down next to me. The waitress, who was standing a few feet away, immediately came over to fill the empty coffee cups in front of us. I quickly put my hand over the top of my cup and signaled that I didn't want any. "Hi, Everyone! I'm only going to be here a few minutes. I already ate."

"Phee's decided to grow houseplants," my mother announced. "Either that or find out how to resurrect her dead ones."

My aunt gave me a funny look and reached into her large embroidered pocketbook, pulling out a large book. "Speaking of death, I have the perfect novel for us. Written at the turn of the last century and translated from Albanian, *The Death Hand from the Crypt*."

"We're not reading it, Ina," my mother said. "We agreed to stick with nice domestic murders this year. Charlene O'Neil, V.M. Burns, Mary Marks, Kathleen Bridge, Stephanie Blackmoore, and John Lamb. I had to get a magnifying glass to read the print in that last godforsaken novel of yours. We're sticking with close-to-home, domestic murders and that's that."

"I don't think we need to find a cozy mystery in order to do that," Marianne said. "We've got our own home-grown murder already. Can you believe it? One of our Sun City West Rec Center board members killed with a bow and arrow. I swear, I'm afraid to take a walk around the neighborhood."

"Has the sheriff's department made any arrests? I haven't heard a thing," Cecilia said as she adjusted the starched white collar on her button-down shirt.

That woman is a former nun if I ever saw one.

Suddenly everyone looked straight at me. Everyone except my mother, who began to slather butter on a piece of toast that was already saturated. I knew in that instant she had told them something.

"Look," I said, "before any of you ask me if I know anything, I don't. Unless you count the fact my boss and his partner were asked to consult on the case. I repeat, *my boss and his partner.* Not me. I'm the bookkeeper. And even if I did happen to come across some information, I certainly wouldn't be in a position to share it."

The ladies made annoying little guttural sounds until Louise finally spoke up. "Okay, okay, enough of the dis-claimer. What do you really know?"

"Honestly? Nothing."

My mother finished slathering the butter on her toast and cleared her throat. "If Phee says she doesn't know any-thing, she doesn't. But the minute she does, I'll let all of you know."

Terrific. Why don't we simply rent one of those comput-erized billboards and have a rolling screen of updates?

I mouthed the words "thank you" to her, followed by a

grimace. "It was nice seeing everyone, but I really should head out. I've got a ton of things to do."

"Don't go anywhere on my account," came a loud voice from behind me. A loud male voice that belonged to Herb Garrett. "Don't any of you ladies leave until you answer this question. Do I look like a murderer to you?"

Dead silence.

Herb continued, "Well? Do I? Or a bowman for that matter? What the hell is wrong with the Maricopa County Sheriff's Department? Do you believe they had the audacity to question me about Sorrel's murder? Well, they did! Sent a deputy right to my door. Claimed I made a threat at the meeting Monday night. What threat? Did any of you hear me make a threat?"

The ladies started muttering and mumbling, but nothing coherent was said, so Herb leaned over the table and kept talking. "According to Deputy Bowman, who, by the way, has the personality of a tomato, I was confrontational at the meeting. Confrontational. Who the heck wasn't? It was an idiotic proposal. Anyway, I thought I'd tell you about that miserable encounter. Don't let me interrupt anything. I only stopped in here to get a dozen bagels since they've got that Saturday half-price special going on."

"Phee's on her way out," my mother said, "so you're welcome to take her seat."

"Nah. Thanks anyway, but I've got a busy morning and a full afternoon. Bill roped me into being on the sign committee for the bocce and lawn bowling tournament. I'm meeting some of the guys to start putting up the posters."

Myrna slunk down in her chair and avoided all eye contact with Herb. The second Herb left, Shirley asked Myrna how the practices were coming along.

"I guess okay. For everyone else. But not me. When it

comes to my turn, I freeze. All I can think about is Sorrel's body next to where my bocce balls landed."

Shirley clasped her hands together. The mauve nail polish I last saw was replaced by a deep sapphire color. "Lordy, Myrna, you didn't kill that woman. You've got to get over it. Think about something else next time you toss a ball."

"I tried. If I'm not picturing the dead body, I'm wondering if someone is going to shoot an arrow in my direction."

Cecilia, who was sitting next to Myrna, put her hand over Myrna's. "Would it make you feel any better if we came to your practices and supported you? You know, like a cheerleading squad without the cheers."

"I couldn't ask you to do that. Really, I couldn't."

I thought I detected a look of relief on my mother's face, but it didn't last.

Myrna looked down and bit her lip. "Actually, it would make me feel better. We practice again on Monday at nine."

What followed was Myrna laying out the entire schedule of bocce team practices and the ladies deciding who would be at each one. It was the perfect time to make my escape.

I stood and shoved in my chair. "Gotta go." I headed to the side door.

Behind me, I could hear my mother yelling, "Call me later!"

Chapter 8

Marshall and I agreed to a late brunch the following day at the Wildflower Bread Company, not too far from where we both lived. It was twenty past ten, and I expected him at my door within the next few minutes. Under normal circumstances, I'd be glancing at the nearest clock anxious for him to arrive, but this time I checked the clock hoping he'd be running late. I needed more time to figure out how I was going to broach the subject of my unofficial interview with Claudia Brinson and my subsequent knowledge about Frank Landrow. Maybe it *was* a love interest gone bad.

My God, I'm working off of my mother's playbook.

The doorbell rang and I nearly jumped. Talk about feeling edgy. I hated keeping things from Marshall and was determined to tell him everything I'd learned once we got to the restaurant.

So much for that scenario.

I managed to blurt out everything the instant he walked into my living room. "I don't like keeping things from you," I said.

"Uh-oh. This doesn't sound good. Are you about to tell me you're seeing someone else?"

"What? No. Of course not. Oh my gosh. No."

"Okay, then what?"

"Remember when I told you and Nate about the garden club and how they were angry at Sorrel as well?"

Marshall brushed some flyaway hair from his face.

"Well, I knew you and Nate were really busy with your own contacts and I sort of managed to have a very telling conversation with one of the garden club members. Please don't be upset. I don't want you to be upset. I don't want you thinking I'm trampling on your territory. I don't want you to . . . oh, no. That's exactly what I'm doing. I've graduated from interested party to road yenta. Just like my mother."

"Calm down, Phee. You're acting as if you committed a crime. I'm not upset. Honest. So, who was this garden club person and what did you find out?"

"Maybe we should sit down. This may take a while."

We moved to the couch and sat inches from each other. If it wasn't a bright Sunday morning with the light streaming in the windows, I would have been tempted to forget about Claudia Brinson altogether. Instead, I gave Marshall the complete rundown, including Claudia's take on Sorrel's relationship with Frank. Marshall looked stunned, as if I'd discovered the root cause of poverty.

"Frank? You said his name was Frank?"

"Uh-huh. Frank Landrow. Why? Does that matter?"

"Phee, I could kiss you!"

Instead, he leaned over and gave me a hug. "The sheriff's department shared some information with us last night. An autopsy of Sorrel's body was performed by the medical examiner. That much we knew. No surprises. The arrow punctured a major artery in the neck. Since a murder investigation is underway, personal belongings couldn't be returned to the husband. The clothing Sorrel was wearing had been placed in a bin, and it wasn't until late Friday when the sheriff's department found a note tucked inside one of her pockets. A note that was signed with a single letter.

"Oh my God! Don't tell me. The letter *F*?"

"You got it. The letter *F*."

"We've got to start paying more attention to my mother. All those years of watching soap operas must have paid off. What did the note say? Did they tell you?"

"They faxed a copy to the office. Do you realize your conversation with Claudia might have pushed this investigation closer to the finish line?"

"Wow. So, what did it say? Was it a love note?"

"I wouldn't go that far. It was more like a warning."

"Huh?"

"It said 'Watch out for stray bocce balls tomorrow. You're liable to trip over one.'"

"That's it? Nothing else?"

"That's it. But it does prove something. This Frank guy knew Sorrel walked around the perimeter of the golf course. She must have told him she'd come across stray balls. Too bad there wasn't a date on that note. It could have been in her pocket from weeks ago. I've got to find out how long Myrna's been practicing with the team, and I've got to have a one-to-one with our Mr. Landrow. Can you give me a second? I'm sending Nate a text and he'll take it from there."

"Um, would you rather cancel our brunch so you can deal with this stuff?" I asked.

"Not on your life. A few hours aren't going to make a difference, but, if you don't mind, I'll take a raincheck on that hike."

Then he gave me another hug, only this one was followed by a fairly decent smack on the lips, before we headed out to the Wildflower Bread Company. Fabulous frittata, great coffee, and wonderful company. I was home by two, with Marshall promising he'd call later and apologizing again for taking off.

"It's too good a lead, hon. We never would have figured out who 'F' was if you hadn't had that conversation with Claudia."

"So now what?"

"Nate has already contacted the sheriff's office, and they're going to follow up on the note by paying a little visit to Frank Landrow. They want Nate and me to stop by later this afternoon for an update."

Another hug, but this time with a longer kiss. This one with hints of cinnamon and nutmeg. I watched as he walked to his car and remained standing at the window for a good two or three minutes after he was out of view. Finally, I snapped out of my daze and decided to make good use of my time.

I threw in a load of wash and began an entirely different investigation—gathering the tax information I needed for the IRS. Sure, the deadline wasn't until April, but I liked to play it safe and have my forms completed by March. It was one of those weird obsessive things ingrained into my mind by my mother before I even knew what taxes were. It had started with my fourth grade homework. I remember my mother in a floral housedress, hands on her hips, grilling me as if I was withholding a state secret.

"When is this project due?"

"In two weeks."

"Good. You'll get it done by next week at the latest."

"But it's not due until a week after that."

"What if you have an emergency? Then what? You'll miss the deadline and fail. Emergencies happen all the time. What if the library gets flooded and you can't get to an encyclopedia? Or what if, God forbid, the power goes out during one of our winter storms?"

"I'll write by candlelight."

"Ah-hah. You could get too close and burn your fingers. Finish that project a week early."

Yep, that was why I was such a nutcase when it came to deadlines. At least my afternoon was productive, and, by five-thirty, I was ready to make myself a sandwich and turn on the TV. No sooner did I open the fridge when my phone rang. Figuring it was Marshall, I answered right away. That'd teach me for not checking the caller ID. As I heard the voice, I saw the name—Harriet Plunkett.

"Oh good, Phee. I was hoping you'd be home. Is Marshall with you?"

"No. He and Nate had to deal with something. What's up?"

"Get a pencil and mark your calendar for Thursday night at seven. Herb's called a powwow and wants all of us to meet. The book club ladies and his pinochle crew. We're meeting at Bagels 'N More. He reserved the large table. Besides, it's not crowded in there at night."

I was still stuck on the word "powwow." "What are you talking about? What do you mean a 'powwow'? And is that a politically correct word to use anymore?"

"It's a strategic planning meeting to deal with that ridiculous board proposal that's coming up next month. Herb and his cronies did some snooping around and found out that four of the eight members on the board are in favor of the eco-friendly park idea. Add Sorrel's vote to the mix and it would've passed. He's worried that the next appointee might feel the same way Sorrel did."

"Do you have any idea who the board will appoint?"

"Don't I wish! No. They'll dig around and scrounge up someone none of us have heard of. They'll introduce that person at the next meeting, swear them in, and voilà! It'll be a done deal. When a board member can't complete his or her term, the board can appoint anyone. No election needed. This is awful."

"So, how's this powwow of Herb's going to help matters?"

"Divide and conquer. Those were his words. Well, actually not his. Someone said them once and I think it made them famous, but anyway, Herb figures if each of us gets in touch with a board member we might be able to sway them in our favor. He plans on divvying up the names. Four of the board members were against her proposal, so whoever gets one of those has to convince them to sway another member."

"Let me get this straight, and, by the way, I think it was Julius Caesar who penned that divide and conquer quote. Herb is asking his buddies and your book club friends to each contact a rec center board member out of the blue and pressure them into changing their vote. That is, if they intended to vote in favor of that ridiculous idea."

"I wouldn't use the word 'pressure.' It's much too negative. We're supposed to use diplomacy. And if we manage to shift enough votes in our favor, it won't matter who the next appointee is."

Thank goodness I was at the other end of a phone line because my eyes were rolling around in their sockets like balls on a roulette wheel. "Okay, I get it. But I don't think those board members are going to be all that thrilled to get phone calls from people about the issue. That's what the meetings are for."

"Who said anything about phone calls? The way Herb has it figured out is really quite clever. We find out their hangouts, their habits, you know, all that stuff, and then unobtrusively bump into them at different places."

"This is sounding worse by the minute."

"In less than a month, the very atmosphere and lifestyle

in Sun City West could change drastically. We need to be heard."

"I know this is hard for you, Mom, but backtrack for a minute. Sorrel Harlan was found murdered on the golf course. If anything at all happens to one of those board members, guess who the number one suspects will be? Let Herb write a letter to the editor or something. Maybe even speak on the local radio station. This plan of his could backfire bigtime."

"You can tell Herb that yourself. On Thursday. At seven. At Bagels 'N More."

"This meeting has nothing at all to do with me. I live in Vistancia, remember?"

"Your mother happens to live here. And if you don't want her moving in with you in Vistancia because her neighborhood got overrun with a brigade of lollipop-licking children and graffiti-tagging skateboarders, you'll come to the meeting."

"Ugh." It was all I could say. My stomach was practically in knots when I hung up the phone. Thirty seconds later, it rang again. I was positive it was her.

"Don't you think you're taking this to the extreme? You make it sound as if everyone under the age of thirty should be put on the no-fly list."

"The what? What are you talking about?"

"Oh my gosh. Marshall. I thought it was my mother. We had a horrible conversation."

"I guess. From the sound of it. No-fly list and all."

I told him about Herb's powwow and the crazy plan he hatched to thwart the eco-friendly park proposal.

"Yeah, you were right to tell your mother to proceed with caution, and, in this case, maybe not proceed at all. Sorrel's death was a homicide, and until the killer can be apprehended, it's best to play it safe. The sheriff's department has already questioned the board members, but they're delving deeper into the matter, and Nate and I may be asked to assist with that part as well."

"Are you saying they suspect a board member?"

"Right now, they suspect everyone."

"How'd it go tracking down Frank Landrow?"

"I'll give you the full-blown version tomorrow, but let's just say this case gets more and more muddled by the minute. Say, I owe you a hike, don't I? How about making a full day of it next Sunday? Heck, we can even start on Saturday night."

"The parks close at eight."

"Who said anything about the parks?"

Chapter 9

It was a typical nonstop Monday, and I didn't get a chance to talk to Marshall until midmorning. He and Nate had client appointments, and I had enough work piled on my desk to keep me out of everyone's hair. Augusta stopped in around ten to let me know she was going to the donut shop during her break and asked if I wanted anything.

"One glazed donut isn't going to kill you," she said.

I figured the sugar would give me energy, which, in turn, would translate to productivity, which could then be construed as calorie burning. I took her up on the offer. What I didn't expect was a two-for-one donut sale that day. I had already consumed the first one when Marshall gave a quick rap on the doorframe. Bits of strawberry frosting clung to my lips and I immediately reached for a napkin.

"You look good in frosting. Don't worry about it," he said.

"This is Augusta's fault. Honestly."

Marshall laughed and pulled up a chair. "Okay, Frank Landrow. Here's the long and short of it—the sheriff's department was unable to locate him yesterday."

"Unable because he wasn't home or unable because of something else?"

"Both. His wife, Eleanor, was home but said he left early in the morning to do some 'soul searching,' whatever the heck that is. She didn't seem to have a clue either, according to the deputy who spoke with her. And that's not all. The deputy said he was never so uncomfortable in his entire life. Felt as if she could look right through his uniform and see him buck naked. Whew. Glad their department got to interview her and not me."

I stifled a giggle, but it was no use. I wound up laughing out loud.

"Go ahead. Have fun with this, but I can sympathize with that deputy. From what he said, this Eleanor Landrow was practically all over him and not at all concerned about the whereabouts of her husband. In fact, she told the deputy that if her husband wound up missing, she'd be really miffed because it would interfere with her pedicure and spa appointment the next day."

"Wow. Do you think she had anything to do with his disappearance?"

"No. Because he came back. Early this morning. Told the wife he spent the night at the Hampton in Glendale."

"In Glendale? Why Glendale? There's a Hampton right across Grand Avenue in Sun City West."

"Said he was driving around trying to deal with things. Who knows?"

"Maybe whoever killed Sorrel has it in for Frank, too, and he's worried. For all we know, he might have been promoting that eco-friendly park idea and someone got ticked."

"The deputy who met with Frank's wife had the same thought. Unless, of course, Frank had a thing going with Sorrel and it was more than platonic."

"Sounds like something right up my mother's alley. You know how she's always coming up with these ideas about jealous wives. If it turns out to be true, I'll never live it down."

"From what the deputy said about Eleanor Landrow, I highly doubt it. Anyway, Nate and I are up to our noses with the archery club. Thirty-six members and, according to their president, none of them have the skills to land an arrow on a target like Sorrel's neck."

"Maybe they weren't aiming for her. What if someone else was the real target?"

"Hmm . . . could be, but I'm not so sure. The home-owners and the garden club members had solid motives to go after Sorrel. I'll stick with that for the time being. Anyway, Deputy Bowman plans to talk with Frank this afternoon, and, since we're consulting on the case, Nate will be sitting in. I've got a full schedule, so I'll hear about it secondhand."

Marshall wasn't kidding about the full schedule. The minute he left my office, his eleven-thirty appointment arrived. I heard Augusta announcing it in that lovely, loud voice of hers. Same deal with the noon appointment. I found out later that five of those meetings were with members of the Sun City West Archery Club, who had agreed to speak with Nate or Marshall in our office, rather than someplace in Sun City West.

None of them were considered suspects as of yet, but some of them weren't taking any chances. According to Marshall, three men brought in their paper archery targets that had been removed from the foam backing. None of them had bull's-eyes. In addition, all five men had alibis for the morning of Sorrel's murder.

Nate's agenda was fairly similar. Targets with no bull's-eyes and decent alibis. By the time he left to meet with Deputy Bowman and Frank, he had interviewed three archery club members.

* * *

The next morning, a letter to the editor of the *Sun City West Independent News* appeared. It was written by the president of the archery club and offered the club's condolences to the family of Sorrel Harlan. The letter went on to explain that the archery club, although committed to marksmanship, valued sportsmanship above all else and stood firm that none of its members would ever jeopardize anyone's safety by shooting a bow and arrow in a public place, such as a golf course.

A few archery club members agreed to meet at Putters Paradise in Sun City West on Wednesday, and that took up much of Marshall and Nate's time. The result of those interviews was the same: a few paper targets and decent alibis.

"It's as if they're all citing the party line," Marshall said when we went out for pizza and wings on Wednesday night. "I doubt Nate and I are going to get much further with the archery club. Sharp shooters they're not."

"Could someone in the club be hiding how skillful they really are?" I asked.

"Nah. I doubt it. Why bother to be in an archery club only to hide how skillful you really are? Why bother to set up a ruse? Keep a low profile? The fewer people who know you can use a bow and arrow, the better. Seems to me, most people in these retirement community clubs are pretty social. It would be hard for some loser loner to pretend otherwise."

"What about motive? Do any of them own golf course homes?"

"Sure. About a third of them. The third with the worst paper targets and the best alibis."

"Too bad Nate and Deputy Bowman couldn't get anywhere with Frank Landrow the other day."

"That's putting it mildly. The guy shut down like a battery at twenty below zero. Wouldn't answer a darn thing. Course, it didn't help any that the wife was in the room."

"Does that mean the sheriff's office will be bringing him in for questioning?" I asked.

"They want to give it a few more days. Meantime, they'll do some background checking on him. Which reminds me, is your mother still planning on joining that powwow tomorrow night?"

"Oh yeah. They're not backing down. I think Herb put more planning into this than most military commanders would. According to my mother, there are five pinochle guys: Herb, Bill, Kevin, Kenny, and Wayne. You know all of them from the play last December. Add Myrna, Lucinda, Cecilia, Shirley, Louise, Riva, Marianne, Constance, my aunt Ina, and my mother from Booked 4 Murder, and you've got fifteen. Herb insists on adding me to the mix because he needs an even number. Sixteen. The way he figures it, two powwow appointees will be assigned to each board member. An even deal. Says two chances are better than one if they're going to convince the board to back down on that proposal."

Marshall leaned across the table and spoke softly. "Please don't tell me you're really going to go along with that plan, are you?"

"I, er, um . . ."

"Seriously, Phee, I don't like the idea of you cornering one of those board members. Heck, I don't like the idea of any of you wrangling with them."

"I'm not thrilled either, but my mother's breathing down my neck insisting her lifetime investment in the house will be reduced to smithereens. Her word. Smithereens. Told me last night the house is her only protection if Social Security and her pension disappear. Muttered something about her and Streetman living in a cardboard box under the I-10 Bridge. You know how she blows things out of proportion. Besides, it's not as if Herb's buddies or the book club ladies would be meeting with those board members in some clandestine place. It would be out in the open, like at a supermarket, or the gas station, or—"

"One of them could very well turn out to be Sorrel's killer. If they felt pressured or cornered and they were convinced you or the others posed a threat, they might be willing to kill again."

"Now who's blowing things out of proportion?"

"I'm just concerned about you. You should know how I feel by now."

I looked at the expression on his face and reached my hand across the table to grab his. "I do. Listen, if it will make you feel any better, I promise to stick to wide-open, highly trafficked venues. Okay?"

"I suppose it will have to be okay."

"I'll give you the details after Thursday night."

"I'm holding you to it. Come on, we've got a pizza to finish up."

Chapter 10

Bagels 'N More looked like a deserted movie set, with the exception of Herb and Bill sitting at the middle table. Two semi-bald men with pouches, only Bill was taller and seemed to carry the weight better. I looked around and sighed. It was the last place I wanted to be on a Thursday night, when my couch and a decent TV lineup were only minutes away. Still, I'd promised my mother I'd be here.

Herb saw me the minute I walked into the place. "Hey, cutie! Where's the rest of your crew?"

"Hey, same could be said about yours."

"At least Bill showed up on time. Kevin and Wayne are on their way over from the men's club, and Kenny's finishing up dinner. He gave me a big spiel about his wife making pot roast and not wanting to miss it."

"The ladies should be here any minute. Oh look! Shirley and Lucinda are coming in the door now." As if a flood gate opened, Marianne, Riva, and Louise also walked in.

They were followed by Myrna, who flung the door open and trounced over to the table, each footstep clomping on the floor. "I just got off the phone with Harriet. She'll be a few minutes late. That dog of hers refused to go outside for his evening walk. She had to coax him with some string cheese."

Everyone turned in my direction.

"Don't look at me. I was never coaxed by food."

Just then Kevin and Wayne walked in alongside Constance and Cecilia. Next to each other, the two men reminded me of Laurel and Hardy. While Kevin was thin and wiry, Wayne was short, stout, and muscular.

The waitress started filling the coffee cups on the table as we waited for the rest of the crew to arrive. My aunt Ina made her usual entrance as if auditioning for Gloria Swanson's role in *Sunset Boulevard*. A faux leopard scarf was draped around her head and neck, and her earrings had more jewels than the ones in Queen Elizabeth's throne room.

She took the chair next to mine, greeted everyone, and gave me a poke in the elbow. "Where's your mother? I thought she'd be here by now."

"Dog problems," I said.

Bill grumbled a quick hello to the women as he poured sugar into his coffee. "Let's get this show on the road. I want to get over to Curley's as soon as we get out of here. We should've held this meeting over there."

Cecilia gave him a nasty look as she reached for her cup. "Then you would've held it without us."

"I'm here! I'm here!" My mother's voice was like an explosion. "Did I miss anything? You'd better not have started this powwow without me."

She rushed over to the table and sat down next to Herb. "Who's missing?"

"Only Kenny and he'll be here any sec. . . . Great! He's coming in right now."

Motioning for everyone to lean into the table, my mother bent her head as if she was rolling dice. "We need to keep our voices low. We can't risk being overheard."

"This isn't the CIA, Harriet," Louise said. "And other than that really elderly couple in the corner, no one else is in here. Besides, my hearing aids aren't working too well, so you'll have to speak up."

My mother furrowed her brow. "If you wouldn't insist on covering your ears with all that long hair of yours, maybe the hearing aids would work."

"Hearing aids don't have anything to do with long or short hair. And since when is below the chin considered long? Anyway, this meeting better not take all night. I received a summons to appear for jury duty selection in the morning, and I don't want to be fined for being late. Jury duty. Of all the rotten things. In two years I turn seventy-five and get automatically excused. I can't bear the thought of getting stuck on some jury. In downtown Phoenix, no less. Why does the courthouse have to be in downtown Phoenix?"

"Will you give it a rest, Louise?" Bill asked. "Damn courthouse is in Phoenix since it's the county seat. Now, if you want to get out of jury duty, this is what you do. When they call your name and you go to the front of the court-room, look at the judge and say, 'Give me an old-fashioned murder case. An old-fashioned murder case.' Pound on your chair if you have to. Then act kind of casual and say, 'Do they still have hangings in Arizona?' It'll work like a charm. They'll excuse you from that jury faster than you can get out of your seat. They'll thank you for your service and get you out the door."

"Are you sure? Because I don't want to wind up on that horrible Darla Marlinde case."

Bill scratched his chin. "The one where she killed her boyfriend by putting the poisonous scorpions in his bed?"

"Uh-huh. It's been all over the news. Along with that

other case. The embezzlement one. So, you're certain your tactics will work?"

"Oh yeah. Haven't been called back since 1998."

Herb glared at Bill and raised his voice. "Enough with Louise's jury duty. If this meeting takes any longer, she'll be sitting on Sorrel Harlan's case. That is, if they ever find her killer. Meanwhile, we need to squelch that insane proposal of Sorrel's before it's too late. Hey, move over Kevin, here comes Kenny. Now we can get going."

As soon as Kenny took a seat at the table, Herb started the meeting or "powwow" or whatever name one can give to a haphazard strategic planning session. No sooner did he get started, Wayne began to complain about his back and Cecilia said her bunions were bothering her. It took all Herb could do to get everyone to focus. A few people ordered bagels and that production lasted longer than an epic poem. Finally, the group accomplished something. And that was because my mother took over, much to Herb's relief.

"We haven't got all night," she said. "It's really simple. There are eight board members and sixteen of us. I'll read off each board member's name and assign two people to that person. Unless someone has a particular board member in mind."

Cecilia waved her hand in the air as if she was back in a third-grade classroom. "I volunteer for Eloise Frable. She goes to my church, and I can always find a way to talk to her during social hour after the Sunday services."

"Good, good," my mother replied. "What about you, Shirley? Did you make hats for any of them?"

"No, but Mildred Saperstein plays mahjong at Palm Ridge on Tuesdays. She's not at my table, but I'll find a way to start a conversation. Lordy, it can't be that hard."

Then Shirley turned to my aunt Ina. "Aren't you in the mahjong league, Ina?"

"I was, but it interfered with the yoga meditation classes Louis wanted us to attend. Never mind, I'll skip yoga, and Louis can meditate by himself for an afternoon or so. Put me down for Mildred."

My mother looked directly at me. "Are you getting this, Phee? Are you writing this down?"

"Huh? What? I didn't know I was supposed to take notes."

"Well, you work in an office, don't you? Who else is going to take notes?"

Rather than start an argument, I rummaged in my bag for a piece of paper, pulled out an old receipt, and used the back of it to write down the names.

"You men have been awfully quiet," Lucinda said as she eyeballed Kenny, who had seated himself next to her. "Who are you going after?"

"Kevin and I will take Harold Stevens. We see that old coot every morning at Putters Paradise. Might as well chew the fat and see if we can get anywhere."

"I'll take Jeannine Simone," Herb shouted. "I mean, if no one else wants to."

"Do you know anything about her?" my mother asked.

"Other than the fact she's drop-dead gorgeous? What else is there to know? I'll figure out something."

Just then, Wayne elbowed Herb. "Well, you're not going to do that on your own. I'll take Jeannine with you."

"Fine. Get that down, Phee."

My mother shook her head. "I'm not so sure it's a good idea for both of you to go after Jeannine. She might think you're stalking her or something. Maybe we should reassign her to the women."

Herb's face turned beet red. "Hell no. I called dibs on her first."

"Dibs? She's not a soccer ball. What's the matter with you? I think it would be better if Myrna and Riva took Jeannine."

Myrna looked up from her bagel. "Not me. I'd rather take Bethany Gillmore. Have Riva do it with Marianne or Constance."

"That's all right with me." Constance stared directly at Herb.

"Well, it's not fine with me. Wayne and I are not going to stalk Jeannine. We'll simply strike up a nice conversation with her. I've seen her at the Friday night bingo games. It's a wide-open social hall, Harriet, so she's not going to feel threatened."

"Goodness, Herb. You're as bad as Streetman when he gets his mouth around a bone. You and Wayne can keep Jeannine but don't mess it up."

Twenty-five minutes later, all the names were assigned, leaving only Burton Barre to my mother and me.

"Um, does anyone know anything about Burton?" I asked.

"Yes," Lucinda said. "He works on the giant summer puzzle at the library every year. Been doing it forever it seems. He's even on the committee to select the puzzle. I read about it in the community newsletter. Of course, it's February, so I don't know if he'll be hanging around the library."

"Don't worry," my mother said. "Phee and I will track him down. She has connections, you know."

If you think I'm going to ask Nate or Marshall to profile this guy, think again.

"And one more thing," she continued. "Don't go asking anyone any questions about Sorrel. We should leave that to the sheriff's department and Phee's office. Then again, if they offer information—"

"Tell them to call Williams Investigations or the Maricopa County Sheriff." The words couldn't come out of my mouth fast enough. "Last thing anyone needs is to misconstrue something."

Bill got up from his seat and shoved the chair into the table. "Got it. No Sorrel. Guess that's it for the night. I'm off to Curley's. Who's going to join me for a brewski?"

"Not yet," Herb shouted. "Sit down. We need to set up the next meeting." Then he turned to me. "So, sweetie, when can you get the hit list to all of us?"

Shirley shushed him as soon as he said the words "hit list." "Lordy, Herb, we don't need anyone overhearing us."

"Ain't no one here except a few old buzzards, and they're halfway around the room. And they'll only hear us if they've got their hearing aids turned up."

Suddenly, Louise, who was seated next to Herb, elbowed him. "That comment had better not have been meant for me."

Herb simply groaned. The next powwow was set for the same time and place the following week. If I was back in Minnesota, I'd be praying for a blizzard. Out here in the desert, the best I could hope for was a monsoon, and they only happened in the summer.

Chapter 11

"I see you survived that little strategic planning committee meeting of Herb's last night," Marshall said when I got into work the next morning.

"Survive is a good word. It's a miracle they were able to accomplish anything. Honestly, their attention spans are as bad as preschoolers. Any little thing gets them off task. The worst was when Lucinda started to put butter on her bagel and Wayne jumped all over her because 'you're supposed to put cream cheese on a bagel.'"

"They didn't mention anything about questioning the board members regarding Sorrel's murder, did they?"

"No. You can relax. They agreed to leave those questions for the authorities. Speaking of which, any news?"

"Yeah. Her toxicology report came back negative. No sign of drugs or alcohol or anything suspicious, and the cause of death was officially listed as the severing of an artery due to an arrow wound to the neck. No surprise there. I know we spoke to the members of the archery club, but we're going to pursue that further. In fact, I'm on my way out the door to meet with the manager of the archery range. He may have some information that the club members are hesitant to disclose."

"Nate going with you?"

"No. He's got appointments all morning and will be leaving early to check on his aunt in Sierra Vista. I think he's hoping she'll recuperate soon from the broken hip so he can return that parrot of hers. Apparently Mr. Fluffy-pants isn't the quietest roommate."

"I don't suppose he is. Still, he's probably a lot less neurotic than my mother's dog. Anyway, I'd better get to work."

"We're still on for dinner tonight, right?"

"Wouldn't miss it."

The rest of the day was relatively quiet until a little past four. I was working at my desk and sat up with a jolt as Augusta pounded on the doorjamb.

"There's a Louise Munson to see you. She wanted to meet with Nate, but when I told her he was out of town until Monday, she said you'll do."

"Louise is one of my mother's book club friends. Tell her to come on in."

I couldn't possibly imagine why on earth Louise would need to see Nate, but the more I became acquainted with the book club ladies, the less I was surprised about anything they did.

Louise charged into my office and pulled a chair close to my desk. "Phee! Thank goodness you're in. That nice secretary offered me coffee, but I'm too wound up to drink anything. Can you believe it? I was selected for jury duty. When I see Bill Sanders, I'm going to wring his neck! That plan of his didn't work. In fact, the prosecuting attorney couldn't get me on the jury fast enough. At least it's not the Darla Marlinde, scorpion-killer case. If I read one more thing about her, I'll go out of my mind. I even let Shirley and Lucinda talk me into buying one of those small, black-light flashlights for my key chain, so I can check for scorpions around the house."

She held her key chain in front of me and pointed to the small cylinder tube with a tiny logo of a scorpion. Scorpions turned all sorts of fluorescent colors under a black light, and that was how they could be spotted. What I didn't realize was how worked up my mother's friends got over some tabloid news. I imagined my mother had purchased a black light, too. God forbid a scorpion got within five yards of Streetman.

"Anyway, Phee," Louise went on, "like I said, it's not that case. It's some other boring thing. The embezzlement one. I'm not supposed to talk about it with anyone, but it hasn't started yet, so I guess it doesn't matter."

She was talking a mile a minute, and I was still at a loss as to why she came into our office.

"Um, is there something I can help you with?" I asked.

"No. Unless you can get me off of that jury. Why did I ever listen to Bill?"

"So, you wanted Nate to see how you can be removed?"

"No, no, that's not why I'm here. I was going to call your office, but I had to pass by on my way back from Phoenix and figured it would be easier if I stopped in."

"Because . . . ?"

I wanted to yell "spit it out, spit it out," but took a breath and forced a smile.

"That jury selection took forever. There had to be at least fifty people in the courtroom, and it was moving slow. I needed to use the ladies' room so I asked the bailiff, I think that's what you call those guys. Well, anyway, I asked him if I could be excused to use the restroom and he said yes."

I gave up thinking I'd get a clear and succinct response to my question, so I leaned across the desk. "Go on."

"Anyway, when I got into my stall, two women came in, and I don't think they realized I was there. I always take the farthest stall because I figure people won't walk that far and the stall might be cleaner."

I let out a long sigh, but Louise didn't seem to notice. "The two women were complaining they'd lost their key witness. And you'll never guess who that witness was."

Now she had my interest, and I sat up straight. "Who? Who was it?"

"Sorrel Harlan. They didn't mention her name exactly, but I know it was her from what they were saying."

"Um, I don't want to sound rude, but weren't you having some problems with your hearing aids?"

"Oh, *that*. Turns out they just had to be cleaned. I can hear a penny drop from a mile off now."

"That's great. Tell me, what did they say?"

Louise pulled her chair even closer to the desk. "Sure. The one woman said, 'Imagine. An arrow to the neck, and boom. There goes our case.' And the other one said, 'We'll be hard pressed to find another witness. We need to get a postponement.' I was hoping it was for my idiotic case, but it wasn't."

"How do you know?"

"Because the first woman said, 'You don't get many eye witnesses to something like that. She saw who did it, and it wasn't our client.' It can't be my case. I mean, how do you see someone embezzle money? It had to be something else. Maybe Sorrel witnessed a murder or tampering with evidence or a robbery. But whatever it was, maybe that's what got her killed and not the golf course proposal. What do you think?"

I think there are more motives floating around for Sorrel Harlan's murder than grains of sand on a beach.

"Uh, I don't really know. Listen, I'll tell Nate and Marshall you stopped by, and one of them will give you a call. Okay?

Meanwhile, please don't say anything about this to anyone. It could really muddy the waters, if you know what I mean."

"When I first came in, you asked if it was about Nate getting me off jury duty. Can he do that?"

"I don't think so, but I don't know. You can ask him or Marshall when you speak with one of them."

"Thanks, Phee. I don't have to report to jury duty for a few days. Who knows what can happen in that time."

She thanked me and headed out the door. A few minutes later, I stood to stretch and get myself a cup of coffee before Augusta turned off the machine for the weekend. While I added some half-and-half to the brew, I heard Marshall's voice.

"Hey, everyone! I'm back. Did you miss me? Whoa, look what time it is. I can't believe I've been gone all day with interviews."

"Phee had an interesting one, too." Augusta seemed unable to keep herself from laughing.

"Really? You'll have to tell me about it."

"It's going to complicate your murder investigation," I said.

"Not any more than anything else. I think we can safely eliminate the Sun City West Archery Club members as suspects. I spoke with the range manager, and he is positive no one in that club has the skills to hit a target so precisely. He went on to say that some members are lucky if they can land an arrow on the side of a barn."

"Gee. They sound as skillful as Myrna's bocce league."

"Here's the kicker, though. The range manager told me there are lots of sharpshooters who don't use a range. They go out in the desert, take a foam target or even a hay bale, and practice. He did mention a few idiots he'd heard of who shoot at cacti, but the fines for doing that, especially with saguaro, are really steep. It'll be nearly impossible to track down those desert shooters. If we're going to get anywhere with this, we'll have to focus on motive."

"Yeah. About that . . . Louise Munson from the book club stopped by, and she added motive number three to your list."

"You mean to tell me there are more people who wanted Sorrel Harlan out of the way, other than the golf course homeowners and the garden club?"

"Yeah. The real perpetrator in some case that's going to a jury."

"Huh? What case?"

"That's just the thing. Louise doesn't know."

I went on to tell Marshall exactly what Louise told me, expecting him to register a fair amount of frustration, but his reaction was quite the opposite.

"It's not going to be too difficult for me to find out what cases are going to the jury in the next few weeks. Of course, it will have to wait till Monday when I can place some calls. Someone might have a stronger motive than property values for doing away with Sorrel. Meantime, I've got some paperwork to catch up on. I'll lock up everything after you and Augusta head out. How about if I pick you up at seven thirty for dinner?"

"Works for me."

I headed back to my desk when the phone rang, and Augusta shouted a familiar clarion call. "Phee, your mother's on the phone!"

Don't tell me Louise called her the minute she left this office.

"Hey, Mom, I was about to head out. Can I call you later?"

"This will only take a minute. I have a very important favor to ask you. I meant to speak with you about it last night, but we were all so caught up in that meeting."

"Okay. What favor?"

"Shirley, Lucinda, and I are going to the chocolate festival in Glendale tomorrow and then out to lunch."

Do not invite me. Do not invite me. Just get on with the favor.

"Anyway, I'll be gone from the house for most of the day, and Streetman needs to go for his midday walk. Can you do it? Can you stop by and let him out? I know you work some Saturday mornings, but you can swing by here afterward."

I tried not to groan. "Yeah. I'll take him out. I'm not working tomorrow."

"That's wonderful. When can you stop by to get a map of the neighborhood?"

"What? A map? I don't need a map. I can walk him around the block without getting lost."

"It's not that kind of a map. I printed off the neighborhood map from Google and made important notes about which houses and lawns to avoid. Some people don't want dogs to pee on their property. In fact, there's a crazy woman around the corner who runs out of her house screaming whenever we approach. I have to drag poor Streetman into the road. Also, the dog has his favorite spots, and I marked those as well. The big jacaranda tree directly across the street, the two small olive trees three doors down, the large red boulder—"

"Seriously?"

"Unless, of course, you'd rather take him to the dog park. His probation's been over for a while, and no one has registered any complaints. He rides like a perfect little gentleman in the car. Put him on your passenger seat. Use a towel if you're worried about shedding."

Given my choices, I opted for the dog park. Last thing I needed was a crazy woman to start screaming at me. I told my mother I'd pick up the dog around one, because I wanted to get some early-morning shopping done.

"That's a good time for the park. It's practically deserted at that time. Doesn't start filling up until three."

She thanked me and asked if I wanted her to bring me back chocolates from the festival. I politely declined. By the time I got off the phone, Augusta had already shut the lights off in the main office and was waiting for me by the door.

We shouted "Good-bye" to Marshall and closed the locked door behind us.

Augusta shook her head as we walked down the block to our cars. "No real leads on the Sorrel case, huh?"

"Too many leads. And they seem to be growing exponentially."

"I figured as much when that nice Mrs. Munson from your mother's book club came in."

"She overheard something at the courthouse when she went there for jury selection," I said.

"The Darla Marlinde case? The scorpion sorceress? That's what the tabloids are calling that woman."

"No, nothing that exciting. Anyway, I'm sure Nate and Marshall will figure it out."

"Just you be careful, Phee. Seems to me, an arrow to the back of someone's neck is just as bad as a deadly scorpion in their bed."

Chapter 12

I didn't want my Friday night date with Marshall to end. A fantastic meal at Firebirds followed by some cozy time at my place. It was tough saying good night, but both of us had full Saturdays ahead. We were still at the kissing stage of our relationship and taking it slow. When I was younger and started dating, I remembered my mother warning me, "Too fast, too soon and it's over." I think I actually used the same line with my daughter. But now, in my mid-forties, I kind of wanted to speed things up.

Saturday morning was a whirlwind of grocery shopping and a quick jaunt to Walmart for replacement toothbrush heads and some bath towels. Mine had that ratty, frayed look about them, and I figured if Marshall was ever going to spend the night, I didn't want him to think I couldn't afford decent towels.

At a few minutes past one, I pulled up to my mother's house and got the dog. It wasn't easy. Most dogs come running to the door playfully or barking. Streetman ran under the couch. I had to resort to the only tactic that I knew worked. String cheese. The second he heard me removing the plastic from the tube, he was right in front of me by the refrigerator.

I gave him a tiny piece, clasped his leash to the collar, and we were off. My mother was right. The dog was a wonderful passenger. He liked being in the passenger seat, even though he was too short to look out the window. She was also right about the dog park. No one was there. We had the whole place to ourselves.

Streetman immediately took care of business as soon as I let him in the gate. He then proceeded to sniff around and claim every rock, bush, and tree in the place. I decided to sit for a few minutes on one of the benches and let the dog mill about. A few seconds later, the gate opened and a stylishly dressed, slender woman with short dark hair rushed over and sat next to me. She was too well dressed for the dog park and arrived without a canine companion.

"I think I'm being followed. Do you mind if I sit here with you for a few minutes?" she asked.

"Um, sure."

I looked at the parking lot, and the only cars that came in were headed to the tennis courts, the bocce and lawn bowling, or the fitness center. "I don't see anyone. Are you sure?"

The woman appeared to be visibly shaken and kept staring at the parking lot. She appeared to be in her early fifties, with flawless skin and deep blue eyes.

"I'm pretty sure." She was still staring at the lot. "It started this morning when I went into Dunkin' Donuts for a cup of coffee on my way to the nail salon. Two men were behind me in the line. A short, stocky man, balding. He kept sucking in his stomach. The other man was short and stocky, too, but with brown flyaway hair and a round face. He was wearing a golf shirt with an insignia for the Sun City West Footlighters. You know, the theater group.

Oh my God. Herb and Wayne.

The woman went on before I could say a word. "When

I left with my coffee and drove to the salon, they followed me. I figured they'd be gone by the time my appointment was done, but, somehow, they reappeared when I went to fill up my car. I didn't want to drive home, and I didn't want to go to the sheriff's posse station. I was afraid the deputies would think I was overreacting. So, since the dog park is so close to the gas station, I thought I'd be safe here. By the way, I'm Jeannine. Jeannine Simone."

"I know. You're on the recreation center board of directors."

"That's right. You must have seen my picture in the monthly newsletter they send. It's a horrible photo. I look like I blew in from a windstorm. Is that where you recognize me from?"

I doubted Jeannine could ever look horrible under any conditions. No wonder Herb insisted on speaking with her instead of another board member. "Actually, no. But I do know, or I have a very good suspicion, as to who those men are who are following you. And don't worry. They're harmless. Idiotic, but harmless."

I went on to explain everything about my mother's book club and Herb's pinochle cronies and how they wanted to sway the board into a "no" vote for Sorrel's golf course conversion plan. "Honestly, I think those two bumbleheads were working up the courage to speak with you. Unfortunately, finesse and manners don't appear to be their strong suit."

Jeannine had all she could do to stop laughing. "I'm so glad I came here instead of going to the posse station. I can't understand why they didn't simply say something to me. Anyway, if you must know, I'm totally against that ridiculous proposal. I don't own a golf course home, but I live directly across from one of the golf courses. Last thing I need to see are cars parked all along the street. There are only a few entrances to the golf courses. That means people will be cutting across homeowners' yards to get into the park. They're not going to feel like walking all the way down a block if they can find a shortcut. It'd be a nightmare."

"Tell me, do most of the board members feel the same about it as you do?"

"About half. That means a tie vote until another member is appointed. I doubt anyone will change his or her mind. Sorrel was able to convince Mildred Saperstein, Burton Barre, Eloise Frable, and our own president, Harold Stevens, to see it her way."

"What about the other members? The ones who were against the proposal? Do you think any of them could have murdered her?"

"With a bow and arrow? Clarence and Barry probably have twenty/eighty vision between the two of them, and Bethany isn't much better."

"They could have hired someone."

"You mean a hitman? I only know about those things from TV shows and pulp fiction. And hypothetically, even if they could, they wouldn't be able to afford it."

"Yeah, I suppose you're right. It's such a baffling case."

"That proposal of Sorrel's was insane. I'll grant you that. But to kill her over it? If you ask me, it seems a bit more, well, personal. She must have really rubbed someone the wrong way or knew something incriminating. Whatever it is, I hope it gets solved before the next board meeting. I'd like to put this thing to rest. Oh, and there's one more thing."

"What's that?"

"Even if the board decided to convert one or more of the golf courses to an eco-friendly neighborhood park, they couldn't do it for at least two years. We have a signed contract with Golfscapes. They're the largest golf course management company in the Southwest. They manage all the big courses, like Pebble Brooke in California and

The Boulders in Arizona, plus a number of retirement community golf courses like ours."

"Wow. I didn't know that."

"It's public knowledge. We have to disclose that sort of information on our financial reports to the community. So, even if Sorrel had her way, she'd still be two years off."

"Did you know her personally? I mean, outside of sitting on the same board of directors."

"No. Not at all. And from the little I saw at the meetings, I'd venture to say she was . . . well . . . different. In an earth mother, hippy sort of way, but you're probably too young to visualize what I'm trying to say."

"Oh, I get it. I have an aunt like that. Sort of."

The gate swung open, and a small apricot poodle ran in. Streetman was at her side in a nanosecond. So far, so good. All he was doing was sniffing her. Still, I didn't want to take any chances. Somehow, if he messed up, it would be my fault.

"I don't think Herb and Wayne are going to make their way over here," I said. "You should be fine. Anyway, I've got to get my mother's dog home." *Before he winds up on probation again.*

Jeannine walked with me to the gate. Once Streetman was safely on his leash, we headed out.

"It was nice talking with you," she said.

"Oh, I didn't even introduce myself. I'm Phee Kimball, official dog sitter for my mother, Harriet Plunkett. She's the resident here."

"Harriet Plunkett? Seems to me I've heard that name before."

Of course you have. It's probably plastered on a billboard somewhere . . .

"Wait a sec. Now I know. She was in that play a few

months ago. *The Mousetrap.* Wonderful performance. Be sure to tell her."

"I sure will. And nice meeting you, Jeannine."

As soon as I got inside my mother's house, I gave Streetman some kibble and left a note on the table:

> *The dog was fine. Met Jeannine Simone at the dog park. Tell Herb and Wayne to quit following her. She thinks they're stalking her. Found out the only ones who support Sorrel's plan are Harold, Eloise, Mildred, and Burton (our guy). No sense having anyone waste time with the others. I'll talk to you this weekend. xx's, Phee*
>
> *P.S. Do you have the yearly financial report for the Sun City West Recreation Centers? I'm curious about something.*

The rest of my day was pretty routine. I decided to make use of the cooler weather and prepared a lasagna for the freezer. Only a few months a year were suitable for indoor cooking as far as I was concerned, and February was one of them. Marshall and I were going to take advantage of the weather as well, with an early morning hike tomorrow at the Hassayampa Water Preserve in Wickenburg, a short drive from Sun City West.

As I opened the oven door and slid the pan of lasagna onto the rack, the phone rang. Instinctively, I answered it. A quick "hello" and I was bombarded.

"I got your note. Didn't I tell you Streetman would be well behaved? The ladies and I had a wonderful time at the chocolate festival. I came home with a giant box of white and dark chocolate-coated pretzels. I'll try to set some aside for you. Oh, about your question. I don't save those old recreation center financial reports, but I'll tell you who does. Herb. Herb saves all that stuff until it piles up. Then he sets it out for recycling. I'll give him a call and see if he still has it. Do you need it right away?"

"Um, not right this minute, but I'd like to take a look at something."

"Is it about Sorrel's murder? Do you think the rec center board was embezzling money and Sorrel found out? That's a real motive for murder, you know."

I had to say this much. At least my mother wasn't dwelling on her usual theory that the jealous ex-lover was the culprit. Never mind if the whole world thought the victim was celibate. As far as my mother was concerned, it was *always* some jealous ex.

"Sort of. But like I said, no big rush."

"Okay. Fine. I'll speak to Herb. I'll also let him know he's lucky Jeannine didn't have him arrested for stalking. Good grief."

"Can you ask him to let the others know that Bethany, Clarence, and Barry were against the proposal? No sense in bothering them."

"When were you planning to run into Burton Barre? I think the library is our best chance. Of course, it's closed tomorrow, but maybe Monday."

"Mom, I'm working. Remember? Plus, I have no idea what this guy looks like, and just because Lucinda said he works on the giant jigsaw puzzle in the summer doesn't mean he's hanging around there all winter. Talk about wild goose chases."

"Burton Barre is a distinguished-looking, African-American gentleman. Well built. Grayish hair. Clean shaven.

He was sitting next to Jeannine at the board meeting when we all suffered through Sorrel's proposal."

"Okay. That narrows it down as far as looks are concerned, but—"

"I'll tell you what. I'll stop by the library Monday and speak with one of the clerks. I know which ones are more in tune with their patrons."

"You mean which ones are the busybodies," I said.

"That's not a socially correct word."

"Oh brother."

"When I find out more about Burton's schedule, I'll call you. We only have a few days until Thursday, and we're not going to be the only ones showing up at Bagels 'N More without having accomplished our mission. It will look especially bad for you, Phee, seeing as you work for an investigative firm."

"As their bookkeeper!"

Chapter 13

I had a hunch about Sorrel's murder, and it had nothing to do with angry homeowners or Frank Landrow's less-than-jealous wife. It was more in line with corporate greed and money. Two strong motives in my book. Still, there was nothing concrete to back up my thinking, so I decided not to mention it to Marshall when we took our early morning hike on Sunday.

"I don't know. I have this bizarre feeling about your mother's friends and the way they go about things," he said as we paused from our hike to sit on a huge boulder and do some bird watching. "I hope they don't get carried away and start asking questions about Sorrel's murder. That could complicate the investigation."

"I know. I know. They all agreed to stick to the original plan of persuading the board to squelch Sorrel's eco-friendly park idea."

"What about you? Weren't you supposed to track someone down?"

"Uh-huh. Burton Barre. I told my mother I had a busy work schedule. Maybe she'll tackle it on her own. She's going to ask one of the library clerks about the guy since he's a regular over there. By the way, how are you and Nate doing with this?"

"Miserably, if you must know. We widened the search for top-notch archers but got nowhere. We've had lots of meetings with the sheriff's deputies to share information, but there are no substantial leads at this point. In fact, Nate got so frustrated that he called Rolo Barnes to look into Marlene Krone and Eleanor Landrow."

Rolo, who always reminded me of a black Jerry Garcia, was our unofficial cypher and hacking expert. He used to work for the Mankato Police Department but found it far more lucrative to freelance. He had a zillion quirks, and, in addition to his regular fees, he liked to be paid with kitchen gadgetry. The particulars varied depending upon whatever diet he was on. Worst was the juicing diet. That one had cost me a fortune when my mother was convinced a book curse was going to kill her and her friends.

"Do you actually think it could be love interests gone wrong? My mother would be all over this if she knew. And, having never met Marlene Krone, she'd come up with a description that would rival Mata Hari."

Marshall laughed. "Let's say there was a love interest between Milquist and Marlene. She'd have a good motive to get rid of the wife. Milquist is one very wealthy man."

"What about Eleanor?"

"She might have suspected her husband of cheating with Sorrel."

"Oh my gosh. It sounds like that horrible Darla Marlinde scorpion killer case. Only with an arrow instead of a stinger."

"That woman's had more TV coverage than most presidents. I'm just glad her case never landed on our laps."

He put his arm around my waist and pulled me in closer

for a quick kiss. "If we're going to get any hiking done, we can't do it sitting on this boulder."

I let Darla Marlinde and Sorrel Harlan slip out of my mind once we got back on the trail. In fact, Marshall and I didn't resume talking about the investigation until dinner and that was only to re-hash what we already knew. Though neither of us were culinary experts, we managed to create a fabulous Chinese stir-fry at my place.

Phoenix might have a plethora of Chinese restaurants, but none, as far as we were concerned, that made the kind of food we were used to in Minnesota.

As Marshall put it, "The only sauce they seem to make is black bean sauce, and if that's the case, we might as well be eating Mexican food."

I couldn't agree more.

Monday morning came way too fast, and my wake-up call made it worse. My mother's voice on the answering machine was loud enough to be heard from the kitchen. I was still in bed and had no desire to pick up the phone, even after four rings. The voice, however, couldn't be ignored.

"Phee! You should be up by now. Don't you have to go in to work? Call me. We don't have to track down Burton Barre. He'll be at Sorrel's memorial service this Wednesday evening. I just read about the service in the morning paper. They're holding it at the Garden of Perpetual Memories behind one of the funeral parlors on Camino del Sol Boulevard. Call me."

It was the "we" in her message that meant trouble for me. I reached over, grabbed the phone, and dialed her back.

"Nice wake-up call, Mom. You know, some people get

to wake up to chirping birds or maybe Westminster chimes, not messages about funeral arrangements."

"It's not the funeral. They already had that. A private affair. This is her memorial service. It's the perfect place to get information. All of those board members will be there. They would have egg on their faces if they didn't show up. You and I can unobtrusively mention our concerns about the proposal to Burton. Plain and simple. I'll let Herb and the book club ladies know about this as well, in case they didn't read it in the morning paper."

"Whoa. Wait a sec. I don't think it's such a great idea to have Herb show up at Sorrel's memorial. Or Myrna either, for that matter. Both of them spoke out quite vehemently at that board meeting. I don't think their attendance would be appreciated at her service."

"Hmm . . . you might have a point. Okay, I'll let everyone know, and I'll tell Herb and Myrna not to attend. So, do you want to meet me there or pick me up? It starts at seven. If you come here directly from work, I can take something out of the freezer for us."

As soon as I heard the words "I can take something out of the freezer," my mind went into a tailspin. Food in my mother's freezer could have been there from the Roman Empire. In an effort to avoid consuming anything she would unearth, I said, "I'll meet you at the memorial service." It was a panicked reaction. Now it was too late. I'd agreed to go, and there was no turning back.

"I can't believe what I did," I whined to Nate and Marshall when I got to the office. "It's bad enough I got roped into those imbecilic powwow meetings of Herb's, but now this? I've got to learn to say no. No. No. No."

"Take it easy, kiddo," Nate said. "You just walked us into a goldmine."

"Huh?"

Marshall smiled and patted me on the shoulder. "He's right. Where else can all those suspects be rounded up? While your mother is busy trying to convince Burton Barre to change his vote, you can quietly listen in on the conversations and see if anything incriminating surfaces."

"Ugh. I stink at that. Couldn't one of you go with me?"

Marshall shook his head. "Wish I could, but I've got a client meeting at six in Phoenix. Possible product thefts at a major company."

I glanced at my boss and waited.

He walked over to Augusta. "Write down memorial service in my appointment book for Wednesday night." Then he winked at me. "Like I said, we're about to walk into a goldmine."

The only "goldmine" I walked into following that conversation was the profit and loss statement for Nate's business. While I couldn't exactly call it a goldmine, his business was doing well. Having a second investigator meant more clients and enough income to balance out the additional costs. I wanted to complete my end of the year preparations early so I would have plenty of time for his tax preparer's deadline. Not too far off from the countdown for my own Form 1041.

As I calculated and recalculated the figures, my mind wandered back to the hunch that had been plaguing me all weekend. Other than the homeowners, someone else would lose bigtime on that proposal. And if I was right, it wouldn't be limited to Sun City West. Once or twice I thought about getting up and tossing my idea in front of Marshall, but the last thing he or Nate needed was some unsubstantiated feeling that came out of nowhere. Instead, I blurted it out to Augusta when I took a break.

"It's possible," she said as she added some milk to her coffee. "Of course, anything is feasible when it comes to murder. I'm thinking this Sorrel woman must have really ticked off someone. My guess is it was personal, not business."

"That's the same thing Jeannine Simone said the other day."

"Who?"

"Jeannine Simone. She's one of the board members. I ran into her at the dog park when I had to take my mother's dog over there. It's a long story."

Augusta sighed and shook her head. "It always is when it comes to Sun City West. Too many complications over there. If it wasn't for the lousy weather, I'd retire up on some mountain in Idaho with a good supply of ammunition and a decent freezer."

"Seriously?"

"Seriously, but not likely. Besides, I hear Idaho has its fair share of loonies, too."

Chapter 14

Nate and I left the office at a little past five on Wednesday and stopped at In and Out Burger for a quick meal before heading to the Garden of Perpetual Memories. We had agreed on In and Out Burger because it was on our way, and, in Nate's mind, unless a hamburger was involved, it wasn't a meal. It also had a huge parking lot, where I could leave my car and share a ride with Nate. It made more sense than following him all the way to Sun City West. He'd drop me off after the service, and I'd be more than halfway home to Vistancia.

The funeral parlor was a few blocks down on Camino del Sol, a large street that was the unofficial business district for Sun City West. Either Sorrel was extremely popular or something else was going on in the area. Cars were parked everywhere.

"Look," Nate said. "How about if I pull into that medical imaging place and we can park there? It's closed for the day and a hell of a lot closer than parking down the street. My guess is the funeral parlor parking lot is packed."

"Works for me. Oh goodness! Take a look. It's Herb Garrett and Bill Sanders. They're crossing the street and heading toward Sorrel's memorial. My mother said she was going to tell Herb to stay home. This is going to be a nightmare."

"Calm down, kiddo. That place is going to be so crowded no one will notice."

Nate was right about the place being crowded, but I wasn't too sure about the reaction Herb would get from Sorrel's husband or some of the board members. I bit my lower lip and didn't say a word as Nate and I walked across the street. The sun was already setting, casting pink and purple hues in the sky. Something I never saw in Mankato.

The Garden of Perpetual Memories was directly behind the funeral parlor. It was a large, lovely amphitheater that surrounded a giant stone fountain on three sides. The fountain consisted of three brownish spheres ranging in size. They looked like small planets that had escaped from their solar systems. Small boxwood beauty plants and lantanas in shades of yellow and red framed the outer circle. Colored bricks, known as pavers, comprised the floor of the amphitheater. Upon close inspection, I saw the names of deceased carved into the red, tan, and brown bricks. I imagined Sorrel's would be next.

The amphitheater offered nothing more than circular stone seating. Hard, cold, stone seating, with torch lighting surrounding the entire place. The glow from the lights was meant to be soothing, but it gave off an eerie effect. If the service ran longer than an hour, most of the attendees would need chiropractic care.

Nate pulled me aside and whispered, "After we sign the guest book, let's get a seat on the end of one of those circular benches. Preferably toward the back. That way we can get a good bird's-eye view of who's here, and, if we need to move, we can do it easily. Judging from that table behind us, with all those plates and napkins, I'm figuring they'll have some sort of reception after the service. And remind me, in case I get caught up in a conversation with someone, to use my iPhone to snap pictures of the pages from that guest book."

I glanced at the table and then back to the crowd. I immediately recognized Claudia Brinson, who was seated with a few other ladies. Probably the gardening club. I was eyeballing the area for my mother when Nate gave me a nudge.

"Say, isn't that your aunt Ina with the long black veil and that strange gauzy dress?"

"Oh my God. You're right. She looks like she just walked off the set for a gothic horror movie. Let's keep our heads low so she doesn't see us. We'll never be inconspicuous if she joins us."

"Too late. Here she comes."

"Phee! I was looking all over for your mother. Don't tell me that dog of hers made her late again."

"I . . . er . . ."

"Never mind. I see her. She's with Shirley and Lucinda near the refreshment table. I wonder what the funeral parlor will be serving. Usually something dismal and unappetizing. Oh! Hi, Nate! How rude of me. Good to see you again. Are you here on official business? The murder and all?"

Nate took her by the elbow and spoke quietly. "I'm here at Harriet's request. Well, Phee is, anyway."

My aunt tossed one of her long braids behind her neck, gave me a funny look, and took off for the refreshment table, where my mother was now joined by Louise and two of the snowbirds, Riva and Marianne.

"I suppose I should let my mother know I'm here," I said to Nate. "Although, I'm sure my aunt Ina has already informed her."

"Go ahead. I'll save your seat."

The place was beginning to look like a sold-out concert. People were streaming in nonstop. In addition to the board members and the garden club, I imagined friends of Sorrel and Milquist were also here, along with neighbors and possibly distant relatives. Other than the few board members' faces I recognized from the other night, no one looked familiar.

Off to the left, near the largest sphere in the fountain, Herb and Cecilia seemed to be having words. I had to pass that way in order to get to my mother, so it was no wonder I heard everything. I also saw Cecilia point a finger at Herb's chest.

"Harriet said she told you it was best for you to stay home. You're a suspect in Sorrel's murder, you know."

"Don't be ridiculous, Cecilia. The deputies cleared me. I was only speaking my mind at that board meeting. There's no law against that. And, by the way, were you able to convince Eloise Frable to nix that proposal?"

"Not really. She said she'd have to weigh the options."

"Maybe I should find her and have a few words with her."

"That's not such a good idea. She might think you're threatening her. Oh no! Myrna just tromped in. Harriet told her to stay home, too."

I turned my head, and, sure enough, Myrna Mittleson walked in and took a seat next to Constance, who must have arrived while I wasn't looking. One thing for sure, the Booked 4 Murder book club was all in attendance. My mother was finishing up a conversation with Riva when I got to the refreshment table. Louise and Marianne were already at their seats.

"Save me a seat, Riva," my mother said. "I need to have a word with Phee."

I smiled at Riva, gave her a quick wave, and pulled

my mother aside. "This place is beginning to look like a sideshow."

"Tell me about it. Did you see Herb over there? I distinctly told him it would be in his best interest to stay home. And Myrna's here, too."

"I know. I know. Don't worry about it. This place is so crowded, hopefully no one will notice. I had no idea Sorrel was so popular."

"Me either," she said. "Listen, I saw Burton Barre in the fourth row by the middle sphere. Keep an eye on him and catch him when the service is over. Everyone will be heading to the refreshment table. By the way, did you see the memorial photo wall behind the fountain?"

"Um. No. Nate and I signed in and looked for seats."

"Check out that photo wall. It's near the refreshment table. It could hold important clues. Don't dwell on Sorrel's baby pictures and all that nonsense. Look at the ones with other people in them. Maybe one of them is her killer."

I had to admit, my mother was pretty sharp when it came to things like that. It made me feel as if I lagged two steps behind.

"That's a good idea. I'll try to snap some of those photos on my phone. Nate's going to do the same with the sign-in book. So, um, maybe you could talk with Burton Barre. You'd be more convincing."

My mother let out a groan as if I had asked her to heave a giant boulder across a stream. "I suppose I'll have to. Shirley plans to corner Mildred. I hope she gets there before your aunt does. Did you see what Ina's wearing? This is a memorial service, not tryouts for *Wuthering Heights*."

The soft piped music that was playing in the background got louder.

I realized that everyone was seated, with the exception

of my mother and me. "Well, the service is about to start. Talk to you later."

Nate got up from his seat at the end of the row and let me in. "That must be the husband sitting off to the side by the podium. I can't tell who's sitting next to him. Wait a minute. Wait a minute . . ."

He pulled out his phone and did a quick Google search. "Ah-hah. Unbelievable. Look at this picture. It's from the back cover of that book Milquist coauthored."

I bent my head and stared at the screen. Then I stared at the woman seated next to Milquist. "It's Marlene Krone all right. She looks just like her photo with that Dutch Boy haircut and those round black glasses. I'll be darned. That's kind of brazen of her. Don't you think? Why on earth would she have a seat in a spot that's normally reserved for next of kin?"

Nate let out a funny little huff that sounded more like a laugh. "Nothing surprises me anymore."

The music stopped and a tall, white-haired man wearing a gray suit approached the podium. He introduced himself as the nondenominational leader of the Peace in Our Time Church and thanked everyone for their attendance.

He read a lovely eulogy for Sorrel and invited her guests to speak at the podium. The recreation center board president, Harold Stevens, spoke first, and told everyone how committed to the community Sorrel was and how unfortunate it was to lose such a fine lady so soon. He was followed by Mildred Saperstein from the board who pretty much echoed the same thing.

Someone by the name of Betty O'Neil from the garden club said a few words as well, mostly about Sorrel's love of nature and her unwavering generosity.

"I'm ready to nominate her for sainthood, how about you?" Nate whispered.

One by one, others approached the podium and shared their stories about Sorrel. As they spoke, the funeral parlor staff began to bring the refreshments to the table. I could see two large coffee urns and platters that I imagined held assorted cookies. I also saw something else—Jeannine Simone running out of the place as if her life depended on it.

Chapter 15

"Nate! Psst! Nate." I tried to keep my voice low. "Did you see that woman? It's Jeannine Simone. She raced out of here as if she was scared to death. Dear God, I hope Herb or Wayne weren't the ones responsible for triggering her fast exit."

Nate sat up and looked around. "Nah. There's Herb off to the left with a few guys. Is Wayne one of them?"

I peered over my shoulder and stared. Sure enough, Herb and Wayne were seated next to each other, and I could see the top of Kenny's head and Bill's familiar baseball cap.

"I wonder what spooked her. It didn't look as if she was being followed."

"Maybe she got a phone call and had to rush home."

If these were ordinary circumstances, I would have agreed, but something in the pit of my stomach told me otherwise. "When we get out of here, do you mind if we stop by her house? Her address will be in the Sun City West directory. I can pull it up on my phone."

"Sure, if it will make you feel any better."

While I was Googling Jeannine's address, I lost track

of the speakers. However, the message was always the same—Sorrel Harlan's unwavering kindness and compassion. The woman who was currently at the podium relayed some anecdote about Sorrel nursing a baby quail before turning it over to the Fallen Feathers Rescue.

"I don't know about you," Nate said, "but my rear end is numb."

Just then, the leader of the Peace in Our Time Church returned to the podium and invited the audience to line up and offer their condolences to Sorrel's husband, Milquist, before proceeding to the refreshments.

"I didn't realize what a long night this was going to be," I said.

"It may be long. Let's make it productive. See what we can learn from the crowd."

The line serpentined around the place, in and out of the benches, as the attendees gradually made their way to shake Milquist's hand. Nate and I had managed to hightail it toward the front of the line, and that was because we were seated at the end of a row. Behind us, I heard someone sobbing. Not those small discreet sounds people often made at funerals or memorials, but loud throat-garbling sobs. I turned to see who it was.

A small man with brownish-gray hair and stooped shoulders was crying into a large handkerchief. Behind him stood an elegant-looking woman wearing a dark black blazer and white slacks. A monochromatic scarf was draped across her neck. She was sporting diamond studs in her ears and appeared to be annoyed.

"Stop it, will you? You weren't even related to her."

My ears perked up, and I gave Nate a poke as I turned my head in their direction.

"The world has lost such a loving soul, and I'm partially responsible. It's a burden I don't think I can bear."

The woman reached into her bag and pulled out a small tube of lipstick. "Honestly. I doubt any of the other members of the garden club are reacting the way you are."

Garden club. That's what she said. The couple behind us had to be them—Eleanor and Frank Landrow. The woman certainly fit the description Marshall had gotten from the deputy. I was dying to tell Nate, but we were standing so close to Frank and Eleanor I was afraid to open my mouth. Instead, I stared straight ahead and tried to focus on what they were saying.

The woman went on. "If I didn't know you better, I'd swear you were having an affair with her. And why do you blame yourself? You didn't shoot that arrow."

"I knew it wasn't safe for her to walk around that golf course, and yet . . . and yet . . ."

More sobs. Suddenly, Nate was saying how sorry he was, and I realized we had reached the front of the line as Milquist Harlan reached out to shake my hand. I muttered something about how sorry I was for his loss as he introduced me to the lady seated next to him.

"This is Marlene Krone, a dear family friend and the coauthor of one of my books. When she heard the news about Sorrel, she drove straight through from Albuquerque and has been here to help me through this. Too bad she can only stay for a few days."

I extended my hand. "Nice to make your acquaintance."

"Likewise."

Her grip was like a Neanderthal's. Or close to it. I wondered if she had squeezed Nate's hand with as much strength. I wanted to linger a bit to see if I could catch the conversation between the Landrows and Milquist, but Marlene had already turned away from me and was extending her hand to Eleanor. I had no choice but to follow Nate to the refreshments.

"Check out these epicurean delights," he said.

"You *are* joking, right? The little sign says 'ORGANIC OAT AND HONEY CAKES AND GREEN TEA.' Guess Milquist and Sorrel must have shared the same taste in foods."

"The cakes look like bricks. Someone could lose a tooth biting into one of them, and it won't be me. Anyway, I've got to get photos of that guest book before they remove it."

Nate slipped into the crowd as I pondered whether or not to grab an oat cake. Streetman's dog biscuits looked more appetizing. I'd decided to give it a try anyway when someone tapped my shoulder.

"Can you believe this is what they're serving? I nearly choked on one of them. And forget the tea."

It was my aunt Ina. Muttering and grumbling about the food selection. Then, as if a lightbulb went off in her head, she gave my arm a nudge. "Phee, do you know which one is Mildred Saperstein? From the board? Your mother will have my head if I don't find that Mildred woman and talk to her about the vote. Shirley knows which one she is, but I can't find Shirley anywhere in this crowd."

"Why do you need Shirley? I thought you knew Mildred from mahjong."

"Only by name. I can't be expected to—oh! There's Shirley now. Talking with Myrna near those bougainvillea bushes."

And like that, my aunt was off. No "see you later" or "have a nice night." I was watching as she made her way to Shirley and Myrna when I suddenly remembered I needed to check out the memorial photo wall. Fortunately, everyone seemed to be gathering around the refreshment table or talking with each other in small clusters. It was now or never. I took the cell phone from my bag and walked over to the large double poster board that read SORREL HARLAN'S CELEBRATION OF LIFE.

My mother was right. Too many cutesy childhood photos. Thankfully, they were limited to the poster board on my left. Without stopping to scrutinize the right side of the board, I snapped photo after photo and quickly returned the phone to my bag. I had just zipped the bag closed when I had the strangest thought. *What if Milquist Harlan is in danger of being murdered, too?* Hadn't Augusta told me that Milquist's family was exceedingly wealthy and he had no heirs? Now I had a second theory floating around in my head, rivaling the first one I had come up with. The one I refused to tell Marshall or Nate about.

"Phee. You look as if you're lost in space. Everything okay?"

It was Nate. Back from his little reconnaissance mission. I pointed to the poster boards. "Look at the photo wall. I've got them all on my phone."

"Good move, kiddo. Can you email them to the office?"

"As soon as I get back to the car. Listen, I had an unsettling thought. What if Milquist is going to be the next target? Maybe it's been about him all along, and Sorrel's murder was the opening act."

"Look at the top benches. See those two men talking?"

"Uh-huh."

"They're plainclothes deputies. Keeping an eye on Milquist. Your thought crossed their minds as well. Marshall or I should have mentioned the sheriff's department surveillance to you. We've both been way too busy."

"Um, speaking of Marshall . . . and I really should've

had this conversation with you a long time ago, but are you all right with the two of us dating?"

"In general, or as your employer?"

My face got warm.

"Relax, kiddo. I'm joking. Marshall spoke to me months ago. Many months ago, to be precise. Had I known you were both interested in each other, I would've encouraged him to ask you out back in Mankato. You're both professionals. Who knows? The two of you could become the next Nick and Nora Charles or Johnathan and Jennifer Hart, although they were amateur detectives, come to think of it."

"You're as bad as my mother. I'm not a detective."

"Not officially. Look, we'd better get going if you want to check on Jeannine Simone."

"Give me a split second. I probably should let my mother know I'm leaving."

"Okay. I'll be waiting by the archway and taking in the crowd."

My mother wasn't too difficult to spot. She was standing by one of the tea urns, holding a small cup. Cecilia and Louise were doing the same. It looked as if all three of them were deciding whether or not to drink the stuff.

"Hi, Mom. I'm on my way home. I'll talk to you later. You can tell me how it went with Burton Barre."

"I'll tell you right now. He gave me the party line. 'Thank you for your input. I'll take it under advisement.' Harold Stevens told Kevin and Kenny the same thing. I swear those board members probably rehearse that line in their sleep."

"Don't get too discouraged. All it takes is one 'no' vote from any of those four members, and the proposal will be shot down."

"Shh! Don't say 'shot down' out loud. You don't know who could be listening. Did you check out the memorial wall?"

"Sure did. Snapped some photos on my iPhone, too."

"Good, good. We can discuss them later."

"There's nothing to discuss. Nate and Marshall will review them. Look, Nate's waiting for me. I've got to run."

"Tell him to look at the photo in front of the Heard Museum. You can thank me later."

It took Nate and me less than ten minutes to drive to Jeannine's house. It was located catty-corner from the Echo Mesa golf course and distinguished by the cluster of date palms that surrounded an elegant fountain. It appeared as if the lights were on in the front room.

"Might as well ring the bell," I said. "She knows me, and I'll introduce you."

Jeannine came to the door within seconds and looked absolutely fine. I felt like an idiot.

I brushed some loose hairs from my forehead and swallowed. "Um, hi! I know this is really odd, but when I saw you rush out of Sorrel's memorial service, I thought something was terribly wrong. I knew it couldn't be those two pinochle-playing friends of my mother's, because they were still sitting in the service. So, I decided to stop by and check on you."

Jeannine gave me a smile and turned to face Nate.

"Oh, I'm sorry, how rude of me," I said. "This is my boss, Nate Williams, from Williams Investigations. He attended the service as well."

Nate and Jeannine shook hands while I tried to get a glimpse of her living room through the partially opened door. No upturned furniture. No signs of distress. I wanted to tell her how sorry I was for bothering her, but she spoke first.

"That was so caring and thoughtful of you. Really. But everything's fine. I got one of those home alerts on my phone, and that's why I rushed back here. The app notifies me if there's a break-in or, God forbid, a fire. In this case, it was a 'glass break' message."

"A what?"

"I have glass breakers installed on the windows. If someone or something breaks the glass, it sounds an alarm. Unfortunately, the darn thing is so sensitive, that half the time when the train goes by or when the fighter jets from Luke Air Force Base make a lot of noise, it signals an alert. I asked the company to adjust the alarm. Anyway, there was no break-in. No nothing. A posse volunteer was already at the house when I pulled in, and we checked everything. Again, I'm really sorry you had to waste your time."

"It's no bother." I was still trying to peer into her living room. "I guess everyone's a tad nervous, given what happened to Sorrel."

Nate took me by the elbow, signaling we should get a move on. He smiled at Jeannine as she thanked us again and closed the door.

"Guess that was a big waste," I said.

"Not exactly. Did you happen to see what she had hanging on her walls?"

"My eyes couldn't get past the weird shag carpeting. Who has shag carpeting anymore?"

"Someone who likes to combine style with texture, I suppose. And what about those framed Indian artifacts of hers? Looked like they were competing for wall space. Oops. Wrong choice of words. Framed Native American artifacts. Arrowheads and beadwork. Hmm, Marlene Krone and Milquist Harlan aren't the only ones interested in indigenous cultures."

"Lots of people collect southwestern art."

"True. True. But not many keep three-foot archery bows in glass display cases, like the one she had off to the left behind the two accent chairs."

"You don't think—"

"Not yet, anyway."

Chapter 16

"I can't imagine what possible motive Jeannine Simone would have for killing Sorrel," I said to Marshall when he got to the office the next day. "But there it was. Right in her living room. A giant bow. Nate saw it clear as could be. I mean, how many people display bows and arrows? Unless she was some sort of aficionado."

"Whoa. Talk about going from zero to a hundred in thirty seconds. Slow down, Phee, and go back to the beginning. Motive. Hers was the same as everyone else's—objection to converting the golf courses. And we don't even know if she can shoot a bow and arrow. As far as the authorities are concerned, there's nothing out of the ordinary to link her with the Harlans."

"So you checked? Or Nate did. You *did* think something might've been going on."

"If an investigation is going to be thorough, every nuance needs to be explored, that's all. Which still brings us to our current status of coming up short. And that bow, by the way, was some sort of ceremonial one. I doubt it could've sent an arrow very far. Oh well, maybe we'll have better leads once we're done studying those photos you snapped last night. I'm about to pull them up on email, as soon as I get into my office. Nate should be along any minute. He'll be busy going through that guest list," Marshall said.

"Take a good look at the photo with the Heard Museum in the background."

"Okay. Why?"

"It was something my mother said, that's all."

"Heard Museum. Got it." Marshall gave me a wink and walked into his office.

Augusta was fast at work at her desk, and I figured I shouldn't be standing around doing nothing when I had a zillion things waiting for me in my office. I was itching to get a good look at those photos and would have done as much last night if I wasn't so exhausted when I got home. Wanting to free up storage space on my iPhone, I copied the memorial wall pics to the office computer on my desk.

The curiosity was killing me. I looked at the time. Nine twenty-three.

Five minutes to peruse these babies isn't going to make a difference.

I pulled up the first photo and took a good look. Sorrel and a few girlfriends in front of a university library. On to the next. Sorrel in the middle of a huge demonstration. Her sign read, TREES AGAINST THE MALL. Judging from the color of her hair and the clothing, the protest was probably during the time she was at college. Two more pictures. Sorrel hiking up a trail who knows where, and Sorrel sitting on some rocks in the middle of a stream. Her hairdo hadn't changed in decades. I did pull up a few photos of her and her husband, mostly outdoorsy ones. The only formal-looking picture appeared to be taken of the two of them at their wedding.

Nine thirty-four. I had to get to work.

I was about to close the program when I decided to

skim through the rest of the photos in order to find the one with the Heard Museum. The Heard Museum, known for its vast collection of southwestern art, was located off of Central Avenue in Phoenix and looked like a gleaming-white, modern-day, Spanish Colonial building with wrought iron gates framing its three front archways. The photo was easy to spot, and, within seconds, I knew why my mother had insisted Nate and Marshall take a look.

Nine-forty. I really had to get to work.

Wasting no time, I pulled up my accounting spread-sheets and tried to get my mind off of Sorrel. Reconciling accounts was one of those rote tasks that gave me a sense of accomplishment, unlike trying to solve a murder case. I must have been at the computer for at least an hour when Augusta rapped on my doorframe.

"There's a hysterical woman on the line for you, and it's not your mother. This lady's convinced there was an attempt on her life."

"Shouldn't she be talking to Nate or Marshall? Or the police?"

"She gave me her name twice, but, with all the crying and gasping, I couldn't figure it out. Anyway, she said you'd understand."

"Thanks, Augusta."

I knew it had to be one of my mother's friends. The description fit all of them. I picked up the phone. "Hello. This is Phee." I waited for a response.

What I got was endless choking and gasping sounds.

"Are you all right?" I asked. "Do you need me to call for emergency assistance?"

"It's a miracle they didn't kill me! I thought I had taken my last breath back there. Ran me off the road. That's what they did. I'm sure someone from the bocce league put them up to this."

Last breath. Bocce league. Woman's voice. I put two and two together.

"Myrna? Is that you?"

"Yes. It was awful, Phee. I was on my way to the bocce court for practice when, out of the blue, this beige blur of a car careened into my golf cart. Next thing I knew, the cart jumped the median and landed in a clump of bushes. Right on RH Johnson Boulevard before you get to Trail Ridge Drive. I'll be traumatized for life. Of all days to take my golf cart instead of the car. I thought I'd save money on gas. Now that golf cart is mangled to the point of no return. And I'm not much better off."

"Um, where are you calling from? The hospital?"

"No, I'm home. The EMTs checked me over after the accident and all I have are some scratches. The golf cart got towed to one of those repair shops on Camino del Sol, and I got taken home by a posse volunteer. Anyway, can you find out which person in that bocce league did this?"

"What makes you think it was someone from the league? Chances are it was one of those crazy speeders that people are always complaining about. Especially on RH Johnson. It's become a shortcut to get to Route 60."

"It was no accident. Ever since Sorrel's body was found near those bocce balls I accidentally lofted, everything's been going downhill. Half the time I can barely throw the ball. I know our league's been talking behind my back. It's not only Bill who doesn't want me in the tournament."

"Okay, that being said, I still don't think anyone would resort to causing the kind of accident that could have resulted in a serious injury or even death."

"Huh? Death? I'll never be able to have a moment's peace until I know for sure."

"I'm not promising anything, but I'll ask my boss to see if he can get a copy of the sheriff's report. Were you able to give them any information other than the color of the car?"

"A beige blur. That's all I saw. I couldn't tell you if it was a van, an SUV, or one of those mini things that are all the rage. Anyway, I missed today's practice. I already called Cecilia to let her know. She was going to watch me today, like we decided at Bagels 'N More. Tomorrow's your mother's turn."

Wonderful. It better not turn into mine.

"Try to take it easy and relax. Like I said, I'm sure it had nothing to do with the bocce league."

"But you will look into it, won't you? I can't afford to hire your company, but I figure maybe you could put your ear to the ground, so to speak, and see what you dig up."

I didn't have the heart to come right out and say no, so instead, I left it with some sort of noncommittal "we'll see where it goes." I stood, stretched, and walked into the front office for a cup of coffee.

"Another murder in Sun City West?" Augusta asked.

"Nah. The hysterical voice should have been a dead giveaway, though. It was a friend of my mother's. The woman got run off the road. She was in a golf cart. Luckily, she's all right."

"Why did she call you?"

"She thinks someone from her bocce league did it on purpose. Long story."

Augusta chuckled. "It always is."

By midafternoon, Nate and Marshall had reviewed all of the names on the guest list and made some discreet inquiries. Still nothing definitive. I was totally immersed in my own work and had completely blocked out those photos until Marshall brought up the subject just as we were closing at the end of the day.

"So, what's your take on that photo in front of the Heard Museum? I know you looked at it. According to the poster that appears off to the side of the photo, the picture was snapped last year."

"How do you know I looked at it? Oh, never mind. I'm wagering it was the garden club, but if you ask me, there was something going on between Sorrel and Frank."

"Huh? How'd you get that?"

"Probably the same way my mother did. Take a close look at the woman seated to Sorrel's right. If looks could kill, Sorrel's body would have been found on the museum grounds and not a year later on the Hillcrest Golf Course."

"I'll definitely need to take another look, but it's getting late and I'm starving. Want to grab a bite to eat and come back here to study that photo again?"

"Absolutely."

"I thought you'd say that. This sleuthing is getting under your skin, isn't it?"

That, or the guy I'm sleuthing with . . .

Marshall had all he could do to hide the sheepish grin on his face. "Anyway, Nate left early in order to track down some of those guests and have a few words with them. Maybe we can make some headway with the photos."

"Um, about making headway, there's something else going on. Myrna Mittleson called me this morning. Her golf cart was run off the road."

Like a daytime drama, I unfolded all of the details, which weren't many. From the beige blur to Myrna's conviction that someone in the bocce league was out to get her, words spewed out of my mouth nonstop.

Marshall looked like he didn't know what to think. "A beige blur, huh? And she expects you to figure out who did this?"

I shrugged.

"We'll put it on the list. Come on. I'm beyond starving now."

We settled for a quick meal at the deli around the corner and returned to Williams Investigations before seven. Marshall ushered me into his office and pulled up another chair so both of us would have access to his computer screen. It took all of three seconds for the image to appear.

"I never shut the computer off. Somehow I figured I'd be coming back here." He leaned into the screen. "Okay, I'm looking at the woman on Sorrel's right, and, yeah, she's got daggers in her eyes all right. Yikes."

"Take another look. Do you recognize her?"

"Vaguely."

"It's Bethany Gillmore. She's one of the recreation center board members. The only reason I know is because I remember Shirley commenting about the outfit Bethany was wearing that first night when Sorrel presented the proposal. She had said something about Bethany needing to tone down the purple a bit."

"For or against the proposal?"

"Against. Now possibly with another motive for murder. It's funny, but Claudia Brinson, the woman I met from a dog park acquaintance, never mentioned Bethany being in the garden club. I think I'll give her a call and see what else she knows. Um, er, that is if you don't mind. After all, it's really your investigation."

Marshall stifled a laugh. "Maybe on paper, but we both know otherwise. Sure. Go ahead. I'm up to my neck checking other leads, not to mention the clients whose cases don't involve Sun City West. Oh, and, before I forget, I'll place a call to one of the deputies and see what I can learn about Myrna's accident."

"I know she'll appreciate it. I know *I* do. Last thing anyone needs is for her to go crazy with this and alienate her entire bocce team. Plus, my mother will get stuck in the middle since she's friends with Bill and some of the other players. What a mess. I'm not even involved with that tournament, and I can't wait until it's over."

"When is that thing, anyway?"

"This coming Wednesday at five. Not the game itself, but the pregame ceremony and introduction of players. They hold a procession that runs from the bocce courts past the dog park and ends in front of the lawn bowling area, where the players will be introduced. The rec center sets up chairs all around the walkway. The actual games begin the next day. It's quite a big deal, according to Myrna."

"I'm not so sure she'll be playing."

"What do you mean?"

"Usually, after an accident, even a minor one, the pain sets in. I'm imaging Myrna's going to feel a heck of a lot worse tomorrow."

"I guarantee it won't stop her. She's hell-bent for leather she's going to participate. In fact, my mother is supposed to watch her practice tomorrow morning."

"That should be a doozy. Speaking of morning, if we don't get going, we'll be sitting right here at dawn."

"Great! It'll give Augusta something to talk about."

Chapter 17

My mother couldn't wait to give me the rundown on Myrna's bocce practice, starting with the fact that the two of them arrived at the courts at the ungodly hour of eight. That gave Myrna a full hour to loft balls before her team arrived. It also gave them something else—a new suspect in Sorrel's murder.

"Would you listen to me, Phee?" my mother said. "I'm serious. He could be our killer."

The "he" she referred to was the golf course manager for Golfscapes, the company that provided all of the maintenance. I gleaned that tidbit during the lunchtime phone call I shouldn't have taken. Between bites of my ham and cheese sandwich, I listened to my mother's accounting of what she and Myrna had seen.

"So, there he was. Whatever his name is. The same man who gave that insipid report at the board meeting. Looked to be in his thirties or maybe forties. Hard to tell with that stubble on his face. Personally, I blame Brad Pitt for that. Ever since he decided to forgo shaving for a few days, every man between eighteen and eighty decided it was stylish. Anyway, this guy was driving around the perimeter of the course and got out of his golf cart to take a closer look at the fence that separates the course from the bocce courts."

"Really? The man got out to look at the fence, and you think that incriminates him? He's in charge of the maintenance."

"Myrna and I thought maybe he was making sure there were no other clues."

"Forget it, Mom. You're going off the deep end with this one. Tell me, have Myrna's ball tosses improved?"

What followed was something between a groan and a sigh. "Maybe a bit. It doesn't matter. She's gotten so rattled about the tournament and getting run off the road she all but took Bill's head off when he got there. Did I tell you Myrna made a list of her league members and stood in the parking lot to see if any of their cars were beige?"

"Um, no."

"Well, she did. And Bill's was the only beige car. A Chevy." I took another bite of my sandwich.

"Myrna raced over to him and started yelling, 'You're the one with the beige car. The beige car. It was you!' And then Bill said, 'What are you yammering about, you crazy woman? What's the matter with a beige car?' And then Myrna said—"

"Mom! I've got work to do. I don't need to hear the entire conversation."

"Fine. Here's the long and short of it. It wasn't Bill who ran her off the road. Turned out he had a dentist's appointment and hadn't gone to the bocce practice. He even made Myrna stand there and wait while he called the dentist's office and had the receptionist speak directly with her."

"Oh brother. At least that tournament will be over in a few days."

"Yes. And you should take advantage of it."

"Huh?"

"All the board members and bigwigs will be there. You never know what you might overhear. Someone knows something about Sorrel's murder. Besides, what else are you doing on a Wednesday evening?"

"Anything but that."

"Think about it, Phee. I'm serious."

I finished the last bite of my sandwich and washed it down with bottled water as the phone call ended. Much as I hated to admit it, my mother did have a point. Those community events pulled in big crowds and people tended to talk.

The rest of the afternoon seemed to speed by. I was so engrossed in my accounting that I didn't even hear Marshall by the door, calling my name.

"Phee. Thought you'd be interested in what I discovered about those cases going to the jury. It took me longer than I expected to find out, but your mother's friend Louise might have opened up the case for us."

"Really? Wow! Tell me."

Marshall plopped himself in the chair next to mine, leaned his elbows on my desk and rested his face in his fists. "Three cases are going to juries. The first one has been making headline news for weeks. The Darla Marlinde case. I half expect that to turn into some blockbuster Hollywood movie, but I seriously doubt Sorrel was a witness. Next is the case I'm sure your mother's friend will have to sit through. It's a fraudulent check scheme allegedly perpetrated by the owners of a small grocery store in South Phoenix. Again, not likely for Sorrel to witness anything there. That leaves the third case. And here's where it gets interesting."

I brushed the hair from my face and didn't say a word.

"This one is right up Sorrel's alley, although I don't

know exactly what she could have witnessed. It's an environmental case that involves the deliberate pollution of the Agua Fria River that feeds into Lake Pleasant. A pesticide company is being accused of dumping raw material into the river. That's something Sorrel could very well have witnessed, given the fact she was such a nature lover. Maybe she was out hiking and saw something."

"This pollution case . . . would it have meant a tremendous loss of money for the pesticide company?"

"To put it mildly, yes. Money and jail time. You name it. And we're not talking some little mom and pop operation. This pesticide company is part of a giant corporation. That means stockholders and everything that goes with it."

"With Sorrel out of the way, the prosecutor might not have had a case."

"Yep. I'd say that was a hell of a good motive for knocking her off."

"So now what? What do you do next?" I asked.

"Start researching that company for its local employees and see if any of them are particularly skilled in archery. Of course, that doesn't rule out the other strong motive coming from the homeowners. One of the things I've learned in this business is people can be pretty loose lipped when it comes to divulging information. That's why opportunities like Sorrel's memorial service can be really telling."

"About those opportunities . . . there's one next Wednesday."

Marshall's eyes crinkled when I mentioned the tournament parade. "Okay, what do you say we mark our calendars for snooping and dinner? Meanwhile, Nate and I have a few days to track down the other leads."

"My mother will be ecstatic. I just hope she doesn't decide to bring the dog. She's gotten it into her head that

Streetman would be more socialized if he was taken to some of these events."

"And?"

"Last I knew, he peed on three people at a patio pancake-breakfast fund-raiser."

"Remind me to steer clear of him, will you?"

Marshall went back to his office, and I was about to pick up where I left off with my accounting, when I remembered what I had forgotten to do yesterday.

My God. I'm getting as bad as the book club ladies.

I'd completely forgotten to call Claudia Brinson and ask her about Bethany Gillmore and the garden club. That photo of Bethany in front of the Heard Museum was disturbing, to say the least. Was she angry at Sorrel? At Frank? I figured Claudia might have an answer, so I dialed her number right away.

"Goodness, Phee," she said. "I don't know why I didn't mention Bethany to you the other day. She's no longer in the garden club. Resigned shortly after our trip to the Heard Museum. I had the feeling something happened on that excursion but could never find out what. Sorry I can't be more help."

"That's okay." I tried not to hide the disappointment in my voice.

"The last time we talked you asked if I thought anyone had it in for Sorrel, and I said no. I mean, up until that day at the Heard Museum, no one gave any indication of anything like that. And I figured if something did happen at the museum, it couldn't've been too godawful or I would've heard about it. There's no such thing as keeping a secret around here. Still, something was off, if you know what I mean."

"I think so."

"Again, sorry I'm not much help."

"You've been more than helpful. If you think of anything else, please call me. You've got my home number and the office."

"Sure thing."

I thanked her again and switched screens to pull up that picture. Something *was* off, and it was driving me nuts. It was as if I had the answer to Sorrel's murder staring me right in the face, but I couldn't see it. Like one of those old "Magic Eye" pictures, I felt as if I was dealing with an illusion and not the real thing.

Chapter 18

With no new evidence and dead-end leads, the investigation moved slowly over the next several days. *Thoroughly,* according to Nate and Marshall, but slowly. By milling about the tournament parade, I was hoping Marshall and I could pick up information that would move the investigation forward. What we picked up instead muddied everything.

Marshall and I took our separate cars and left work early in order to get to the parade before five. I worked through my lunch hour to make up the time, even though Nate said it wasn't necessary. In spite of the snowbird traffic, we made it to Sun City West with fifteen minutes to spare.

The parking lot that linked the recreation center buildings with the dog park, the lawn bowling area, and the bocce courts was packed, forcing us to park across the street in one of the empty church parking lots. As we walked to the bocce courts, we immediately spotted Shirley and Lucinda, who were headed our way.

"Better speed up our pace," I said to Marshall, "before one of those two keels over."

A few seconds later, the ladies had caught up. Shirley grabbed me by the arm and pointed to the left side of the dog park near a small greenbelt. "I think that's your mother over there, isn't it? Thank the good Lord she left the dog at home. Said something about the event being too stressful for him, but if you ask me, she didn't want to risk another leg-lifting episode. We should've agreed to meet in a designated area. Lordy, this is absolute chaos. Who would think watching people throw balls at pins or at other balls would be so popular? Oh look! The lawn bowling leagues are lining up."

To the far right, a few yards from the bocce courts, a sea of white engulfed the entire sidewalk. White shirts, white slacks, white shoes. Green, red, yellow, and blue sashes tied around the waists indicated the leagues. At least I figured as much. There had to be at least fifty players. Behind them, another lineup was taking place. This was less coordinated, and the players were sporting polo shirts and assorted slacks in various lengths, ranging from capris and pedal pushers to full length. It was easy to spot Myrna, given her height, coupled with that upswept hairdo of hers and those bejeweled glasses she always wore. I craned my neck to see if I could find Bill, but it was impossible.

"We'd better make our way over to my mother, or we'll never hear the end of it," I said to Shirley.

"You go ahead, honey. Lucinda and I want to wish Myrna luck."

Then, without another word, she and Lucinda elbowed their way toward Myrna.

"Unbelievable," Marshall muttered.

"Huh?"

"These friends of your mother's. They don't stop at anything, do they? Come on. I see an open space. Let's make a run for it."

My mother had managed to secure a prime location, not only to watch the procession but to sneak through the dog park and exit on the other side, close to the board's seating area for the presentation.

"You didn't miss anything," she said when Marshall and I stood next to her. "They're just starting the parade."

If there was such a thing as organized confusion, this would have been it. The small groups and clumps of players were suddenly in two straight lines, walking steadily ahead as the spectators cheered and applauded. Occasionally someone yelled out something to one of the players, and he or she responded with:

"Don't forget we're having brisket tonight at Tootie's house," or

"I thought that was next week," or

"I remembered your clean socks, Dennis," or

"I can't stop now!"

Marshall leaned over to me and whispered, "If this is what I have to look forward to in the next twenty-five years, I'm moving off the grid."

When the lineup was down to the last half dozen people, my mother, Cecilia, Riva, and Constance made a beeline across the dog park, where the other book club ladies were waiting. Marshall and I raced to keep up as the women crowded onto a few small benches that Herb Garrett was apparently guarding.

"You owe me big time, Harriet," Herb shouted. "I had all I could do to fend people off! Why didn't you come here in the first place, like we talked about?"

"Because Myrna needed to know we were here, cheering her on. I didn't want her to wait until she got into the presentation area."

I'd never seen anyone roll their eyes and their head at the same time, but Herb did.

"Never mind. It's about to start. That blowhard, Harold Stevens, is taking the microphone."

The lawn bowling and bocce league players formed three semicircles around the podium as Harold Stevens welcomed the leagues and the audience to the grand tournament. Beginning with the lawn bowling, he introduced each league's team captain, who, in turn, introduced their players. Thankfully, the players only waved a hand in the air to acknowledge the recognition. Applause followed.

"At least they're not having everyone speak," I whispered to Marshall.

"My God, if they did, we'd be here for the next millennium."

When the lawn bowling introductions were completed, the bocce ones began. Four or five board members sat dutifully in their chairs. A few of them tried to stifle yawns as the endless list of names was read.

Louise gave me a poke in the arm and gestured to the parking lot. "I guess Myrna got her golf cart back. Surprised they could fix it so soon."

"Huh? What?"

My mother's hearing rivaled most species of bats, and she quickly responded. "What are you pointing at, Louise? That's not Myrna's golf cart. They won't have hers fixed for weeks."

"Well, it sure looks like hers. How many red and white striped carts are there in Sun City West? I thought she had the only one that looks as if Ringling Brothers designed it."

Marshall looked across the parking lot to where Louise was pointing and told me he'd be right back. Before I could respond, he took off, leaving me stuck listening to the mind-numbing roll call. Then Myrna's name was read out loud, and, without warning, the woman standing next to me let out a deafening shriek that would rival a varsity cheerleader. Apparently, Myrna had at least one fan.

"Where'd Marshall go?" Louise asked when the next name was read.

"Um, he had to check on something. He'll be right back."

Wrong choice of words. Given Sorrel's bizarre murder, coupled with the tendency for my mother's friends to over-react, what followed didn't surprise me.

"Check on what?" Lucinda shouted. "Does he think the murderer is here?"

Cecilia must've heard the word "murderer" and filled in the rest. "The murderer is here! Where? Where is he, Phee?"

"He's not here. I mean, there's no murderer here." I tried to shout, but no one heard me because they were louder. Louder and hysterical.

Shirley kept yelling "Lordy, Lordy" while Lucinda kept telling everyone to "keep their heads low."

Herb, who had left the bench area in order to join his cronies nearer to the podium, returned along with Kevin and Wayne. "What are all of you yammering about? We won't be able to hear them introduce Bill, and that's the only reason we came here."

"Sorrel's killer is running around loose," one of the women shouted.

"No!" I yelled. This time really loud. "No killer. No nothing. Everything's fine."

Herb shook his head, made a grunting sound, and walked back to the other benches, followed by his buddies.

My mother, who was in the middle of a conversation with Louise, stopped midsentence. "Look what you started, Phee."

"What? Huh?"

All eyes were on me as if I, somehow, orchestrated the fracas, when, in fact, I did everything to quell it. "I, er, um—"

"Oh, never mind. Here's Marshall now. We can ask him ourselves." My mother didn't wait for a response from anyone. She immediately charged him like a defensive tackle. "Is there anything going on we should be worried about? Out with it!"

"The only thing I'd worry about is if this presentation goes on much longer," Marshall said.

A few "hmmphs" followed as the ladies turned back toward the podium. Marshall tapped me on the arm and motioned for me to step away from the crowd. We wedged ourselves into a small alcove in the stucco wall that separated the lawn bowling from the dog park.

"What's going on? Where'd you go?"

"To check out that red and white golf cart. I thought if what Louise said was true, then Myrna's golf cart might have been mistaken for that other one. I had a feeling the accident was intentional, but she wasn't the intended victim."

"And?"

"And I was right. Our buddy Deputy Bowman ran the plates for me. That red and white golf cart is registered to Milquist Harlan."

"My God! His body's going to turn up somewhere if we don't do something."

"The sheriff's department is already on it. They've notified the deputies who are patrolling this event, and they're sending someone to the house in case anyone is home."

"There is no 'anyone.' It was just Sorrel and him. And if the golf cart's here, so is he. Unless that Marlene Krone is still staying with him. I doubt he left her at the house alone but who knows? I hate to think my mother might be right with those far-fetched theories of hers, but, in this case, she might be right. That Marlene seemed a little too close for comfort, if you ask me."

"Listen, they're still droning on and on with the list of participants. What do you say we make our way around the perimeter to see if we can find Milquist?"

"I'm game. Anything's better than this."

We kept our backs to the stucco wall and scanned the crowd. No sign of a dowdy, middle-aged man with a young gold digger at his side.

"Why do you suppose Milquist would be at this event anyway?" I asked. "I mean, it doesn't really sound like something he'd be interested in."

"It's not something we're interested in and look at us. He must have a reason. That golf cart is only a few yards from here. It's not as if he intended to use the swimming pool or the billiards. Those buildings are too far off."

"Yeah, I suppose you're right. And he doesn't own a dog, as far as I know, so that leaves the dog park out of it."

We skirted around the crowd, first on the right-hand side and then backtracking to the left. There was no way we could get close enough to the podium to look directly at the participants and fans.

"I recognize a lot of people here," I said, "but no Milquist."

Marshall took me by the elbow and ushered me toward the sidewalk. "I've got a better idea. We should've done this to begin with. Let's wait by his golf cart. This presentation is bound to be over soon, and he'll need his ride home."

I barely heard the word "home" because a thunderous applause came out of nowhere, and, the next thing I knew, we were tousled and jostled as the crowd started to disperse.

Marshall let go of my elbow and grasped my hand. "Geez, talk about timing. How fast can you move?"

"Fast enough."

Is this what Lot's wife felt like when she was fleeing

Sodom and Gomorrah? I figured as long as I didn't turn back, I would be okay.

"Drat!" Marshall shouted. "Someone's already in the golf cart."

We stood there, our mouths wide open, as we watched the golf cart cut diagonally through the parking lot and out to the main road.

"So much for that," I said. "Now what?"

"Now we walk to the church parking lot and grab my car. I've got Milquist's address programmed into the GPS. Let's see if he makes it back there."

"In one piece?"

"At all."

Chapter 19

"What if it's not Milquist driving that golf cart?" I asked as we pulled out of the parking lot and headed east on Meeker Boulevard.

Marshall chuckled. "We'll find out soon enough."

The Harlans' house was situated in the middle of a cul-de-sac off Deer Valley Road, the newest phase of the development. And not only that, but they lived in one of the ritziest sections, known for spacious yards, boulder and waterfall features, and houses that boasted stone veneers. I couldn't take my eyes off the place. "Guess the family timber industry left them well off, huh?"

"Yep. I suppose. The house even has a separate golf cart garage. If Milquist did drive directly back here, he must've arrived only a few minutes before us. I'll knock on the door and see. No sense both of us getting out of the car."

Marshall walked to the front door. Sure enough, Milquist was home, and Marshall waved for me to join him. Oddly enough, Sorrel's husband didn't seem too surprised to see us.

"The sheriff's department left a note on my door asking

me to call them. I was about to do that when you rang the bell," he said. "Does your visit have something to do with their note?"

As soon as Marshall said yes, Milquist invited us in, but not farther than the foyer. Marshall explained the entire incident with Myrna's golf cart and seemed to study Milquist's face for a reaction. If he had one, it had to be as subtle as hell.

"So, you understand," Marshall went on, "that the sheriff's department and my office are concerned that whoever killed your wife might have you in their sights as well. I'm sure the sheriff's department will explain further when you call them."

Milquist proceeded to chew off a piece of fingernail all the while staring at Marshall. "I don't know what else they can explain, unless they plan to provide me with security. Are they going to do that?"

"Unfortunately, I rather doubt it. I know they had deputies at your wife's memorial service, but that was a one-time thing. Have you received any verbal or written threats? Anything at all that made you feel as if you were a target?"

"No. Nothing of the sort."

Marshall took a quick breath while I tried to be discreet about glancing into the rest of Milquist's house. The foyer opened up into a sitting area, but nothing seemed out of place, and there was no sign of Marlene Krone. Maybe she had already driven back to Albuquerque.

"Mr. Harlan," I said, "was there a particular reason you went to the lawn bowling and bocce tournament parade today?"

The man looked as if I'd asked him to divulge national security information. "Er, well, it was on Sorrel's calendar since she was a member of the board, and, well, I don't know, I guess I figured maybe I'd run into someone who might have information about her death. Stupid thing. I know."

"Actually, it might've been a dangerous thing," Marshall said. "Crowds and all. Listen, if I were you, I wouldn't be driving in that red and white golf cart. It's too obvious if someone does indeed have you in their sights. Use your car. Besides, in case of an accident, cars are safer. Those golf carts can be demolished in a second. Myrna was lucky she only suffered a few scratches."

Milquist looked down as if he was the culpable one. "I'm sorry that lady got injured. Especially if I was the intended victim. And, for the life of me, I can't imagine why. It's not like Sorrel or I had any enemies. Grant you, my wife did have her moments and her causes, but to murder her over something like that? And why come after me? I don't have anything anyone would want."

I was beginning to feel uncomfortable and didn't know what to say. Thankfully I didn't have to.

"We're working hard to find those answers for you, Mr. Harlan," Marshall said. "Meantime, keep your doors locked and stay out of crowds. Give the sheriff's office a call, will you?"

Milquist nodded and closed the door behind us.

I waited until Marshall and I were a few feet from the car before I said anything. "I think he's hiding something, but what, I don't know. An affair with that woman? Marlene? Too obvious, don't you think?"

"I'll tell you what I do think. My mind will be sharper and clearer once I've had something to eat. What'll it be? Pizza? Burgers? Mexican?"

"Honestly, Marshall, I could do all three."

"What do you say we take both cars and grab a pizza in Surprise? That should be a safe enough spot away from—"

"My mother and her friends?"

"I was about to say 'the tournament crowd.'"

"I think we'll be safe. Curley's will pack in all the men, and Bagels 'N More and the Homey Hut will get the women. As far as the gossip goes, it'll be a tie."

"Much as I hate to admit it, that gossip keeps bringing us closer to the clues we need to solve this darn thing. If Louise hadn't thought the golf cart was Myrna's, I never would've noticed it in that crowded parking lot. Milquist may be our key player after all."

"Meaning?"

"Nate and I will have to keep tabs on the guy. And if he is a target . . . oh geez, I probably should go back in there and warn him about suspicious beige vehicles. I'll only be a second. You might as well wait for me in the car."

I made myself comfortable and took out my cell phone to see if I had gotten any calls. To prevent me from getting distracted while driving, I kept it on mute. Sure enough, there was one voice mail. My mother.

"Where'd you disappear to? Thought you and Marshall might join us at Bagels 'N More. Maybe another time. Myrna's team plays at eleven tomorrow. Too bad you're working. Call me later."

Whew. I was off the hook for now. I slipped the phone back into my bag as Marshall got in the car.

"I think I made Milquist even jumpier. He wouldn't let me inside this time and kept glancing at his watch. I asked if everything was all right, and he said 'yes.' Look, I know I'm starving, but ten more minutes isn't going to make a difference. Let's drive around for a while and swing back here. I'll bet anything we'll find a car parked in front of his house."

"Marlene's?"

"That would be too easy. So, shall we take the scenic route?"

Marshall drove past Palm Ridge Recreation Center and the ponds that housed Sun City West's waterfowl. We paused for a few minutes to watch them and then returned to Milquist's cul-de-sac.

"My God, you were right. Whose Mercedes is that?"

"We'll know soon enough. At least it's not beige. I'll snap a quick photo of the license plate and hope Bowman is still in a good mood."

I didn't say a word as Marshall took the picture and drove out of the cul-de-sac, pulling over farther down the street to make the call. I held my breath while he waited for Deputy Bowman's answer.

"Edmund Wooster."

"Edmund Wooster? The guy Sorrel replaced on the board? The one who left for personal reasons?"

"That's his car, according to Bowman."

"Wow. I wonder what on earth he would want to see Milquist about?"

"It could be as innocuous as dropping by to offer condolences. Or . . ."

"Or?"

"I genuinely don't know. Let me put it this way—Edmund Wooster is now on my radar screen. Come on. Let's get that pizza before something else turns up. I'll get you back to your car, and we'll go from there."

Nothing turned up between the time we ate our pizza and the next morning. Unless I counted the annoying, late-night phone call from my mother.

"Phee, I thought you were going to call me. Don't you ever check that cell phone of yours? I even left a message on your landline."

"Um, sorry about that. I forgot to check them."

"Why did you and Marshall rush off? Was he on to something?"

I knew the rumor mill would go crazy if I told her Milquist had the same golf cart as Myrna, so I glossed it over. "No, nothing like that. The usual stuff investigators do in those situations."

"I suppose you want to know why I called. I figured you would've forgotten about Herb's next powwow. It's tomorrow night at seven. Same place. At least I spoke to Burton Barre about the proposal. Like I told you before, I didn't get anywhere, but I spoke to him. This meeting's going to be a big nothing. I'm sure the others got the brush off, too."

"Maybe Herb can cancel the meeting. I mean, why waste everyone's time?"

"Because you never know what someone might've found out. The proposal is one thing, Sorrel's murder is the other."

"I thought the deal was no one was going to broach that matter with the board members."

"Not directly, no. So, are you coming?"

"I suppose. But it better not drag out longer than an hour or so. Oh, one more thing. Would you have any idea if Edmund Wooster and Milquist Harlan knew each other?"

"Why? Is it important? Is Edmund a suspect?"

"No. I mean, I don't know. Um, I kind of thought of Edmund, that's all. Leaving the board so suddenly and then Sorrel being appointed to replace him."

"Tell you what. I'll make some calls tomorrow and let you know when I see you at Bagels 'N More. Nate and Marshall are welcome to come, too."

"Okay, Mom. Have a good night."

It was a no-brainer in my book. Nate and Marshall might have had the Maricopa County Sheriff's Department and hacker extraordinaire Rolo Barnes at their disposal, but my money was on Harriet Plunkett.

Chapter 20

Nothing on paper linked Milquist Harlan to Edmund Wooster, at least according to Nate and Marshall. They'd both been hard at work long before I got in. Marshall had to take off on another case, and Nate was busy with background checks, so I didn't have much time to speak with either of them.

At a little past noon, when I returned from grabbing a sandwich at the deli, Augusta informed me that my mother had left a message.

"Don't look so panic-stricken. It's a good message. She said to tell you Myrna's team won and they're up again tomorrow. If they win again, they'll be in the finals on Saturday."

"She didn't insist I be there, did she?"

"No. Guess you're off the hook."

"For the bocce tournament. I'm still stuck going to their strategy meeting tonight. You know, their plan to chip away at the remaining board members who still want to go ahead with Sorrel's eco-friendly park idea."

"If I were one of those board members, I'd either change my vote or abstain. If some nutcase was responsible for killing Sorrel over property values, those other guys are sitting ducks. When your mother called, I half expected her to tell me someone else was murdered."

"Bite your tongue. But come to think of it, not all of the board members were at the parade last night."

For the life of me, I tried to visualize who I'd seen seated behind Harold Stevens. Definitely Jeannine Simone. She was hard to miss. Barry Wong was there, too, and so was Clarence McAdams. All of them were adamantly against converting the golf courses. So that left the "yes" votes, or the sitting ducks, as Augusta pointed out. Maybe that was why they weren't there. After all, who wanted to be a sitting target? Then again, it didn't seem to faze the board president.

I dreaded another evening listening to people argue over whether or not mayonnaise belonged on a bagel or if the tax got counted into the tip. Still, my mother's book club friends and those pinochle men were a wealth of information. It was simply a matter of asking them the right questions, and I planned to do just that.

Instead of chitchatting with Augusta or surfing the Internet during my afternoon break, I wrote down the names of all the suspects, coupled with the key motives for Sorrel's murder. Then I plotted them on what best could be described as my own "Richter Scale," only instead of using words like "minor" or "massive," I used terms ranging from "lukewarm" to "boiling." By the time I finished, it was like looking at a treasure map with too many pieces missing. I read it over three times before getting back to my real work.

At the lukewarm end of the scale, I had written "jealous lover." Next to it, I wrote Frank and Eleanor Landrow's names along with Bethany Gillmore, whose nasty look in that Heard Museum photo still plagued me. Moving further up the scale to "warm," I added Hawaiian shirt guy, Russell (Spuds) Baxter, with the notation "et al." for the golf course homeowners. Using that Latin abbreviation somehow gave credence to my list. I went on with "pesticide company pollution" for the Agua Fria dumping that Sorrel might have witnessed. To me, they seemed to have the most at stake. I made a mental note to ask Nate and Marshall what, if anything, they were able to learn about those employees and their archery skills.

At some point in the afternoon, Nate headed out on business and Marshall returned for less than a half hour. He, too, was mired under with interviews and promised to call me later that night after the soiree at Bagels 'N More.

I had more than enough time to go home, change into comfortable jeans, and check my mail before driving over to the restaurant. I also had a few minutes to reread my Richter Scale list. This time, I added Jeannine Simone's name under "tepid," a new category. That was because she owned a bow and arrow, decorative or not. It was beginning to seem as if everyone in creation was on that list, yet I had the nagging feeling I had forgotten something.

The parking lot at Bagels 'N More seemed to have more cars than it did the prior Thursday. Either my mother or Herb had managed to commandeer more people to attend the powwow, or there was some weekly special going on that attracted more customers. One step through the door and I got my answer. That bowling tournament had brought in crowds from the neighboring retirement communities, and, with the late games, it seemed as if those lawn bowling and bocce leagues wound up here.

The T-shirts gave them away. DESERT PALM ROLLERS, LA LOMA LAWN BOWLING LEAGUE, and CHAPARRAL VILLAGE BOCCERETTES.

Bill was muttering about it as I got closer to the middle table, where my mother's crew had set up camp. "Darn it. We should've worn our T-shirts."

"Hi, everyone!" I plunked myself down between Myrna and my mother. "Did I miss anything?"

"No," Herb said, "but you'll have to keep your voice low. Bad enough we have to worry about the Sun City West tongue waggers. Now we've got 'em from all over the place."

He waved his arm in the air to further illustrate the point he was making, but the waitress mistook it as a sign we were ready to order.

"Not yet," Myrna said. "We're not done with the menus."

This crew had been coming to Bagels 'N More long before the first George Bush was in office. I had no doubt they could recite the menu from breakfast bagels to early bird specials without pausing for air. Besides, how many ways could bagels be prepared? I didn't say a word and waited while they studied the selections. My aunt Ina couldn't make the meeting because she and my uncle Louis had tickets to a ballet in Phoenix, and Riva was home with a sore throat. Other than that, the rest of the book club was there—my mother, Shirley, Lucinda, Cecilia, Louise, Myrna, Constance, and Marianne. As for the men, they weren't about to miss a night out either. Even Kenny decided to forgo his wife's cooking in order to be here. I later learned she planned on making liver and onions, not one of his favorites.

Kevin, who was sitting on the other side of Myrna, gave her a poke on the arm. "Heard you didn't botch things up at today's game."

"Keep it that way, will you?" Bill added before Myrna had a chance to reply.

My mother gave both men a searing glance and cleared her throat. "We came here to discuss that other matter, not the tournament. But before we do, does anyone here know why Edmund Wooster would be paying a visit to Milquist Harlan?"

Then she looked at me. "Sorry, Phee. I didn't have time to make those calls."

"Don't know about that," Wayne said, "but I do know one thing. He didn't resign from the board for personal reasons. He resigned due to a conflict of interest."

A collective "huh?" followed as Wayne continued, "Yeah. And too damn bad. At least he was against that ridiculous proposal. None of this would've happened if he'd stayed on the board."

"Forget that," my mother said. "What was the conflict of interest? Spit it out, Wayne, we haven't got all night."

"I was at the podiatrist's office this morning. Lousy bunion won't go away. They were really backed up in there and somehow I got into a conversation with a guy who happens to be Wooster's neighbor. Seems our old board president got offered a job with Golfscapes."

"That mega, golf course maintenance company?" Myrna asked. "Oh, and before I forget, the other day I thought their manager might've been the killer because of the way he was snooping around by the fence near where Sorrel's body was found. But guess what? They were measuring for a new fence and got it installed in time for the tournament."

I whispered to my mother. "Didn't I tell you it was going to turn out to be something like that?"

"Shh. Yes, you did. Enough already."

Herb sat up in his chair and gave the table a quick pound with his fist. "Can we please get this meeting back on track?"

The waitress appeared at that moment, and it took another ten minutes for her to get the orders straight. I was sure she was real thrilled with all those separate checks, too.

"Okay," Herb continued, "where did we leave off? That's right, we were just getting started. So, um, Harriet, would you like to take over?"

My mother didn't wait to be asked twice. She immediately scrambled for a list she had stuffed into her pocketbook. "We crossed off the four no votes—Bethany, Clarence, Jeannine, and Barry. And yes, Wayne, Edmund Wooster would've been the fifth if he'd stayed on the board. So, that leaves Harold, Eloise, Mildred, and Burton. I can tell you right now that Burton was tight-lipped. Said he'd consider it. Big deal. I say that all the time. And if I'm not mistaken, that's what Harold told Kevin and Kenny, right?"

"Yeah, that about sums it up," Kevin said.

Cecilia looked up from her cup of coffee and made a soft *tsk* sound. "Eloise was pretty noncommittal, too. Rambled on about the good old days when everyone met at her neighborhood park in Brooklyn. I reminded her this was Sun City West, and she said she knew perfectly well this was a golf community and that people would go to extremes to keep it that way."

"What about you, Shirley?" my mother asked. "Did you and Ina have any better luck with Mildred Saperstein?"

"I don't think she's going to cast a vote. Lordy, no. Poor thing's afraid to leave the house. Said she didn't want to be the next victim. Apparently, she thought Sorrel's plan was a good one. Then Ina went and told her to stand up for her rights. Good grief! Talk about shooting oneself in the foot. What on earth was your sister thinking?"

I shot my mother a look. We both knew what my crazy aunt was thinking. Women's rights, self-expression, women's empowerment, ban-the-bra, and anything and everything that had to do with the women's movement since the first suffragettes.

"Did anyone ever figure out what happens if it's a tie vote?" Herb asked.

Kenny and Kevin both said "yep" at the same time, and Kevin explained. "Yeah, we asked Harold when we spoke to him. If the vote is tied, the proposal doesn't pass. It's put on hold until they decide to reintroduce it. And a new appointee is incligible to vote for thirty days."

Bill slammed down his coffee cup, nearly spilling it all over the table. "Oh hell no! This damn thing could go on indefinitely. I was hoping for some good news."

"Well, I've got good news," Louise announced. So loud, in fact, people from the other tables turned to listen. "This afternoon I got a message on my answering machine from the Maricopa County Office of the Jury Commissioner. My case was settled out of court. I don't have to appear for jury duty. And, I'll be excused for the next eighteen months. If that's not good news, I don't know what is."

That left two cases going to jury trials. The highly publicized Darla Marlinde scorpion killer case and the Agua Fria River pollution one. Marshall was pretty certain Sorrel was the witness for the pollution case, but he was still gathering information. His workload and Nate's had seemed to escalate with this murder. Too many loose ends. This past week both investigators were knocking themselves out reviewing employee records from that pesticide company to see if anyone had archery skills. Since the company was housed in Maricopa County, the sheriff's department had no problem getting a subpoena to review the records and including Williams Investigations as partners in the process.

"Good news for you, Louise," Herb said, "but we're still far from it regarding those eco-friendly parks. Hey, getting back to Wooster, why on earth would Golfscapes hire him? That kind of came out of the blue, don't you think? And what's taking so long with our food?"

"The food's on its way," Myrna said. "And just because Golfscapes didn't confer with you first doesn't mean it came out of the blue. For all we know, Edmund Wooster could've had his eye on a job with them for months."

"Doing what? What does he know about golf course maintenance?" Cecilia unwrapped the silverware from the paper napkin and proceeded to polish it, all but tearing the napkin apart.

Wayne seemed anxious to explain. "More than you think. According to that neighbor of his, Wooster used to be a bigwig for a similar company in California. That company went belly-up in the recession, taking a huge chunk out of Wooster's pension. Guess he needed the money. Boy, I bet it must've really rubbed him the wrong way when little miss eco-friendly got appointed to the board."

Cecilia gave her teaspoon a final wipe with her napkin and looked up. "It's not nice to speak of the dead that way."

"What way? I didn't say anything wrong. It's not like I called her a four-letter word."

At that moment, the waitress arrived with the first tray of food, and, as if on cue, everyone stopped talking. When the woman left to get the next tray, my mother went back to her original question.

"So, no one knows why Edmund would've paid a visit to Milquist?"

"Probably went to offer his condolences," Marianne said. "If he hadn't resigned from the board, Sorrel might still be alive. Maybe he had a guilty conscience."

Herb bit into his bagel sandwich and tried to talk at the same time. "Doubt it. The guy must've had another reason."

The rest of the food arrived, and, for a good five or six minutes, all I heard was chomping, slurping, and chewing.

"Hey, Myrna," Kevin broke the silence. "Did they ever find the car that ran your golf cart off the road?"

Myrna shook her head. "No. We don't have traffic cams in Sun City West, and all I saw was a beige blur."

"Yeah, a beige blur that wasn't mine." Bill leaned in to face Myrna.

"I said I was sorry, didn't I?"

Lucinda wiped a smudge of cream cheese from her lip. "Beige? You said beige? The Sun City West maintenance vehicles are beige. Beige with our new logo plastered on the sides."

Suddenly, the table went quiet, and I felt someone kick my ankle.

"Maybe they weren't just measuring fences that day." My mother leaned over toward Myrna. "What if that arrow really was intended for you?"

Myrna gasped.

Shirley let out a "Lordy, Lordy" that got everyone's attention, and the table erupted in absolute verbal chaos.

I grabbed my mother by the wrist and whispered, "Now look what you've done."

To which she replied, "I was only thinking out loud."

I tried to prevent her from saying another word by offering her some of my bagel crisps, but she brushed them aside and continued, "That shooter could've been aiming for Myrna. No offense, Myrna, but you're a fairly large target, and the bocce court is what, a few yards away from where Bill found Sorrel's body? For all we know, Sorrel could've been bent over, looking at something. That little stream . . . wildflowers . . . she was in the garden club, after all. When she stood up, she deflected the arrow, and it went right into her neck."

"My God, Harriet," Herb shouted. "That's ridiculous."

"Ridiculous? Then how do you explain the other attempt on Myrna's life? The golf cart incident?"

Myrna's face had turned a sickly greenish color, and, for a second, I thought she was going to pass out on the table. Much as I didn't want to share Marshall's findings regarding the golf cart, I felt I had no choice.

"It might have been a case of mistaken identity. At least that's what Nate and Marshall think. Look, don't go sharing what I'm about to tell you with anyone. It could compromise the murder investigation. I mean it! Milquist Harlan has a golf cart that looks exactly like Myrna's. Red and white stripes. According to the golf cart shops, that model was never popular and the style was discontinued. So, whoever killed Sorrel might be gunning for Milquist as well."

The color started to come back to Myrna's cheeks, and she took a sip of coffee. "It still doesn't make me feel any better. I don't think I'd better play in tomorrow's match."

"You can't do that," Bill said. "It's too late to find anyone else, and we'd have to forfeit the game. Heck, there'll be a big enough crowd around the courts. No one's going to try anything stupid."

As things turned out, the only one trying anything stupid was me.

Chapter 21

Our office order for toner hadn't arrived yet, and, in spite of shaking and re-shaking the cartridge, it gave out before I left work yesterday. I offered to stop by Office Max on Friday morning and pick up another one on my way in. I thought it would only take me a few minutes, but the place was packed. That was why, when I arrived forty minutes later than usual, I had missed Nate, who was out on a case, and learned from Augusta that Marshall was behind closed doors with a "cougar." So much for getting a chance to tell him about last night's debacle at Bagels 'N More.

"Marshall's with a cougar? He's in his forties," I said. "I thought cougars only pertained to women who went after younger men."

Augusta didn't flinch. "He *is* younger, compared to her. And let me tell you about her. If her clothes were any tighter, she'd pass out. And that perfume . . . do you smell it? I'll have to fumigate the office later."

"Um, yeah. I thought maybe the cleaning service used a new floral cleanser, heavy on the floral. Guess you'll have to give his office a real airing out when she leaves."

"I've opened the front windows already."

As I started for my desk, Augusta stopped me. "Don't you want to know who it is?"

"Why? Do I know her?"

I usually didn't get involved in Nate's or Marshall's cases outside of Sun City West, and the only reason I got roped into those was because my mother seemed to have a grip on the cord. I studied Augusta's face and knew it was bad news. She couldn't hide that wicked smile that was getting bigger and bigger.

"The cougar behind the door is Eleanor Landrow. Wife of Frank Landrow. Thought you might be interested."

"Eleanor Landrow? What on earth does she want with Marshall?"

"I think she got him by default. Nate was already out the door when she arrived."

"No appointment?"

"Uh-uh."

"Geez, I'm dying to know what's going on."

"Shh. You won't have to wait long. His office door's opening."

I immediately raced to the copier and started to install the new toner, but it was difficult keeping my eyes off of her. Augusta was right. The woman was wearing tight, black leggings with an equally tight, low-cut, black tank top and a sheer, white, open tunic. It was a wonder she could breathe. If that wasn't sufficient, she wore dangling gold earrings and a gold choker chain. The perfume, that had started to fade with the open windows, came back full force.

Eleanor had draped herself over Marshall's arm as he walked her to the door. I tried not to make eye contact with Augusta for fear one of us would burst out laughing and undermine the professionalism Nate and Marshall worked so hard to attain. I all but stuck my head into the copier as I listened to Eleanor.

"I can't possibly thank you enough. That Deputy Bowman was no help whatsoever, and I need to know the truth about my husband and that woman. Frank is being very tight-lipped about the whole thing. But like I explained, I had my suspicions. I don't need Sorrel Harlan's ghost hanging over my head, if you know what I mean."

Marshall opened the front door for her and stepped outside, making it impossible to overhear what he was saying. I didn't want to appear like a busybody, so I quickly finished up at the copier and raced into my office.

"You don't have to scurry off like that, Phee," he said as he stepped inside. "And, Augusta, you can stop pretending to be looking at your computer screen."

"That obvious, huh?" I walked back to the main office.

"What's obvious is I've got to throw these clothes into the wash as soon as I get home, that is, if I can make it through the day. I smell like a French whorehouse. Pardon me."

I caught a quick whiff and stepped back, almost bumping into the doorjamb to my office. "Um, not that we were eavesdropping, but we couldn't help overhear what Eleanor was saying. Do you really think there's some validity to that? An affair with Sorrel? I don't get it."

Augusta seemed in a hurry to put in her two cents. "Seen stranger stuff back home. Maybe this Frank guy got tired of being with a well-kept woman and wanted a dowdy, homely girl instead. They don't require as much maintenance."

Marshall's jaw dropped. "It's not like we're talking about a car or a house. And as far as an affair goes, we don't know. Not yet."

"So, you're going to follow through on it?" I asked.

"It's all part of one big puzzle. Plus, we're still waiting for Rolo Barnes to get back to us on Eleanor and Marlene. So, as long as my washing machine doesn't conk out, I'll see where this takes me."

"Before you go back to work, I need to tell you about last night. The meeting . . ."

"I'm afraid to ask."

"It's about Myrna's golf cart accident. Lucinda pointed out something. All of the Sun City West maintenance vehicles are beige. Any chance you could—"

"Bother Deputy Bowman again?"

"Uh-huh."

Marshall gave me a wink, muttered "you got it," and headed straight for his office.

"Dowdy, homely girl?" I said to Augusta.

"You never know what men find attractive these days."

Attractive or not, I seriously doubted Frank and Sorrel were having an affair, but that didn't mean they weren't involved in something else. I had no sooner booted up my computer to pay some office bills when Augusta told me I had a call.

"Your mother, Phee."

Of course. More predictable than the tides.

"Why do you have a cell phone if you're not going to use it? Never mind. That's not why I called."

"You scared Myrna half to death last night. Next time you think out loud, don't!"

"Myrna will be fine. It's the Milquist and Edmund thing that's been on my mind. Condolences, my foot. Something's going on, and you need to find out what it is."

"Uh, isn't that what the sheriff's department and my boss are doing?"

"Not fast enough. Listen, I'll bet you anything Milquist and Edmund are in cahoots about something, and that's what got Sorrel killed."

Oh goodie. We've stepped off the jealous lover theory and onto a wackier one.

"Look, Phee, if you could get into Milquist's house and snoop around a bit, you might be able to uncover something."

I tried to keep my voice down, but it wound up sounding sharp and shrill. "You mean like breaking and entering?"

"Ah, I wouldn't exactly put it that way. Forcible entry is a crime."

"Any unwanted entry is a crime. Even if the guy left the doors and windows wide open. It's a crime!"

"You can't find evidence if you don't look."

"That's why they have subpoenas. And laws. And exactly *what*, if I might ask, am I looking for?"

"Oh good. You're considering it."

"Um, er. No. Not at all. And I need to get back to work."

"You won't have to break in. You'll go inside under another pretense."

"If this is going to be like that dumpster diving thing a year or so ago, you can forget it."

"Nothing like that. Cecilia uses the Happy Housecleaners twice a month. Some of those women are very chatty, and, come to find out, the Happy Housecleaners also clean the Harlan house."

"Oh my God, no! I am *not* pretending to be a housecleaner! I only pretend to do that in my own home."

"Hold on. I know for a fact they'll be there tomorrow morning at eight. If I'm not mistaken, you swapped another

Saturday morning. You're not working tomorrow so you can do this. Cecilia already talked to the woman in charge, and she agreed to have you spend time there watching them work in order to decide whether or not to hire them for your own house. Which, by the way, wouldn't be such a bad idea."

"It won't work. Milquist knows who I am. Remember? The memorial service?"

"For your information, Milquist won't be there. According to the Happy Housecleaners, he prefers to be out of the way. That company is licensed, bonded, and insured, so he doesn't have to worry about them going through his things."

"No, he has to worry about an unlicensed, un-bonded, and unwarranted person going through his stuff. And I don't think my personal liability insurance covers snooping in other people's homes."

"Do you want this murder solved or not? There's nothing to worry about. As far as anyone knows, you're checking out a cleaning service. Very benign."

"What about Marlene Krone? What if she didn't go back to New Mexico?"

"If she happens to be there and she catches you pilfering through something, tell her you're checking to see how well dusted the area was."

"Mom, for the last time, I don't know what I'm looking for, and, for crying out loud, this has disaster written all over it."

"Disaster is better than murder. Call me when you get home."

"Aargh!"

My groan was so loud, Augusta, who had gotten up to make herself a cup of coffee, walked over to my door.

"That bad, huh?"

"You won't believe it. My mother actually wants me to snoop around Milquist Harlan's house tomorrow under the pretense of observing his cleaning service. She even had her friend make the arrangements."

"Milquist. That's the husband of the deceased, right?"

"Uh-huh."

"The husband is always the first suspect."

"He was out of town at a writers' conference when she was murdered."

"Still doesn't mean there wasn't collusion involved. What does your mother want you to look for?"

"That's just the thing. She has no idea and neither do I. Besides, if the guy was hiding something, it would probably be on his computer, and it's not as if I could shove in a flash drive and start copying files. That only works in the movies."

"You never know. There might be papers floating around, incriminating photos, all sorts of stuff. When you really give it some thought, it's not such a preposterous idea. The authorities would need search warrants and reasonable cause to check out the place. All you're doing is observing that cleaning company at work."

"There's another dilemma. Nate and Marshall. I hate going behind their backs. They're the detectives, not me."

"True, but if you tell them, then they become part of an unauthorized search. Far be it for me to tell you what to do, but if you want to put a stop to those annoying phone calls from your mother, you may want to take her up on this one."

"If I get arrested, you're the person I'm calling to bail me out."

"You're not doing anything wrong."

Augusta made her coffee and returned to her desk. I glanced at the closed door to Marshall's office, and, for one brief second, considered bursting in and spilling the beans. I didn't. Instead, I called my mother back and said one word, "Fine." I hoped I wouldn't regret it.

Chapter 22

The Happy Housecleaners' sky-blue van with a logo depicting cloudlike dusters and smiling faces was parked in Milquist's driveway when I arrived. I parked on the street and headed for the front door, pausing every second or so to admire the gorgeous stone pavers that created a swirling path to the entrance. The colors blended perfectly with the stone veneer of the house.

Carefully manicured rosemary bushes and boxwood beauties graced the pavers. *Must be nice having money.* I rang the bell. A young, dark-haired woman in her late twenties or early thirties answered the door. She was wearing jeans and a light blue polo shirt that sported the same logo I saw on the van.

"Hi! I'm Gracie. You must be Phee. Glad you could watch us in action today. We're always hoping to impress new clients. And, of course, our existing ones."

New clients? Is this a done deal? What did my mother do? Am I going to wind up with an expensive housecleaning service?

I thanked her and followed her into the house. This time, I made it past the foyer. Gracie motioned for me to follow her into the kitchen, chatting all the way.

"There're three of us here today. Me, Rosa, and Zia. Her real name's Jalisa, but everyone calls her Zia."

"Uh, do all three of you always work together?"

"Not always. Depends on the job. Some places are real terrors, if you know what I mean. Absolutely filthy until we arrive. Those houses can get up to five of us working."

I couldn't imagine a place so disgusting it would require five housecleaners. Then again, not everyone had a mother like mine, insisting on the "white glove" treatment. Gracie explained that each cleaner worked in a different area, and she was starting on the kitchen.

"Feel free to move about the house but please don't touch anything. Zia's doing the bedrooms, and Rosa started on the upstairs bathroom. This is one of the few houses in Sun City West that has an upstairs area. Just a sitting area, really, and Mr. Harlan's office. Oh, there's also a balcony that overlooks the yard. Nice, huh?"

Nice didn't begin to cover it. The Harlan house was spectacular. While the exterior was desert Southwest, the interior looked more like one of those Pacific Northwest houses I'd seen in travel magazines. Massive wooden furniture, large stone fireplace, beamed ceilings, leather couches, and artwork that showcased the flora and fauna of that region. I supposed it would make sense, given Milquist came from a family that made its fortune in the timber industry. And while I was tempted to take my time and admire the place, I knew I'd better start rummaging around, beginning with the guy's office. I'd seen my share of detective movies, and the office was always the place where incriminating evidence turned up. Of course, those detectives knew what they were looking for. I was as clueless as anyone could get.

"Um, uh, I guess I'll go upstairs and see how Rosa's

doing in the bathroom. My shower always gets dingy on the bottom and nothing seems to work on it."

Wow. This is the first thing I've said that was true.

"Hey, Rosa and Zia!" Gracie shouted. "That lady friend of Ms. Flanagan is here."

I thought I heard both of the cleaners yell out "Okay" or something to that affect. I headed up the circular staircase, another feature that stood out in this dramatic home. Rosa was scrubbing the toilet when I got to the top of the stairs.

"Hi! The trick is to spray on the cleaner and then let it set for a few minutes before scrubbing."

I really had no intention of watching the poor woman toil away in the bathroom and had to think fast. "I see. You know, in order for me to see how well you ladies clean, it might be a good idea for me to, well, check the other rooms before you get there. Kind of a before and after."

Rosa didn't seem the least bit fazed. "That makes sense. The little den is to the left, and it goes right into the office. Upstairs rooms get very dusty in Arizona, and the corners seem to attract all sorts of unwanted dirt. Dead insects, too. You'll be surprised how nice those rooms look when I finish. You can see what they look like now and come back in a little bit. Maybe see how Zia and Gracie are doing."

"Sounds like a plan to me. Thanks, Rosa."

I breezed through the den, which consisted of a small couch, large flat screen TV, coffee table, and indoor corner fountain with LED lighting, and stepped into Milquist's office. It was like going back in time to the turn of the century—the twentieth, not the twenty-first. A massive wooden desk with built-in cubbies took up most of the room, leaving little space for the bookshelves and armoire. Papers were strewn everywhere.

How are you going to dust this, Rosa?

An Acer PC and laser printer took center stage, and I

could see that the setup was Wi-Fi. Must be Sorrel had had
her own computer or tablet. Pretending to check for dust,
I leaned over the desk to make it appear as if I was taking
a better look at the windowsill. Beneath me, I saw what
Milquist was working on—another book. The papers were
numbered, and the content dealt with the eating habits of
the Anasazi civilization. Handwritten comments were
everywhere. Marlene's maybe?

Moving away from the desk, I perused the bookshelves.
Tome after tome about the Southwest, as well as a collection of James Burroughs's naturalist books dating back to
the mid-1800s. I surmised Milquist was into conservation-
ism, along with his late wife.

I noted a few knickknacks on the bookshelves and the
desk. Rocks. Shells. A dried pine cone. Nothing that shouted
out, "Hey! I'm a clue to Sorrel's murder."

Just then I heard footsteps and knew Rosa had entered
the den. I turned away from the desk. "I see what you mean
about the dust. It's everywhere."

Unable to poke around any further in the office, I
headed downstairs. Zia was in the master bedroom, and
Gracie was still in the kitchen. I opted for the bedroom.

As I walked in, Zia was finishing up making the bed,
having changed the linens. She looked up and explained
the process before I could say anything.

"Hi! As soon as I arrive, I strip the beds and throw the
linens in the wash. It takes about forty-five minutes. Then
I put them in the dryer, and when they're done, I fold them
and put them in the linen closet by the hallway bathroom.
Very efficient that way."

My eyes were darting around the room as I tried to
process what I was seeing. A monstrous bed, oversized
dresser, and nightstands with glass globes instead of lamp-
shades. Wooden relief wall hangings and metal sculptures

of animals gave the room an African safari feel. A large flat screen TV faced the bed. No sign of feminism anywhere. Of course, I had no clue regarding Sorrel's decorative tastes.

"You, uh, mentioned stripping the beds. I take it you mean guest rooms, too."

"Oh no, miss. I've never had to change the linens in the guest room. Only Mrs. Harlan's room, rest her soul."

"Mrs. Harlan's room? They have, I mean *had*, separate rooms?"

"Oh yes. Her suite is across the hall. I haven't started in there yet, except for stripping the bed. I'm on my way over there now. Look around this room and the en suite. This model house has two en suites and three bedrooms."

Zia pointed to the master bath. "Rosa cleans the upstairs bathrooms and the powder room downstairs. I do the en suites."

"I see. I'll be sure to take a good look," I said as Zia left the room.

I glanced at the master bath, and she was right. It was gleaming. It was also as masculine as hell. No cute little soap dishes or fancy towels. Plain beige ones on either side of the double vanity. Shaving stuff, an electric toothbrush, and a box of tissues completed the scene. I went back to the bedroom for another look, still uncertain of what it was I was after.

The room reminded me of a motel, and, in that instant, I did something I never thought I would. I opened the drawer to the nightstand that housed the phone. If someone were to call Milquist while he was in the room, he probably had a pad and pen in the drawer. Motel 101.

Sure enough, I was right. In addition to cough lozenges and a few crumbled-up tissues, a small white pad and a few pens were in the drawer. I picked up the pad and studied it. Reading all of those Nancy Drew books as a kid paid off.

I could see the imprint from a note he had written. He must have pressed down hard when he wrote because the indent from the first word stood out—Frank.

Quickly, I tore off the sheet and stuffed it in my pocket. Then I raced out of the room and over to Sorrel's, where Zia was in the middle of making the bed. I could tell she was uncomfortable.

"This is the first, the first . . . This is the first time the sheets have been changed since Mrs. Harlan was killed. We only come here once or twice a month."

I didn't know what to say and stood there staring. Finally, I managed to say something. "This room is very different from Mr. Harlan's."

What an understatement. The room had a gorgeous oak canopy bed with rope designs that matched the armoire and nightstands. Stained glass lamps were everywhere—dragonflies, birds, lizards, you name it. The artwork on the walls was a change, too—watercolors and lithographs of garden scenes.

"Zia, how long have you been cleaning for the Harlans?"

The girl looked up and stared for a moment. "At least three years. The Harlans are steady customers."

"Um, not that it's any of my business, but I'm curious. They have separate bedrooms."

"Shh. Not my business either, but I don't think they were interested in each other like man and wife."

"Because of the separate bedrooms?"

"Look at the bedroom doors. They have locks on the doorknobs."

"Most bedrooms do. I think that's standard for houses."

"Take a good look. The lock on Mr. Harlan's door is small, but it's a keypad door lock. Who has something like that on their bedroom door?"

Who indeed? What was this guy hiding? Especially from his wife. His office was upstairs, not in the bedroom, and if he were to bring a woman home, surely Sorrel would've noticed. There had to be something else. Something else in that bedroom. At first I thought it might've been hidden ledgers, but those could've been locked up in a security safe, no need to lock a door. Then, the weirdest idea came into my head.

"I almost forgot to ask. Do you clean the clothes closets, too?"

"Just the floors. We vacuum and mop them. You can go back and see how nice Mr. Harlan's closet looks."

I didn't need to be asked twice, but it wasn't the floor I was interested in inspecting. It was his wardrobe. What if the guy was a cross-dresser and Sorrel found out? What if she threatened to expose him and he had her killed? I couldn't get to that closet fast enough.

Shirts. Men's shirts. Pants. Men's pants. Jackets, suits, ties, shoes. No sign of women's clothing anywhere. I started to leave the room when I realized something. Not every piece of clothing went into a closet. Without wasting a second, I pulled open the first drawer in the oversized dresser. Men's underwear. But who puts underwear on top of a towel? Someone who had something underneath it.

Sure enough, I had uncovered two pairs of black extra-large lingerie. Too big for Sorrel and much too big for the petite Marlene Krone, with her Dutch Boy hairdo. This was Milquist's private little stash, and I'd wager there was more, only I didn't have time to inspect further. Last thing I needed was Gracie to get suspicious about the length of time it was taking me to observe the housecleaning. I thanked Zia and scurried to the kitchen.

I had to admit the Happy Housecleaners were doing an

amazing job. From dusting plantation shutters to removing grease from the stovetop, they didn't seem to miss a thing, and I felt guilty for beguiling them. As Gracie turned off the water to the sink, I heard myself asking, "Do you prefer cash, check, or credit cards?"

Chapter 23

"You did *what?*" my mother asked when I got home and gave her the news.

"I hired the Happy Housecleaners for you and paid for their first two-hour service. Consider it a gift."

"I don't need a housecleaning service. You could perform open heart surgery on my floors."

"I felt guilty lying to them. I had to make it right."

"Tell you what we'll do. I'll call them and change it to your aunt Ina's house. You know what a discombobulated household she runs. We'll tell her it's an early anniversary gift for her and Louis. Once she gets used to the Happy Housecleaners, I'm sure she'll hire them on a permanent basis."

"I paid for two hours. They'll need more if they're going to tackle her place."

"Fine. I'll add on an hour. So, what did you find out? Was there a connection between Milquist and Edmund?"

"None that surfaced. Um, can I call you back later? I've got to take care of a few things."

"Call me in the evening. Myrna's team is in the finals, and no one wants her to choke at the last second. I'll be at the bocce courts this afternoon. You're sure about Milquist and Edmund?"

"Yeah, I'm sure."

Part of me was dying to tell my mother about Milquist's little secret, but that was the last thing I was going to do. One call to Shirley or Lucinda and it would be spread around the community like a virus. Besides, I had a real clue sitting in my pocket, and I was itching to read it.

Without giving my mother a chance to say anything else, I hung up and took out the indented piece of note-paper. Every amateur sleuth since the discovery of dirt knew how to decipher messages by rubbing a pencil over the indents. I held my breath and rubbed. What emerged on that paper surprised me. It was going to save Marshall a heck of a lot of time, if he didn't kill me first. I picked up the phone and called him.

"You're not going to like this. Well, actually, you are. But maybe not the way I found out. But then again—"

"Phee, if this is supposed to be some sort of riddle, you're driving me nuts."

"Frank Landrow wasn't having an affair with Sorrel."

"How do you know?"

"Here's the part you're not going to like. I found a note, well not exactly a note, I found the indented paper that was underneath a note Milquist had written to Frank."

"I'm almost afraid to ask how. Please don't tell me you did anything that could've put you in danger or compromised the investigation."

"Technically, no. And taking a piece of paper from someone's house isn't exactly theft, is it?"

"Someone's house? You were in Frank's house? Milquist's house?"

"Maybe I should just read you the note. Milquist wrote it. And I'm sure the Frank is Frank Landrow."

"Phee, I—"

"Just listen. Here goes: 'Frank, This should be enough for you to keep her out of my hair. PayPal to Garden Guy like planned. Must get my book finished. Milquist.' Garden Guy has to be Frank. And Milquist sent him money using Paypal. I'm right, aren't I? Milquist was paying Frank to keep Sorrel out of the way so he could finish the book he was writing. Frank wasn't having *an affair* with Sorrel, he was being paid to keep her company. Unless . . . Oh my God. I never thought of it any other way, unless . . . unless Milquist paid Frank to kill her. It can't be, can it? He seemed so broken up at the memorial. Unless it was an act."

"Where did you find the note?"

"Um, this is the part you're not going to like. It was in Milquist's nightstand. Not the note itself, the next sheet of paper on the pad."

Silence. Too much silence. I held my breath and waited. It seemed to take forever before Marshall spoke.

"You went into his nightstand? I know your mother and her friends get crazy ideas at times, but I was hoping, praying, you wouldn't get caught up in them. Especially if it means breaking the law."

"No laws were broken. Not really. Taking a piece of notepaper hardly constitutes theft. And I left everything exactly as it was in the drawer."

I wanted to tell him it wasn't as bad as rummaging through Louis Melinsky's underwear drawer when my aunt Ina and I were trying to find clues about his disappearance, but I kept my mouth shut.

"Suppose you tell me what you were doing in Milquist Harlans's house? How'd you get in there?"

"You can relax. I was invited."

I went on to explain about the Happy Housecleaners

and the one golden opportunity I had to scope out the place. "You have to admit, you'd never have gotten a search warrant to do what I did, and that's not all I found out."

"Why stop now? Do tell."

"Milquist is a closet cross-dresser. I guess that's what they call it."

This time it wasn't silence at the other end. Marshall was trying to contain himself and keep from laughing. "Don't get this wrong. I'm pretty ticked at you for putting yourself in that situation. What if Milquist had walked in? Then what? In case you've forgotten, no one's been removed from the suspect list."

"I know. I know." I tried to sound contrite, but I wasn't sure I was pulling it off.

"That note can't be used as evidence, you know. It was obtained illegally. Your prints are all over it . . ."

"It's still a clue. And a damned good one. So, are we still on for tonight or are you really that angry with me?"

"Angry enough that I get to choose the restaurant. Okay?"

"Deal. Seven thirty?"

"Yeah, I'll pick you up. And, Phee, promise me you're done snooping for the day."

"I promise."

My friend Lyndy called a short time later, and I reiterated everything that had transpired. Whiny voice and all. "You don't think I did anything that awful, do you?"

"Not at all. You were lucky you didn't get caught red-handed with that drawer open, but let's face it, you've got a certain 'in' with those connections of yours in Sun City West. Think of it like a gift. You're going to find out stuff those detectives would be hard-pressed to ferret out. Just be careful. Okay? Nate and Marshall carry guns, you don't."

"My gosh. You're beginning to sound like my mother's friends."

"That bad, huh? I'd better keep my mouth shut then. Call me if you find out anything else. This is better than a Sue Grafton novel."

Lyndy Ellsworth always had a way of making me feel better, and, at that moment, I needed it. We'd met at the Vistancia swimming pool when I first moved here and had been good friends ever since. She was my age and a widow with no children. Her relatives had convinced her Arizona would be a much better place to start over rather than staying in the cold Northeast. The great news was that she and I clicked immediately. I finally had a confidant who understood what life was like with wacky relatives. Lyndy was the soothing voice at the other end of the phone and the purse-guarding savior in dire situations like the one I faced with a murderer at the Stardust Theater not too long ago.

While Lyndy was on board with my escapades, I wasn't a hundred percent sure Marshall would be willing to overlook the way I acted on my hunches. I tried not to dwell on it as I threw in a load of laundry and tidied up my house. Spending the morning watching the Happy Housecleaners made me realize my own place desperately needed sprucing up.

When Marshall rang the bell at quarter past seven, I wasn't sure what to expect. My first husband, Kalese's dad, had been moody and unpredictable. I took a deep breath and answered the door. Before I could say a word, Marshall stepped inside and gave me a hug. A long hug. The warmth spread as our necks touched, and I knew I had no reason to worry.

"I don't care if it's two in the morning. The next time

your sleuthing goes beyond the usual questions and spying from a distance, would you please let me know?"

"I'll try."

"Since it's my choice for dinner tonight, we're going to combine business with pleasure."

"Huh?"

"You can relax. We're meeting Nate at a Mexican joint in Peoria. Rolo Barnes did his homework when it came to Eleanor Landrow and Marlene Krone. Nate wants to go over everything with me, and, since you're almost a de facto investigator yourself, not to mention the vested interest you have in the Sun City West community, it wouldn't be right to exclude you."

"Did Nate say that?"

"Not in so many words. Hey, before I forget, can you show me that note you found?"

"I typed up the message since it's hard to read. Hold on. I'll get both papers for you. They're right over here on the counter."

Marshall took a look at the original and scratched his ear. "Geez, a handwritten note. Don't these guys know we're in the twenty-first century? Then again, notes like this can't be traced like email. I don't think this was anything more than what it says. Milquist paid Frank to keep Sorrel busy enough so she wouldn't interfere with the book her husband was writing. The question I have is, what kind of connection do Milquist and Frank have? It wasn't anything we considered initially. Maybe Nate will have a different take on it when he sees the note."

"Think he'll be really upset with me?"

"If you keep up this stuff, maybe. He'd feel awful if anything happened to you. Anyway, I'm still perplexed about Milquist and Frank's relationship."

I was dumbfounded, too. I knew from Claudia Brinson

that Frank and Sorrel were good buddies from the garden club. As for Milquist? I wasn't so sure he even liked plants. Maybe Rolo Barnes managed to dig up some info while he had Eleanor and Marlene in his sights. I grabbed a jacket and my bag and we were out the door.

The restaurant Nate had picked was one I'd never been to—La Mariposa off of Bell Road. It boasted the usual Mexican décor, with papier-mâché animals and multi-colored sombreros on the walls and ceilings. The nice thing about the place was the privacy it offered—separate booths that didn't bump up against each other and large vases with tall plants serving as barriers between the booths. That meant we could hold a conversation without worrying about being overheard.

Nate was already at the place when we arrived. "This isn't your ordinary Mexican restaurant. Four different salsas for the complimentary nacho chips."

He didn't mention a word about my little escapade at the Harlan residence, probably figuring Marshall had already said enough to me. As soon as the waiter had taken our orders and left the table, Nate began.

"I had to listen to Rolo extoling the virtues of eating un-processed foods before he finally told me what he found out about Eleanor and Marlene. Pretty mundane stuff, when it comes to Marlene. She teaches anthropology at the University of New Mexico and designed a new research program. She and Milquist met online, believe it or not, when he contacted her regarding coauthoring a book."

"What about Eleanor?" I asked.

"Now we're getting somewhere. Eleanor's attributes aren't limited to . . . how can I put this?"

"Her sex appeal?" I blurted out.

"Yeah, that, too. According to Rolo, our dear Mrs. Landrow's ride to a bachelor's degree at the University of

Southern California was funded in part by an archery scholarship from the National Field Archery Association. Of course, that was quite a few decades ago. Hard to say if she kept up her skills."

I gulped the ice water that was in front of me. "Oh my God! It's probably like riding a bicycle. Once you learn, you never forget. She could be our killer. Did you tell Deputy Bowman?"

"Slow down, Phee," Nate said. "If Eleanor was jealous of Sorrel and wanted to kill her, why would she wait all this time to contact our office to investigate the possibility of an affair? Why would that matter now? If she was the killer, she already did it. Evidence of an affair or not."

Marshall leaned his elbow on the table and rested his head in his fist. "I'm not so sure. She might be covering her ass. Pardon me, Phee. It's a fairly common ruse for a murderer to pretend to be interested in seeking out the truth when they already know it."

"You see," I said. "She could be our killer. Although, I have to admit, I find it hard to imagine a woman like Eleanor would ever believe her husband capable of having an affair. Especially with someone who was so, well, *plain*. And I don't buy Augusta's theory either. That the guy got sick of being with a gorgeous woman and turned his sights to one who wasn't."

"Augusta's theory?" Nate said. "Good grief. Who hasn't rendered an opinion?"

Just then our waiter arrived with the first course, tortilla soup. Crushed tortillas floating in a chicken broth with chile peppers, onions, and hominy. It smelled out of this world, and, for a moment, we all stopped talking and started eating. When Nate finished his last spoonful, he leaned an elbow on the table, made a fist and propped his head on it. Then he looked directly at Marshall and me.

"Frankly, I don't buy it. Unless someone keeps up with those particular archery skills, it would be impossible to land an arrow with that kind of accuracy. I was hoping we'd get somewhere with that employee search from the pesticide company, but that pulled up a whopping zero."

"Tell me about it," Marshall said. "I thought those interviews would never end. And all that the employee records revealed were a few letters of reprimand for minor things like continued tardiness or inability to work well with others. Their background checks came back clean, too. And none of them had any archery skills whatsoever. Even if Sorrel had witnessed the illegal dumping of waste, it would be impossible to prove anyone from the pesticide company was responsible for her death."

Nate looked at the table and sighed. "It's a circle that keeps getting wider and wider. Golf course homeowners, possible witness to a crime, an affair gone wrong . . . It's been my experience that when the list of suspects starts to expand, we're better off tightening it up."

"I'm not sure I know what you mean," I said.

"It's simple. We go back to Sorrel's closest group of family and friends."

I was so engrossed in the conversation, I hadn't noticed the waiter returning with our food. My order of shrimp chimichangas looked and smelled spectacular, as did the dishes Nate and Marshall ordered. Enormous slices of seared beef and pork, grilled vegetables, and three different kinds of rice to augment the bowls of refried beans and onions. My boss was right. This wasn't ordinary Mexican fare.

My mouth was watering at the first mouthful of my chimichanga when I heard a voice that made me drop my fork on the plate. "Oh God, no. Do you hear that voice? It's my aunt Ina!"

Short of ducking under the table or throwing the cloth

napkin over my head, it was too late. My aunt and uncle were being escorted to their table by the hostess and immediately spotted us.

"Phee! What a nice surprise! Isn't this place wonderful? We've invited your mother to join us numerous times, but, apparently, Louis and I dine too late for her."

"Yes, it's nice seeing—"

"Nate! I haven't seen you or your partner in ages. Are you working undercover? Did I spoil your sting or whatever it is you're doing?"

"All we're doing is eating, Ina. Nothing else."

"Come on, Ina dear," Louis said. "We don't want their food to get cold."

"It was good running into both of you," I said. "Maybe we can all come back here for lunch or something." *I hope she doesn't take it literally. I'm only being polite.*

"Yes, we will."

Louis gave her a nudge. "Come on, Ina dear."

Her feathered green boa, along with those two long braids of hers, bounced off her shoulders as she continued to their table.

When I was sure she was out of earshot, I said, "That could've been a lot worse. My uncle Louis was probably hungry."

It was bad enough looking up from my meal to discover my flamboyant aunt headed my way, but I was totally unprepared for the interruption that took place over dessert.

"Whoever thought of frying ice cream?" Marshall said as the waiter placed three giant bowls of chocolate, vanilla, and strawberry in front of us.

I was about to reply when, out of the blue, Herb, Wayne, and Bill appeared in front of our table. All of them talking at once.

"You didn't order anything with the *Sriracha* sauce, did you? You'll have heartburn all night."

"I almost had heartburn watching Myrna toss those bocce balls today."

"Yeah, but she didn't foul things up. The team made it to the finals tomorrow."

My ice cream slowly started to melt in the bowl, turning to slosh under my spoon. If the men kept it up, my dessert would become a drink. I decided to hurry things along by getting to the point. "Hi, guys. So, uh, I guess the bocce team has a chance of winning, huh?"

Bill grunted as he spoke. "If Myrna doesn't louse things up tomorrow morning, we'll walk away with a trophy. It's down to two teams. I told her to quit looking at the damn golf course and pay attention to the game."

"Give her a break," Wayne said. "She's still rattled over that murder. Hell, so's everyone else. I heard they had to put extra security on the golf courses, and I'm not speaking about more of those golf marshals. They actually hired a security company to drive around. Not that it'll do much good if they're at one end of the course and Robin Hood is at the other."

I looked at Nate and Marshall. "I didn't know the rec centers added security."

"They didn't have a choice if they expected business as usual." Nate turned to face the men. "Say, isn't that the hostess over there waiting for you?"

Herb stretched his neck and gave a nod. "Geez, we'd better get to our table before they give it to someone else. This place gets really busy on the weekends."

The three of them thundered off as I stared at the gloppy mess in my dessert bowl. "So much for polite conversation. It's like they pick up a conversation out of nowhere and keep going. My mother's friends are notorious for doing that."

"Yeah, well, speaking of notorious, don't look now, but the third act is coming through the door." Marshall's spoon sunk deeper and deeper into his bowl of ice cream. "It's like a Marx Brothers movie."

"Actually," Nate said, "more like a Bing Crosby and Bob Hope road film. Only instead of Dorothy Lamour, we're looking at Eleanor Landrow."

"Yeah," I said. "But that's not Frank."

Like my aunt Ina, Eleanor had to pass our table in order to be seated at hers. She took the arm of the gentleman who was escorting her and brushed by us, offering only a slow nod in Marshall's direction. She moved farther away.

For the life of me, I couldn't imagine who the guy was. "Her escort seems kind of familiar. Like I've seen him before, but I can't place him. Did you guys recognize him?"

Nate, who was still staring at Eleanor's silhouette, suddenly turned to me. "Uh, sorry, kiddo. I guess I was too busy looking at the lovely Mrs. Landrow."

"It's hard not to," Marshall said. "If that dress was any shorter or tighter, it would be a bathing suit."

I had to admit Eleanor Landrow looked stunning in a sleeveless, dark teal sheath with a single strand of pearls. No wonder the men didn't notice her dinner partner. But her perfume was hard to miss. Perfume. I suddenly had a thought.

"Nate, you said Rolo found out Eleanor used to be quite accomplished with a bow and arrow. If she was the killer, would any residue of her perfume still linger on the arrow? Could forensics identify it?"

"I don't think it would. Unless she soaked the thing in it, it's very doubtful. Interesting thought, though."

Marshall gave me a pat on the arm and smiled. "Forensic evidence or not, I think I'll have a little chat with our

Mrs. Landrow this week. She'll want to know if we've learned anything more about her husband's relationship with Sorrel."

"You're not going to tell her about the note I found, are you?"

"Hardly. It was evidence obtained illegally. Which won't happen again. Will it?"

I took a breath and let out a sound that was more like a whine, but I didn't say a word.

Chapter 24

I got up early, went for a jog, which turned out more like a brisk walk than anything else, and got back to my house just in time to hear the tail end of my mother's message on the answering machine.

". . . let me know. Okay? The final round starts at eleven."

The final round. It had to be the bocce tournament, and, from what Bill said last night, his and Myrna's team were one of the two finalists. No doubt, my mother wanted me to go there. Since Marshall and I didn't have plans for the day, and Lyndy was going to be tied up taking her aunt to Costco, I thought it might not be such a bad idea. After all, the finals were bound to bring in lots of people. People who tended to talk.

"Do you want me to meet you at the bocce courts or pick you up?" I asked when I returned the call.

"Why don't you pick me up? That way you can visit with Streetman for a few minutes. It's important he become more socialized. After careful consideration, I've decided it's best if we start with one-to-one contacts so as not to stress him. He can be somewhat unpredictable in crowds."

Oh, he's predictable all right. Ask anyone within a two-foot radius of his leg.

As for socialized? The dog had a better social life than most celebrities. Dog park excursions. Neighborhood walks. Trips to Dairy Queen for special treats. And if that wasn't enough, my mother figured out her bank's drive-thru window offered complimentary dog treats that didn't interfere with his sensitive stomach.

"Fine. See you at quarter after ten."

My mother and I arrived at the bocce courts in time to squeeze into the benches that Shirley and Lucinda held for us. I didn't expect to see so many people in attendance.

"Cecilia, Louise, and Riva are on the other side," Lucinda said. "Look, there's Myrna now. Let's stand up and wave to her."

A quick jab on my back and I was out of my seat like a jack-in-the-box, waving stupidly at Myrna.

"Lordy, that girl looks nervous," Shirley said. "And I suppose Bill isn't making things any better. He's whispering in her ear right now."

"She'll be okay," Lucinda said. "Myrna's a trooper."

The Scorching Rollers from Fountain Hills were up first, having won the coin toss. The back of their lime-green shirts read, ROLLING INTO THE GOOD LIFE AT FOUNTAIN HILLS RETIREMENT VILLAGE, while the front had some sort of logo featuring a lizard tossing a bocce ball. Underneath were the words, SCORCHING ROLLERS BOCCE TEAM.

They seemed polished and relaxed, unlike the Sun City West team. I watched as one of their players tossed out a small white ball and proceeded to follow up by aiming a larger bocce ball at it. This process seemed to go on indefinitely as the teams took turns. Once all the balls had landed, someone measured and recorded the distances.

"Do you have any idea who's winning?" my mother asked.

"No," I replied, "but it can't be all bad. Judging from what I can see and hear, Myrna's not having a meltdown, and Bill's not grumbling loud enough to disturb anyone."

We continued to watch the game as Shirley and Lucinda had a side conversation that seemed more interesting than what I was watching. In retrospect, it wasn't so much of a side conversation as it was Lucinda complaining to Shirley.

"I can't tell you how annoyed I am. I rearranged my schedule so I could be home every afternoon at two in order to follow that trial. I had it all planned. The trial from two to four and then Telemundo, unless, of course, the trial went longer. I could always DVR *Amor bajo el cielo.* I switched all of my appointments to the mornings. The dentist. The nail salon. My internist. Do you think I want to get up that early? Now I'm stuck. Why on earth did they postpone that trial?"

Lucinda didn't give Shirley a chance to answer. "You know what I think? I think her lawyer quit. That Darla Marlinde seems like an awful you-know-what to me. Anyway, they'll have more about it on the news tonight. Louise should be thankful she didn't wind up on that jury."

The Darla Marlinde case. That's what Lucinda was grousing about. The news media was playing it up as if it was a blockbuster movie. "Will there be justice for the scorpion killer's victim?" Justice? From what I'd seen, Darla Marlinde was already tried and found guilty by the media. Now all they needed were ratings. I leaned back and watched the game as one of the Fountain Hills players tossed the ball.

Back and forth, the game went on and on.

At one point my mother offered me some bottled water she had in her bag, but I wasn't thirsty. "Are you sure? You might be thirsty later."

"If I'm thirsty later, I'll get something to drink. Looks like Myrna's up next."

"You're sure about the water?"

I was looking at my mother and didn't see what happened on the bocce court. Nevertheless, I heard it. Along with the entire West Coast. Myrna was screaming her lungs out.

"Help! I've been hit. There's blood dripping down my cheeks. Help! It felt like an arrow. The shooter! The shooter got me. He must be somewhere on the golf course. Help!"

While the other players rushed to Myrna's side, the posse members who were on duty raced for the fence that separated the golf course from the miniature golf and bocce courts. All I could see was a crowd around Myrna. Then, as quickly as the crowd had gathered, it dispersed.

The next voice we heard was Bill's, and he was even louder than Myrna. "You weren't shot with an arrow, and that's not blood dripping down your cheek. A fast-falling wad of goose poop landed on your head, that's all. Goose poop."

Myrna stopped yelling and ran her hand through her hair. Next thing I knew she raced out of the bocce court and headed right to the parking lot. I thought back to that day in the dog park when Cindy Dolton asked me to tell my mother about the geese and their unwelcome presents on the benches.

"Um, I might've forgotten to mention this. Not that it matters, really. But, be careful where you sit at the dog park. The geese are active this time of year. Cindy Dolton asked me to let you know."

My mother looked at me as if I had come off a spaceship. "You could've warned Myrna, you know."

"What? Warned Myrna? How was I supposed to know a bird was going to drop its . . . its . . . crap on her head?"

By now Cecila, Louise, and Riva had left their seats and were walking toward our bench. The activity on the bocce court had stopped completely.

"Lordy, Lordy. This is a mess," Shirley said. "I think that girl just forfeited the game. One of us should follow her home and make sure she's all right. Those goose droppings are big, and it probably did hurt her head. After what happened to Sorrel, it's no wonder Myrna thought she was shot with an arrow."

"Phee and I will check on Myrna." My mother glanced back at the bocce court. "Poor woman's probably a basket case. Oh look! They're leaving all the balls on the court. Guess they're going to continue with the game. Someone's walking over to the microphone by the activity building."

Sure enough, a voice came over the loudspeaker. "The game has been temporarily halted. We're calling it rainout conditions. The game will resume in ten minutes. All players are to return to the bocce courts in ten minutes, or your team will forfeit the game."

Before any of us could say a word, Bill charged out of the bocce court area and headed across the parking lot.

"Let's hope, for his sake, Myrna didn't start the car," Riva said.

Either Bill was particularly fast or Myrna particularly slow, but the two of them were face-to-face about twenty yards from us. Impossible to hear what was being said. Not so much for how they were saying it. Hands in the air from both Myrna and Bill.

"Do you think he'll convince her to keep playing?" I asked.

Cecilia shook her head. "I don't think so. Bill's on his way back and Myrna's still standing there. Maybe we should do something."

"Like what?" someone asked.

Just then, Myrna strode through the parking lot toward the courts. When she got closer to us, she shouted, "I hope a freaking owl drops a load on his head!"

"Looks like the game is on," my mother said. "Quick! We'd better get back to our seats before someone takes them."

The game resumed as if nothing had happened. Well, not exactly nothing. Myrna was still pretty shaken up, and, no matter how hard she tried, her tosses landed those balls out of bounds. In the end, the Sun City West Bocce Team would be taking home the second-place trophy.

"Aw, what the hell, Myrna. You did what you could," Bill shouted as the final announcement was made. "Not everyone's cut out for bocce ball."

"You try playing with bird poop in your hair!" she yelled back as she hurried over to us. "It was horrific. Simply horrific. I could've sworn I'd been hit."

"It's understandable Myrna," my mother said. "We thought you were positively gallant."

Gallant wouldn't have been my choice of words, but it was a word Myrna needed to hear.

"Thank you. I don't know what I would've done if you weren't all here to cheer me on. At least the awards dinner will be indoors."

I pulled my mother aside as Myrna continued to chat with the other ladies. "Awards dinner? You didn't say anything about an awards dinner. Is that going on tonight? You didn't make reservations for us to attend, did you?"

"No, of course not. Not yet. The dinner doesn't take place until sometime in April. They have to order the trophies, have them engraved, that sort of thing. Plus, each team gets to select its most valuable player."

"Oh, thank goodness. Count me out. O-U-T. Out."

Myrna had apparently said her good-byes to the others while my mom and I were talking. In fact, I was so intent on making my point about the awards dinner that I didn't notice Myrna standing right next to me until she cleared her throat.

"I wanted to thank both of you for the moral support. This has been grueling. Absolutely grueling. At least it's over for now and we can go back to playing bocce for the fun of it again. Although, I don't want to go on those courts until they catch that killer. Are they getting any closer, Phee? Does your boss tell you anything?"

"Only that they're working on it and making headway. I'm sure it'll be solved in no time."

"One can only hope. Meanwhile, I intend to keep Lucinda company this week watching Telemundo."

"I didn't know you understood Spanish."

"I don't. She translates as it goes along. We were planning on watching the Darla Marlinde trial, but it's been postponed. Between you, me, and the lamppost, I think the witness for the defense bailed out. That's why they need a postponement."

My nose crinkled automatically. "What makes you say that?"

Myrna took a deep breath and looked at my mother. "Remember that big Ponzi scheme trial a few years back? What the heck was his name? Oh yes. Romero Samson. That thing had to be postponed so many times because all the witnesses for the defense kept disappearing, and Romero's attorney insisted his client was being framed." Then she turned to me. "That was before you moved here, but I think it's the same thing. Why else would they postpone the trial? Without witnesses, they've got nothing."

Witnesses. Nothing. I was staring at Myrna, but my mind was elsewhere. I remembered something Louise had said about the day she reported for jury duty selection. Louise had inadvertently overheard some lawyers moaning about a trial postponement because their witness had been killed. And the cause of death sounded a heck of a lot like Sorrel's. So much so, in fact, that Nate looked into those dockets. There were three pending trials. Louise's was one of them, and it was settled without the need for a trial. That left the Agua Fria case and the Scorpion Murder.

Given Sorrel's penchant for nature, Nate and Marshall had made the assumption she might have been the key witness for the dumping of pesticides in the water. As a result, someone working for that company would've been a prime murder suspect. Especially if he or she had archery skills. But, after days and days of research and interviews, not a single shred of evidence could be pointed at any of the employees. They were about as handy with a bow and arrow as I was with a double boiler.

My heart beat faster as the realization hit me. Sorrel wasn't a witness for some environmental trial, she was a key witness for the Darla Marlinde scorpion murder, and that's why someone got her out of the way.

I grabbed my mother by the arm. "Uh, shouldn't we be getting going? I mean, doesn't Streetman have to be walked or something?"

"He's fine. He was out a little while ago."

Myrna must've gotten the hint because she muttered

something about wanting to get home so she could wash
her hair. My mother promised to call her in the morning.

"What was that all about? Are you in a hurry or something? I was going to suggest we go out to eat," my mother
said.

"I may have figured out who killed Sorrel. Well, not
who, but who would've had the best possible motive."

"Tell me once we get back to your car. You never know
who's listening."

Chapter 25

I wasn't about to call Marshall when I got home from the bocce tournament. Not until I had done my homework on Darla Marlinde. And that took longer than expected. The whole evening, in fact. Internet searches, social media, photos, videos . . . from the *Huffington Post* to *The New York Times*, Darla was all over the news. I imagined if I went global, she would've appeared in every major newspaper from Barbados to Barcelona.

The girl was sensational, if nothing else. A deep red-haired bombshell with large brown eyes and the most seductive expressions I'd ever seen. She'd dated a series of rich and powerful men, mostly in the sports industry, until she latched her claws on Phoenix's most prominent tech giant, Marc Yost from Metronics, Inc. When that relationship soured, the next claws Mr. Yost found latched to his skin were those of the deadly bark scorpion. And more than one. According to Augusta, who seemed to know more about scorpions than most of us, "The venom went through that guy like prep medicine for a colonoscopy." From what I read, Marc Yost was dead within hours, according to the coroner's report.

The night desk assistant from Marc Yost's condo in

Paradise Valley had seen Darla and Marc enter the place on a Friday evening, and he was certain he'd seen her leave sometime before dawn the next morning. Alone. With a large designer bag. DNA evidence indicated she'd been in the bedroom. The bed, to be exact. That didn't raise a red flag, where I was concerned, since the two of them were dating. But somehow, she became the prime suspect in his murder, accused of planting more than one bark scorpion in Marc's bed. The nagging question I had was how Sorrel Harlan figured into any of this. What had she seen? What did she know? If I could answer that, I'd know how she wound up with an arrow through the neck.

As tempting as it was, I waited until the next morning before blurting everything out to Nate and Marshall as they were fixing their coffee.

"Good morning. Where's Augusta? I don't want to repeat this. Never mind. Myrna's team lost. The goose poop threw her off. Long story. Listen, I think Sorrel may have been a key witness in the Darla Marlinde case, and that's what got her killed. Not the pesticide dumping. Not the golf course homeowners. Not some affair she might or might not have been having. It's the Darla Marlinde thing. I just know it."

Nate set his coffee cup on the counter and walked toward me. "Whoa, kiddo. Did you put a triple shot of espresso in your coffee? Slow down."

"Who brought in espresso?" Augusta walked through the doorway.

"No one," we all seemed to reply collectively, at which point Marshall took over.

"Phee's all worked up because she's convinced Sorrel Harlan was a key witness in that scorpion killer case."

Augusta's mouth opened slightly as she gave me a

funny look. "Really? What makes you think that? What did you find out?"

I slowed down long enough to reiterate the entire scenario from yesterday, which really had nothing to do with the scorpion case except for the fact Myrna had mentioned why she thought the trial was being postponed. Nate wasn't that convinced.

"It could be anything, kiddo. Delayed forensic reports. Witnesses recanting their original statements Change of attorneys. Anything."

I wasn't about to give up. "Listen, Louise definitely overheard that comment. 'An arrow to the neck, and boom. There goes our case.' Sure, it made much more sense for it to be the one involving the pesticide company, but that didn't pan out. Maybe Darla Marlinde was framed by someone who knew how to shoot an arrow."

"Talk about walking into a mess," Marshall said.

I kept looking back and forth at Nate and Marshall. "But you will do it. Won't you?"

The corners of Nate's mouth formed a small grin. "Augusta, get Deputy Bowman on the line for me, will you? And one more thing. Phee, whatever you do, do not go chasing after anything that has to do with Darla Marlinde. Understand?"

As if Nate's directive wasn't enough, Marshall had to add his two cents. "This is serious. Darla Marlinde has all sorts of questionable and dangerous connections. Promise me you'll leave this alone."

"Okay, fine." I grabbed a K-Cup of Coffee House Coffee and put it in the machine as the men proceeded to their offices.

"You're not really going to leave it alone, are you?" Augusta whispered.

"For now. Besides, I've got some other loose ends I need to figure out."

"Like?"

"Like what happened at the Heard Museum. If Bethany Gillmore wasn't giving Sorrel the evil eye in that photo, I don't know what she was doing. And what about the relationship between Milquist and Frank? And what was Edmund Wooster really doing at Milquist's house?"

"You've got the common denominator, Milquist. Now all you need is to figure out the equation. That shouldn't be too hard for you."

"I work in accounting, not algebra."

"It's all math, isn't it?"

I sighed and headed to my office, where I buried myself in work until lunch. Nate and Marshall had taken off, but I wasn't sure if they were following leads on Sorrel's murder or the other cases they had. With only Augusta and me in the office, I decided it would be a good time for me to order lunch in and do a little sleuthing on my own.

When I last spoke with her, Claudia Brinson from the garden club couldn't give me much information on that photo taken at the Heard Museum. There was no sense calling her again. I'd be much better off going directly to the source—Bethany Gillmore. I placed the call before I had time to think it through. As soon as I mentioned where I worked, Bethany made an assumption I was an investigator. I didn't bother to correct her.

"I really don't want to talk about this over the phone," Bethany said. "Could we meet someplace? Maybe a coffee shop?"

We agreed to meet at a Starbucks in Sun City West as soon as I got out of work. Actually, I had intended to call Bethany when I first saw that photo of her at the Heard Museum, but I'd never gotten around to it. Now, it seemed even more pressing, and, for some reason, I felt compelled to let Augusta know.

"Should I wait until she tells me what was going on that day at the Heard before I tell her I'm not an investigator?"

"Way I see it, information gathering is information gathering."

"Well, I intend to tell Bethany the truth. That I handle the bookkeeping. That my mother and her friends are unnerved about the murder and need to feel safe again."

"You said you're meeting her at Starbucks?"

"Yeah. Why?"

"Oh, nothing. Starbucks is a good choice. Very public. Very busy. You should be fine."

"What do you mean?"

"For all you know, Bethany's the killer. Wasn't she going to be a 'no' vote on the golf course proposal?"

"The sheriff's department was supposed to do their homework regarding the board members. I mean, if any of those people had a background in archery, wouldn't those deputies know about it?"

"Depends how thorough they are. Like I said, you should be fine. Just don't order a double shot of espresso or you'll be all twitchy."

Nate and Marshall were in and out for most of the afternoon, pausing to meet with a few clients in between. I gave no indication of my plans for coffee with Bethany, and I knew Augusta wouldn't say anything either. If I turned up anything, I'd let them know later.

At a little past five, we headed for the door and turned off the lights. At that moment, the phone rang.

"Want me to take it, Mr. Williams?" Augusta asked.

"Hold on a sec. Let the machine get it. If it's important, I'll pick up."

The four of us stood there like mannequins listening to a

voice I hadn't heard in quite a while, Deputy Bowman's rather unpleasant partner, Deputy Ranston. The man reminded me of a Sonoran Desert toad. In both looks and personality.

"Nate or Marshall, give me a call when you get in. A stolen car just turned up in El Mirage. A beige Chevy Equinox that looks like it collided with something red. That golf cart maybe? Call me."

"Oh my gosh! The beige blur! They found the car that ran Myrna's golf cart off the road. It has to be that car," I said.

Nate motioned for us to head out the door. "I'll give Ranston a call from my cell. No sense all of us hanging around."

Marshall could probably see the look on my face and would know what it meant. I had to give him credit. The guy was really getting to know me.

"I'll call you this evening, Phee, okay? And please don't say anything to Myrna. Or your mother. Or anyone in that book club for that matter." Marshall stared at me.

"Mums the word," I replied. "I wouldn't think of it."

Augusta kicked the edge of my shoe as we stepped out the door. It wasn't accidental.

Chapter 26

With a soft lavender and purple hat, a vivid purple scarf, and a muted bluish-purple sweater, Bethany Gillmore was easy to recognize. I remembered Shirley mentioning something about Bethany overdoing it on the pansy purple when we attended that first recreation center meeting.

I walked over to the corner table and introduced myself.

Bethany was already sipping some sort of foamed drink. "Why don't you get some coffee and we can talk? It's pretty quiet here this evening."

It took me all of three or four minutes to place my order and return to the table. I thought Bethany might be nervous or uncomfortable, but she seemed relaxed and eager to chat.

"I suppose your office wants to know what I know about Sorrel, since we both served on the same board. Is that it?"

I squirmed in my seat, hoping she didn't notice. "Sort of. It has more to do with the garden club."

"Oh, *that*. I'm no longer in the garden club."

"But you were in the club the day you all visited the Heard Museum."

Bethany put her coffee cup down and didn't say a word, forcing me to keep talking.

"At Sorrel's memorial, a photo from that day at the museum was on display, and—"

"Oh dear Lord, you might as well know, I despised that woman. She was so self-righteous, it made me nauseous. But I didn't kill her, if that's what you're thinking. I've never held a bow and arrow, and I don't know anyone who has."

"Um, er, no. I'm not thinking . . . I mean, my office isn't thinking that. Not at all. But something was going on, and it might be important."

Bethany looked around the room and waited until all of the customers were a good distance from us before she spoke. "I've known Frank Landrow since he first joined the garden club. A kind, considerate man, who happens to adore his wife, even if she's a bit of a flirt with really expensive taste. Then along came Sorrel, and, somehow, he got caught up in her tree-hugging causes."

"Huh?"

"Sorrel was always into some environmental effort to save the world. Anyway, it got worse. She dragged Frank into her peace and tie-dye schemes to the point where he was practically tethered to her. He stopped participating on our garden club committees and wouldn't even take part in our annual plant sale, except for distributing flyers. Too busy, he told us. But it was Sorrel. I knew it. I finally couldn't take it any longer, and, when she went to use the ladies' room at the Heard, I had it out with her."

"Oh my gosh. I bet that didn't go well."

"You bet right. She told me that Frank, and I quote, 'had more idealistic goals than to burden himself with the trivialities of your garden club.' That photo was taken a few minutes after we left the ladies' room, and I was still steaming."

"I can imagine."

"There's more. I finally was able to corner Frank alone. And that's when I learned the truth. It was a business arrangement of sorts. Eleanor's extravagant spending was putting a major strain on the Landrow finances. Somehow, Milquist got wind of it and was paying Frank to keep Sorrel occupied. I figured her own husband couldn't stand her, so he had to pay someone else to put up with her. Guess he was too old-fashioned for a divorce, huh?"

Wow! Guess my discovery in Milquist's drawer is right on the money.

"Bethany," I said, and stood up to retrieve my coffee from the counter. "Do you know how Milquist and Frank knew each other?"

"Don't you know? Oh, I suppose not if you're asking me. They belonged to the same country club. Not the same membership status, but the same club."

"What do you mean?"

"The Landrows are social members. The Harlans were, I mean, he still *is,* a proprietary member. Big difference."

On my gosh. This is beginning to sound like Downton Abbey *with the upstairs-downstairs classes.*

Two men, who looked to be in their thirties, brushed by our table, and Bethany stopped talking momentarily.

When they started to place their orders, she continued, "I suppose you're wondering how I know all of this. From Frank. That's how. When he started telling me about the arrangement he had with Milquist, he unloaded everything. After losing an undisclosed amount of money at one of the country club's card games, Frank was approached by Milquist with a proposition to buddy up with Sorrel, so to speak. And, since Eleanor was so preoccupied with her own activities, it seemed a relatively harmless thing for Frank to do. Until it got out of hand."

I took another sip of my coffee and almost wished it was something stronger. "Out of hand?"

"I believe so. That's what Frank was starting to tell me at the Heard when Sorrel reappeared. Then he clammed up, and I walked away."

"Do you have any idea what he might've been referring to?"

"Wish I did. It might shed some light on who killed Sorrel."

"What about Eleanor? Didn't she resent all the time her husband spent with Sorrel?"

"I don't think so. At least Frank didn't think so when we spoke. Eleanor's schedule was always jam-packed. Clothes shopping. Spa days. Workout days. Beauty parlor days. The only time she wasn't indulging herself was when she went to visit her brother."

For a split second, I wondered if that could've been the man she was with at La Mariposa's the other night. "Her brother?"

"Yeah, according to Frank, the guy's had all sorts of jobs around the valley. Some more embellished than others. He's a prima donna like his sister. Frank's not too impressed."

"Do you know what the brother's doing now?"

"Concierge services for a high-class condo in Paradise Valley. Frank has as little to do with him as possible. Let's face it, Paradise Valley is the Mercedes of neighborhoods in the Phoenix area, and Eleanor's brother is probably raking it in. Meanwhile, Frank's struggling to keep his wife happy."

"What an awful situation. I really feel bad for him. At least I can understand why he took Milquist up on that offer."

Bethany stared into her coffee. "I suppose."

"Oh, and one more thing. If you do find out what Frank meant when he said things were getting out of hand, would you call me?"

"Sure. Have you got a card?"

A card. A business card. Of course I had one. It said WILLIAMS INVESTIGATIONS, SOPHIE KIMBALL, ACCOUNTANT.

I reached in my bag and handed her my card. "There's something you should know. I'm not an official investigator, but I do help out on their cases. I handle their accounting."

Bethany gave me the oddest smile. "Then you probably know more than any of them. Nice meeting you, Phee."

I was off the proverbial hook. Stretching the truth always made me uncomfortable. We'd only been at Starbucks a little while, but I was famished and couldn't wait to get home. Funny, but I kept going over Augusta's words the entire drive back to my house. "Common denominator."

At least I knew for certain what the relationship between Milquist and Frank was all about. Still, I needed to find out how Edmund Wooster fit into the mix. *If* he fit in. Then there was the little cliffhanger Bethany tossed my way. What had gotten out of hand?

The blinking light on my answering machine was the first thing I noticed when I walked into the kitchen.

I'm not dealing with that now. I'm going to change into sweats, make myself a sandwich, and then press the message button.

A half hour later I looked at the caller ID to see if it was my mother plaguing me about something, or Marshall calling me, like he said he would. It was a fifty-fifty crap shoot and thankfully, Marshall won out. His message was short and to the point.

"Are you in the mood for company tonight? Give me a call."

I had already washed off my makeup and put on my

rattiest pair of sweats. The ones with holes in places I'd rather not mention. Technically, it wouldn't be as if Marshall hadn't seen me dressed down, so to speak, but I'd seen homeless people in downtown Phoenix who looked better than I did. Still, I was dying to know what he found out about the beige blur that nearly killed Myrna. I pushed the redial button and waited.

"Hey, Phee. When you didn't return my call right away, I figured you'd made plans for the evening."

"Uh, not really. I just stopped for coffee on my way home."

"Coffee? You must have the caffeine jitters by now."

"Fine. I'm going to wind up telling you anyway, so I might as well tell you now. I was having coffee with—"

"Please tell me it was with a friend of yours and not a suspect."

"I don't have a list of suspects in front of me, so I really couldn't say for sure."

"Just spit it out already, will you?"

"Bethany Gillmore. From the rec center board. I was curious about that photo from the Heard Museum. Anyway, you knew I was going to call her. I decided to see her in person, that's all."

"And? Did you find out anything?"

"I'll tell you when you get here. That is, if you still feel like coming over."

"Have you eaten?"

"Just a sandwich. A small one."

"Well, don't eat anything else. I'll pick up something and see you in a little bit."

The "something" turned out to be a double order of chicken wings, Arizona style with all the fixings from jalapeños to melted *queso*. In the forty or so minutes between the end of the call and the time Marshall arrived, I had changed into jeans and a decent shirt. I'd also reapplied a tad of makeup, mainly blush.

We dove into the meal as soon as he got here and didn't talk about the case.

When we were left staring at a pile of chicken bones, Marshall finally said something. "Okay, now that we've made history of those wings, suppose you tell me about your meeting with Bethany Gillmore."

I wasted no time. "I was right all along. That note from Milquist's nightstand? She confirmed it. He was paying Frank. Kindred spirits, my you-know-what. But big deal. This isn't getting anyone any closer to finding out who killed Sorrel. What did Nate learn about that Chevy Equinox? Did they catch the car thief?"

"Oh, they caught him all right, and it had nothing to do with Myrna, Milquist, or Sorrel, for that matter. Seems it was some sort of gang initiation and Sun City West was a prime area for stealing a vehicle. Myrna was just the unlucky one who happened to get run off the road. The theft took place a while ago, but the owner didn't know it. The owner was an eighty-year-old woman who was visiting relatives in Palm Springs. The woman lives in an apartment complex where they have carports, not garages. An easy spot for a would-be gang member to steal a car. And that's exactly what happened."

"So, it wasn't a case of mistaken golf cart identity. And Milquist wasn't the target."

"Correct on all counts. The driver had no clue who Milquist was. And when the sheriff's deputies questioned the guy about a murder connection, the kid all but fainted. Confessed to grand theft auto but swore on his life he never killed, or attempted to kill, anyone."

"Well, I guess Myrna will be relieved."

"Maybe. The kid had no insurance. Big surprise there.

Nate plans on stopping by Milquist's place to let him know what transpired. Especially since we put him on edge about the similar golf carts."

"What a bummer. I was kind of hoping there'd be a link between that accident and the killer. Doesn't this frustrate you no end?"

"It's what investigating's all about. You've got a lot of dangling cords and until you put a knot on the bottom of each of them, the case is still wide open. The good news is we've tied some knots."

"And added more cords. I forgot to tell you about the last thing Bethany said. Frank believed things were getting out of hand."

"Out of hand? What's that supposed to mean?"

"Darned if I know. Bethany didn't know either. Oh, and there's one more thing, but I don't think it has anything to do with any of this. Eleanor has a high-maintenance brother who works in Paradise Valley. Concierge services."

"You're right. I think we can forget about that little tidbit."

"What about that other business? Maybe Sorrel was into something that went too far and that's what got her killed. Frank's probably sitting on top of all of this!"

"Calm down. Either Nate or I will have a chat with Mr. Landrow, okay? Now, will you relax for a bit and concentrate on something other than this case?"

He reached across the table and gave my wrist a squeeze. Neither Sorrel, Milquist, Eleanor, or Frank were mentioned the rest of the night.

Chapter 27

The more I thought about it, the more I was convinced that Sorrel was murdered as a result of something she uncovered regarding Darla Marlinde. That arrow to the neck had to be a professional hit and not some amateur archer who struck it lucky, so to speak. The investigation, in spite of all the work Nate and Marshall were doing, not to mention whatever it was the sheriff's office was up to, still wasn't yielding results fast enough. As if I wasn't painfully aware of it, my mother made sure I got the message loud and clear.

"What's taking your office so long?" she bellowed into the phone.

I was still dripping wet, having just stepped out of the shower, and the only reason I took the call was because I thought it might be Marshall. He'd left his wallet here last night. Said it was too bulky when he sat on the couch.

"I've got to get to work. Can I call you later?"

"This will only take a minute. If Sorrel Harlan's murder isn't solved soon, it's going to cost us an arm and a leg. The rec centers have already added additional security to the golf courses. That doesn't come cheap. And it's not only the golf courses. People are afraid to do anything outdoors. I've even heard some of the snowbirds talking about relocating next winter. You know what that means, don't you? Less income for the community and rising prices for the rest of us. What's taking them so long?"

"My God, Mother. I can't answer that."

"Well, when you get into the office this morning, light a firecracker under your boss. Oh, and did I mention your aunt Ina has decided to take a sojourn to Belize until the matter has been resolved? She said the stress was too much for her and Louis. Especially since they live on a golf course."

"Fine. Firecracker. Belize. Golf course. Got it. I'll call you later."

I hated it when my mother was right. The case *was* taking too long. And what harm would it really do if I did a little sleuthing on my own after work? It wasn't as if I planned to meet with mobsters or gunrunners. I was, in Augusta's words, about to do some "information gathering."

Paradise Valley, with the highest per capita income in the state, was a forty-five-minute drive from the office. If I took the highway. And if traffic was light. Otherwise, it was at least an hour. Still, I figured I'd have lots of daylight ahead of me when I got to Marc Yost's condo. Convinced that Sorrel was indeed the key witness in his murder, I had to see for myself what she could've possibly discovered.

Bless the Internet. I had already written down the address for the deceased's condo and planned to engage whatever tenants wafted my way.

"I'm telling you this, Augusta, because if anything happens to me, I want someone to know my last location."

I had pulled Augusta aside as soon as I got into work. She was early, and my boss, along with the guy I was dating, were both running late. "Here's the address. It'll save time that way."

"What are you figuring is going to happen?"

"I don't know, but I can't stand another day of my mother's nagging. Plus, I think I'm really on to something. It was the Darla Marlinde case that got Sorrel killed. Nate and Marshall think so, too. At least I think they think so. Anyway, you know how long those investigations take. Protocol and all."

Augusta's face was expressionless. "I'd give you my Glock, but you're not licensed to carry. I've got pepper spray in my bag if you want that."

"Uh, no thanks. I'd only wind up spraying myself."

"So, what do you think you're going to find?"

"That's the thing. I don't know. But Sorrel saw something. She had to. I plan to snoop around the building and see if I can get anyone to talk with me. Shh. Here comes Nate."

"Good morning, ladies." Nate walked in. Then, he looked my way. "Hey, kiddo, I don't know what you said to your boyfriend, but he's on his way over to speak with Frank Landrow."

"I, um, er—"

"Don't apologize. Someone has to keep Marshall on his toes."

Nate shuffled off to his office, and I bolted to mine. Marshall and I didn't cross paths the entire day and that was just as well. I didn't know if I could keep my after-work plans to myself. At least I had the foresight to leave his wallet with Augusta, who gave me an odd look and tucked it into a desk drawer.

"You're sure about the pepper spray?" she whispered as we headed out at the end of the day.

"Yes. I'm sure. Thanks anyway."

"You might want to keep Marshall's number on speed dial just in case."

"Thanks for the vote of confidence. I'll be fine."

"By the way, I gave him his wallet while you were out to grab lunch. Guy turned as red as a beet. He left before you got back."

"Thanks, Augusta."

Terrific. Augusta's got us pegged.

I had jotted down a few questions in the event I was actually able to speak with one or more of the condo tenants. In the back of my mind, I kept hearing Marshall scold me for interfering with an active investigation. I chose to ignore it as if it were a hallucination.

Whenever I'd seen real estate listings with words like spectacular, elegant, and priceless, I knew they were exaggerating. In the case of Marc Yost's condo, they weren't. I had Googled the address, and, since another unit in the complex was for sale, I'd gotten all the specs on the building. The structure itself, a massive French Provincial, looked more like a palace than a residence. Behind it was a panoramic view of the Camelback and Mummy Mountains. I imagined the price Marc Yost had paid was worth every penny. Too bad he didn't get to enjoy it longer.

I loved my KIA Sportage, but, with the exception of a landscaping truck off to the side of the complex parking lot, my car stood out like an eyesore among the Audis and BMWs. I parked it next to a Mazda convertible and stared at the shiny, candy-apple-red vehicle. Unlike Minnesota, where people only drove convertibles with the tops down in the summer, it was too hot to do that in Arizona. Convertible owners here only enjoyed the open air in the winter. Off to the left, I saw some fancy-looking garages. Probably extra cost for the tenants. I glanced at the Mazda again. Way out of my price range.

As I got out of my car, I happened to notice a small green decal on the upper left-hand side of the Mazda's

windshield. It looked like the one I had. Left over from
when I worked for the Mankato Police Department in
accounting. As hard as I tried, I couldn't scrape it off my car.
The Mazda owner seemed to be in the same fix. Although
the edges were torn, I could still read PARKING PERMIT
METRO on the sticker.

Not wanting to waste another second, I walked around
the grounds while it was still light. The botanical gardens
had nothing on this place. A few ponds, ranging in size
from smaller koi pools to larger and grander ones with waterfall features and swans, took my breath away. Especially
the ones with the swans.

There were benches and small tables nested under
mesquite trees. Every last bit of shrubbery was perfectly
manicured. As I continued my walk around the place, I
noticed a gardener trimming the bougainvillea. He paused
occasionally to glance at the swans. A perfect opening for
me to start a conversation.

"They're beautiful, aren't they?" I motioned behind me.

"Beautiful and delicate. I hope these survive."

"What do you mean? I thought they'd be all right in this
climate."

"The climate, yes, but not the coyotes. This is the third
pair the company has purchased. All because some of the
tenants want to look at elegant birds, not geese or ducks.
Oh, excuse me. I shouldn't have said that. Please don't
report me. I need my job."

"Please. Don't worry. I'm only a visitor. And I agree with
you. Defenseless birds shouldn't be placed in jeopardy."

"You're the second visitor to say that. There was another
lady who came here a while back. Part of one of those environmental change groups. She had a petition for the removal
of swans from unprotected habitants like ours. I guess her
organization had a list of complexes that had swan ponds."

*Am I hearing him right? Environmental change group?
If that doesn't smack of Sorrel Harlan, nothing does.*

"That other lady. Do you remember what she looked like?"

The man shrugged. "Sorry. Not really. Only that she was middle-aged. Clunky shoes. She got here really, really early to get signatures. Guess she wanted to talk to everyone who walked out of the building to get to work."

"Like how early?"

"I got here at five-thirty that day. Usually I work the afternoon shift, but there was a change in the schedule. Anyway, she was already sitting on the bench by the entrance. She must have gotten here while it was still dark out in order not to miss anyone. She asked if I'd sign the petition, and I told her I couldn't. I didn't need to sign anything that could jeopardize my job. That's all I know. Maybe the desk assistant can help you. It was the same day they found the dead man in the condo. Of course, that was later in the afternoon."

The same day? Holy cow!

My heart was racing as I thanked him and headed straight for the entrance. The desk assistant was sitting at a counter that housed a computer monitor and a phone. The guy's small tan backpack was slung over the chair. Behind him was a locked glass cabinet with assorted keys. Probably for tenants who locked themselves out. With the intense light streaming in, the guy was wearing dark glasses, so I couldn't get a good look at his face. From what I did see, he appeared to be young. Thirtyish maybe. Wearing khakis and a button-down dress shirt. Deep blue.

His iPhone lay on the counter next to his set of keys. The key fob was hard to miss. I recognized it as one of those "Scottsdale Switchblades," where the key flips out at the push of a button. The silver Mazda insignia identified it. I figured his car had to be the convertible parked in front. Fancy car for a desk assistant. I asked him if he remembered Sorrel.

"Sorry, lady. I don't remember anyone with petitions."

"Then you must've seen her by the entrance when you got out of work."

"I clocked out at five, like usual, and there was no one in front. The day guy came in as I was leaving. I work a twelve-hour shift from five at night to five in the morning. It stinks."

I figured Sorrel must've arrived a few minutes after the night guy left and the day guy arrived. Maybe the day guy noticed her.

"The day guy? Do you know his name? His number?"

"Sorry. We're not allowed to give out that information. You can always email our management—Dream View Properties, Inc."

I wrote down the company name, even though I already knew it. "You're the night desk assistant?"

He looked at me as if I was batty. "Uh-huh. That's what I just said."

"Oh, dear. You were here the night Marc Yost was killed. How awful. How tragic."

The guy looked around as if the place was being bugged. "I was here. At this desk when he was murdered. It wasn't as if I saw anything."

"But you did see Darla Marlinde leaving before five when you called it quits for the day, didn't you? That's what you told the police."

"Hey, who are you? I don't have to answer any of this."

I held out my business card, careful to keep my thumb over the word "accountant." "If you must know, I work for a private investigator in the Phoenix area."

"Well, I told the police everything. I saw her coming. That was around eleven. I saw her leaving. Alone."

"You said you work a twelve-hour shift. Couldn't you have missed something? Or someone else coming in after she left? Maybe you had to use the restroom."

"That would've only taken a minute or two."

I looked around the place and noticed the obvious security system. "Was anything found on the security footage?"

"The video system was installed after the murder. The tenants were all freaked out, so the company had a state-of-the-art system installed the next week."

"I just have one more question. According to the police reports, you said you saw Darla come in with Marc. Are you sure it was him? I mean, were they holding hands or walking really close to each other?"

"I didn't really notice. I was mainly looking at her. She's kind of hard not to look at, if you know what I mean."

Oh, brother. What is it with these men? "So the guy she walked in with might not have been Marc?"

"Hey, don't go putting words in my mouth. I don't need to file a new report with the police."

Oh my God! Isn't this what they call an "element of doubt?" "Think again. Did you see anyone else coming and going that night?"

"Sure. Lots of people. And they were all tenants. I already told the police."

I tried to sort this out while thinking what I should ask him next. If Darla Marlinde walked into the building and Marc wasn't the guy who was with her, then who was he? And what if Marc wasn't in the condo at all? What if the guy she came in with had nothing to do with her? He could've been another tenant. Maybe Darla went into Marc's condo alone, stayed there, waited for him, got exasperated, and left before five? After all, that was the story she'd told the police according to the tabloid stuff I'd dug up, as well as some legitimate news articles. Of course, they didn't believe her because the desk assistant had said he saw the two of them walk in together around eleven.

But the desk assistant wasn't really sure, was he? He was too busy ogling Darla and not paying attention to the guy who walked in with her. Suppose Marc arrived later, after Darla left. And suppose it was someone else who killed him? Someone Sorrel had seen. Or what if it was the desk assistant himself? After all, he did have access to all of the condo keys.

Suddenly, I began to get nervous. At about the same time, some clouds formed overhead and the intense glare in the lobby dissipated. The desk assistant took off his shades and placed them on the counter. I got a good look at his face and froze. It was the same man who was at La Mariposa. The one who was with Eleanor Landrow. Her brother! It had to be. Bethany said he was in concierge services in Paradise Valley. This was Paradise Valley, all right, but the guy had exaggerated about his job. If he lied about that, maybe he lied about the night Marc Yost was killed. And the parking sticker I just saw! The first few letters spelled "Metro." What if it was Metronics? That was Marc Yost's company. Could Eleanor's brother have been a disgruntled employee? My mind was spinning out of control. I had to focus back on the timeline for Marc's murder.

There was only one way to find out. That petition of Sorrel's! If Darla Marlinde had signed it on her way out of the building, which would have been any time before five, then maybe, a bit later, Marc Yost signed it on his way in. I mean, he *had* to get back in because his body was found later that day. Scorpions and all. His signature on the petition would prove he was alive when Darla left. She'd be exonerated.

My pulse began to quicken, and I had to move fast. I had to find the gardener and ask him if he remembered what that petition had said. Who was it for? What organization? If I could figure all of that out and link it to Sorrel's killer, I would solve two cases.

"Um, er, this is all the information I need for now, Mister . . ."

"Burrier. Trevor Burrier."

"Thank you, Mr. Burrier. We'll be in touch if we need you."

I made a mental note to find out what Eleanor Landrow's maiden name was as I raced out the doorway to find the gardener. Thankfully, I spotted him by a cluster of palm trees. It appeared as if he was spraying something on the ground.

"Watch your step!" he shouted. "I'm spraying insecticide. Hold on. I'll walk over to you."

I stood absolutely still as the man left the sprayer by a large banana palm and took a few steps my way. "If I don't keep up with the crickets, those bark scorpions will get worse."

"Crickets?"

"Yeah, it's a major food source for scorpions. There really isn't an effective way to kill the scorpions, especially since so many of them nest in the palms, but, by eliminating their food source, many die off or migrate elsewhere. So, what was it you wanted?"

"I was wondering about something. By any chance, did you see what that swan petition said? What was the name of the organization?"

"I only got a quick look, so I could be wrong, but I think

it was AZ Bird RR or something like that. Listen, I need to finish spraying before it gets dark."

I thanked him for his time and practically ran to my car. The Google search for AZ Bird RR could stand to wait for a few minutes while I did something only my mother would condone under the circumstances—snoop around the Mazda convertible.

I already knew the car belonged to Trevor. It was the only Mazda in the lot. My SUV was tall enough to block the view should the guy step out of the building, but I had to act quickly. I leaned over the convertible and opened the glove compartment. Scads of paperwork, a few pens, and some icky tissues. My mother would've been appalled at my not having Clorox wipes with me. She had a point.

Next, I lifted open the small rectangular compartment directly behind the gear shift. In my car it was a catch-all for everything. I was hoping Trevor's would be the same, although I didn't know exactly what I expected to find. A microfiber cloth. More pens.

What does this guy do, collect them?

Wads of old gas station and fast-food receipts and a small flashlight. That was something I always intended to put in my car. A flashlight. But I never got around to it.

I shoved everything back and started to close the compartment hatch when something caught my eye. It was the logo on the flashlight. Only it wasn't a flashlight. It was a black light with a scorpion on it. Same as the one on Louise's key chain. In less than ten seconds, an ironclad theory crystalized in front of me.

Trevor Burrier killed Marc Yost and framed Darla Marlinde. Putting the blame on Darla would've been a pretty easy thing to do since she and Marc were notorious for highly publicized fights in all sorts of fancy restaurants and hotspots. Trevor must've used that black light to locate the bark scorpions behind the condo. All he would've needed was some sort of glass jar and a pair of cooking tongs. Even a tweezer, if he wasn't squeamish. He had that small tan backpack. It could easily conceal a glass jar. He had motive, and he had means. Opportunity came when Marc got back to the condo after Darla left but before Trevor's shift ended at five. All Trevor had to do was grab that black light, go outside for a few minutes, and help himself to some bark scorpions. After all, the gardener said they were plentiful. When he was sure Marc had crashed for the night, or morning in this case, Trevor took the keys to the condo, snuck in, and dumped the scorpions in Marc's bed.

It was the perfect crime. Except for one thing. How on earth was I going to prove it? I didn't even have circumstantial evidence. Lots of people, including my mother's wacky friends, had those scorpion lights. Just in case, I grabbed my iPhone and snapped a quick photo of the black light as it sat in the Mazda's gear shift compartment. Then I took a photo of the "Metro" parking sticker before walking to the rear of the car for the last image I needed—his license plate.

Chapter 28

It was getting late and the gardener had already pulled out of the parking lot. Only a few minutes of daylight were left. I quickly Googled AZ Bird RR and came up with "Arizona Bird Rescue and Rehabilitation." It was part of a larger organization that specialized in saving wildlife. I kept scrolling past the organizational information and photos of rescued birds until I got to the "contact us" part of the page. I was still getting used to mobile searches as opposed to the ones I conducted on my desktop computer.

They had an office in Phoenix. And one in Tucson, too. The Phoenix office was actually located on Mill Avenue in Tempe, near Arizona State University. Office hours were Monday–Saturday from nine to five, with special evening hours from seven to nine on Mondays, Tuesdays, and Thursdays. Hurray for being in a college community.

I went to Google maps for the shortest route and headed over there, trying to ignore the rumbling in my stomach. It felt like it'd been ages since I'd last eaten. According to the address, AZ Bird RR was smack dab in the middle of the college business district, and that meant lots of eateries.

I pictured subs, pizzas, gyros, burgers, and anything with carbs. And unlike my mother's community, those places wouldn't close at eight.

Mill Avenue was bustling with activity when I got there. It took me two swipes around one of the blocks to find a parking space, and I had to use every bit of skill I could muster to parallel park. The good news was that AZ Bird RR was adjacent to a sub shop, and I had every intention of chomping into a loaded sandwich once I was done speaking with someone from the bird rescue.

Posters of water fowl, raptors, and roadrunners were plastered on the walls of the small storefront agency, along with signs encouraging people to save the birds and donate now. Three desks, each with a computer, seemed to take up most of the space. A shared printer sat on a two-drawer metal file cabinet. A girl, who looked as if she was still in her teens, was busy at one of the computers. Her short, spiked hair with emerald-green highlights matched the green T-shirt she was wearing.

She spoke up as soon as I walked in. "Hi! Are you here to sign one of our petitions? Or volunteer maybe? We have volunteers of all ages, you know. Arizona Bird Rehabilitation and Rescue isn't a college organization."

Volunteers of all ages? My God, do I look ninety to her? And what about Sorrel?

"Actually, I was looking for someone who might assist me. Are you the only person working tonight?"

"Clarisse is, but she went out to get something to eat. I know Clarisse handles the accounting, but if it's something other than that, I can help."

"I'm actually here about the petition to rehome swans that are in unprotected areas."

"Did you want to sign it or contribute to the cause?"

I took a quick breath and pulled out my business card, careful once again to conceal the word "accountant." The girl gave the card a cursory glance and looked up as I spoke.

"I'm Phee Kimball and, like the card says, I work for Williams Investigations. We're looking into the murder of one of your volunteers. Her name was Sorrel Harlan, and she was getting signatures for the swan petition."

The girl looked horror stricken. "Murdered? One of our volunteers? That's terrible. Oh my God! Were any birds killed?"

Birds? She's worried about birds?

"Um, no. No birds were killed. But we may have a lead on who killed Sorrel, if we could see the petition she was carrying. Can you do that? Show me the petition?"

She crinkled her nose as if I'd asked her to walk across a bed of hot coals.

I pressed further. "This would be a tremendous help to the investigation. After all, I'm sure your agency would want us to locate the person who was responsible for murdering one of your volunteers."

"Okay. But here's the problem. That file cabinet over there has lots of swan petitions that haven't been sorted yet. I don't have the time to go through each one. Can you come back in a few days?"

By now my stomach was working overtime, and I had all I could do to ignore it. "How about if I sit over there and sort them. Do they have the volunteers' names on them?"

"Volunteer initials are put on the bottom of each sheet with the date." She walked over to the cabinet. "You sure you want to do this now?"

"Absolutely."

"By the way, my name's Sydney."

"Nice to meet you, Sydney. And thanks."

Sydney handed me a stack of petitions that dated back three months. Fortunately, I knew the date in question so once I sorted out the petitions Sorrel turned in, it made the process go faster than I had expected. It took me less than twenty minutes to find the sheets with her initials on them.

"Wow! That was quick. You sure you don't want to volunteer here? It's a wonderful cause, saving birds."

"I'm sure it is, but I work full time. Maybe someday. When I retire."

Who was I kidding? But, it sounded good. I checked each page carefully to find the date in question—the date Marc Yost was found dead. Sorrel had managed to garner two pages with signatures. I held my breath and crossed my fingers. Literally. Sure enough, I spied Darla Marlinde's signature. It was in the middle of the page. I scanned down. No sign of Marc Yost's. I had one page left. Again, I crossed my fingers, hoping Sydney wasn't looking my way. I had "amateur" practically stamped on my forehead.

So as not to miss anything, I held the palm of my hand under each signature and scrutinized it carefully as I went down the page. Then I saw it. Three signatures from the bottom, and it took up two lines. It was almost as illegible as those doctor signatures on prescriptions, but the capital *Y* and the small *o* and *s* in Yost gave it away. The capital *M* wasn't too bad either. Judging from the way Marc signed the petition, he was either in a tremendous hurry or really wasted. It didn't matter. Unless there were throngs of people signing that petition all at once, the guy was alive and well after Darla left the condo. Way too many signatures in between.

Then I had another thought. Suppose Darla *had* put scorpions in Marc's bed before she left the place? No. Even the most stoned drunkard would've noticed those crawly things when they climbed into bed. I was positive Marc's murderer was Trevor Burrier.

"Sydney, I found what I was looking for. Is there any way I could make a copy?"

Again, the crinkled brow. "I guess it would be all right. But the original must stay here."

The original. Only an original document would be admissible in court. I knew I couldn't leave with it, but I wanted to make sure no one else did either.

"Um, what happens to these petitions when your agency has enough signatures?"

"Oh. They get filed with the state and appear on the voting ballots."

Duh. I should've known that. Unlike Minnesota, Arizona was known for a plethora of proposals that appeared on the election ballots. Those petitions wouldn't be destroyed, they'd be archived somewhere, and that was just as bad.

"Do you have a timeline for the swan petitions?"

"We've got plenty of time. It's only March. We won't be turning anything in until summer."

My pulse returned to normal. "That's good. Very good. For the swans, I mean. I'm sure you'll get more signatures."

Sydney made me a copy of the two petition pages, and I also used my iPhone to take my own pictures of them. Feeling guilty for stretching the truth, I handed Sydney a twenty dollar bill and told her it was a donation for the swan cause.

As I started to leave, Clarisse came in, and I could smell the garlic and onion on her breath. By now, I was one step away from dying of hunger. I thanked Sydney and headed straight for the sub shop next door. I'd order all the fixings. No one was going to smell my breath tonight.

Chapter 29

I arrived to work on time, but, apparently, everyone else had gotten there earlier. Augusta was already seated at her desk.

"I'm alive and well as you can see," I said to her as soon as I walked in the door.

"Shh. Come on over. You need to know something."

By the look on her face, I knew it was grim.

"What?"

"It took two days, but the police department in Paradise Valley got the Darla Marlinde information to Deputy Bowman, and he just faxed it to Mr. Williams. Mr. Williams and Mr. Gregory are in Mr. Williams's office right now going over it. Statements, timelines, you name it, they're pouring through it right now to see if you were right. If Sorrel was a witness. I don't think they're going to be too happy you went over to that condo last night."

"Yesterday you thought it was a good idea. You said 'information gathering is information gathering.'"

"That was before the whole kit and caboodle was served up to Mr. Williams this morning. I overheard him saying he was glad you were staying out of it."

"Really? He said that?"

"Yep."

"That's great. That's just great. I'm going to lose my job and my boyfriend."

"What exactly happened yesterday? What did you find out?"

I leaned over her desk, and, keeping my voice as low as I could, I told her everything.

When I was done, she grabbed my wrist and shook it. "You cracked that case wide open, Phee. This Trevor guy killed Yost and framed Darla. The only witness was Sorrel. She saw Yost alive, and Trevor had to get rid of her, so he got his sister Eleanor to shoot her with a bow and arrow. Eleanor being a top marksman and all."

"That's what I figure, too, but the only evidence I have is the petition. Besides, until I can find out Eleanor's maiden name, I won't be a hundred percent certain. I tried a Google search last night and got nowhere. Talk to me when you catch a break. I've got to get to work."

I booted up my computer in record time and started on the tax filing information for the business. I needed something cut and dry that I could do automatically. I also needed time to figure out what I was going to say to Nate and Marshall. I was running scenarios through my head when Marshall knocked on the doorframe and walked in.

"What's the matter? You look like you've seen a ghost."

"What? No. You caught me off guard, that's all. I've been working on the taxes."

"Uh-huh. The taxes. Well, I wanted you to know I spoke with Frank Landrow about what you said the other day. You know, 'things getting out of hand.'"

"Oh yeah. That."

"Turns out Sorrel was into more causes than you could shake a stick at. Poor Frank got dragged along into some of them, and he was getting frazzled. The horse rescue up in Williams, the abandoned dogs in Wittman, and, get this, a swan rescue. And you'll never guess where that was."

There was a reason I didn't play poker. I'd never be able to pull off the face. I pretended to be looking at my computer screen as if, somehow, the tax information would save me. "Um, was Frank there, too?"

"I didn't even tell you where it was, and, no, Frank wasn't there. Listen, maybe I should stop back later. You seem to be really involved with the taxes."

"Oh, what the hell!" I pushed my chair back from the computer, opened my desk drawer, and pulled out the copies I made from the swan petition. "I know Frank wasn't there. I know all about it. And before you lose your temper and say something we'll both regret, although I'll probably regret it more than you, I went to Paradise Valley after work yesterday. To Marc Yost's condo. I knew Sorrel must've seen something, and that's what got her killed."

"I know. I know exactly where you were."

"Augusta? Augusta told you?"

"Phee, I'm a licensed detective. That means I come with some skills. And no, Augusta didn't say anything. And you were talking with a possible murder suspect. You could've gotten yourself killed."

"How do you know all of this?"

"When you raced out of work yesterday without so much as a 'good-bye,' I knew something was off. And Augusta was acting even cagier than usual. I knew you couldn't leave the Darla Marlinde case alone because you were certain Sorrel had witnessed something."

"So you followed me? You followed me all the way to Paradise Valley?"

"You would've noticed my car if I did. Instead, I called

in a favor from an off-duty police officer who lives near there. His car was parked in front of Marc Yost's condo."

"They must pay well in Paradise Valley. All those cars were Audis or BMWs."

Dead silence for ten seconds.

"He also followed you to Tempe. So you might as well tell me every single thing beginning with those papers in your hand."

"You're not angry with me?"

"Angry? I'm furious. Interfering with an open investigation. Talking with possible suspects who could be dangerous. My God! We've had this conversation before!"

"Marshall, I—"

"Look, it's a matter of trust. If I can't trust you or believe you, how on earth is our relationship going to work?"

Aargh. The trust thing. The last time that subject came up, it was with my ex-husband, and I was the one asking the questions. This time I didn't say a word.

"And whatever you do, don't start to cry. It won't help."

"I wasn't going to cry. And no matter what I say, it won't be right. And you can be as angry with me as a hornet, but can you do it after Sorrel's killer is caught and Darla Marlinde is exonerated?"

"Whoa. Darla Marlinde? Innocent? You'd better start from the beginning."

At that moment, Augusta decided to take her break and charged into my office. "Before you or Mr. Williams go off the deep end and fire Phee, I need to say something."

Marshall's mouth couldn't get any wider. "Who said anything about firing Phee? The only one going off the deep end is you, Augusta. Calm down."

Augusta folded her hands in front of her chest and stood as if she was at attention. "Like it or not, Phee's able to get more information from witnesses and suspects than either you or Mr. Williams. Face it, who would you talk to? The sweet girl next door or a couple of investigators who look like G-Men?"

"G-Men? Good grief. I'll make a note to remove the white shirts from my wardrobe. And once again, no one's firing Phee."

"Hrrmph" was the only sound Augusta uttered as she left my office.

"So," Marshall said, "tell me why you think Darla Marlinde is innocent."

"Because Marc Yost wasn't in his condo that night. And Darla left before he staggered in there the next morning. I can prove it."

I showed Marshall the petition and went over the timeline with him. "Look, I know you and Nate got the police reports from Paradise Valley, but, unless I'm wrong, there's probably no mention of that swan petition or any interviews with the gardener. Marc's body wasn't discovered until later in the day when his office hadn't heard from him. The only credible witness the police had was the desk assistant. Who actually happens to be the real murderer. Am I right?"

"Possibly. There were other witnesses, according to the police report. Two tenants, on their way out of the building, saw Darla Marlinde getting into her car and driving off. They didn't say anything about Sorrel being in the vicinity."

"No, because they probably figured it was too inconsequential, and no one would have thought to ask if some environmental lady was there getting signatures for a petition. If you have their names you can check them against the petition. That is, if they agreed to sign it."

More guttural sounds emanated from Marshall. I knew

he was seething about what I had done, and yet, he was also genuinely excited about the direction in which the case was going, even though he refused to acknowledge it.

He ran his fingers through his hair and bit his lip. "Part of me wants to say we might be jumping to conclusions but the other part is yelling you might be right."

He said "we." Does this mean he believes me?

"There's more. I'm positive the desk assistant is Eleanor Landrow's brother. It was the same guy I saw her with that night at La Mariposa. I'll wager a week's pay Eleanor's maiden name is Burrier. Rolo Barnes should be able to find that out in a nanosecond. And I've got the motive, too. When Trevor Burrier realized Sorrel was the only person who could vindicate Darla Marlinde, he had to do something about it."

"You're suggesting he found out who Sorrel was, learned she lived in the same community as his sister, and, together with his sibling, plotted and carried out that murder on the golf course."

"Yes. Yes, I am."

"Too far-fetched."

"As opposed to what else? No one's been able to track down anyone with the archery skills to pull off something like that. Only Eleanor was that accomplished."

"When she was in college! That was years ago."

"I'm sticking with my theory, even if you're not."

Marshall scratched his head and pulled over a chair. Either he got tired of standing or he was about to lecture me again. "I hate saying this. I really do."

Oh hell. Here it comes. We're through.

"Darla Marlinde may be spending her last night in police custody. You really did uncover some strong evidence that will turn her case upside down. I've got to meet with Nate, and we've got to share this with the sheriff's department as well as the Paradise Valley Police Department."

"What about Sorrel's murder? I'm positive both murders are connected. They *have* to be."

"If you're right, the police may get a confession out of Trevor Burrier, but I wouldn't count on it."

He walked to the door. "Please tell me you're done sleuthing in Paradise Valley. I'm going to run out of favors there."

"I plan to stay home tonight."

"Good. And keep your door locked."

He closed my office door as he left, and I didn't find out what had ensued with Trevor Burrier until the next day. I did realize one thing, though. I had to come clean as far as my boss was concerned. He deserved that and a whole lot more.

Chapter 30

It sounded as if an air raid siren went off in my bedroom, and I couldn't reach the phone fast enough. Darn it! I had turned the volume up last night and forgot to lower it.

"Phee! Did you see the news? Williams Investigations is all over the news! Streetman got me up early this morning, or I never would've seen it."

"Huh? What? What time is it?"

"Five forty-five."

I reached over to my alarm clock and shut it off. "What's going on? What's on the news?"

"The Darla Marlinde Scorpion Killer Case. She didn't kill him after all. The real killer was apprehended in the middle of the night. Williams Investigations uncovered some important evidence that broke the case wide open. What the heck were they doing working on the Darla Marlinde case when they should have been finding out who killed Sorrel Harlan!"

It was early and I was groggy, but I was still able to process everything my mother was saying. The Darla Marlinde case. That's why Marshall and Nate disappeared shortly after my conversation with Marshall yesterday.

"Um, I don't know. Let me call you later."

"Better yet, meet me at Bagels 'N More when you get out of work. The ladies and I are going to be there at five-thirty. Five forty-five the latest. Plenty of time for you to drive over. What do you say?"

"Okay. Fine. Bagels 'N More. Five-thirtyish."

She hung up as I threw my legs over the bed and stretched. I got washed up as quickly as I could and turned on the TV as I made myself a cup of coffee. Sure enough, the Darla Marlinde case was exploding all over the news.

Trevor Burrier confessed to everything. Everything, that is, except killing Sorrel Harlan. He was adamant he had nothing whatsoever to do with her murder. According to the news commentaries, and they were on every channel, Trevor Burrier was a data analyst who used to work for Marc Yost's company, Metronics, Inc. About a year ago, Trevor was let go for unspecified reasons. As a result, his income plummeted, and the only job he was able to secure was that of a desk assistant.

When he realized Marc Yost lived in the very condo where he worked, Trevor wanted to get even, so he plotted a way to terrorize Marc and frame Darla Marlinde. I had been right all along. Why then, wasn't the guy admitting to killing Sorrel? It made no sense to me. I took a quick breath, threw on my clothes, and drove to work. Nate was the only one in the office when I walked in, and he immediately threw his hands up in the air.

"Okay. Okay. I admit it. Darla Marlinde wouldn't be a free person this morning if you hadn't snooped around over there. But seriously, kiddo, these exploits could get you in serious trouble, not to mention, killed."

"I know. I know. And I really am sorry about not being upfront with you."

"Snooping around Sun City West is one thing. And, to

be honest, the wealth of information you get from doing that really comes in handy, but as far as high-profile cases go, it's dangerous territory."

"Augusta thinks I should carry a gun."

"Dear God. Only a gun? I'm surprised she didn't insist on an automatic rifle and a few hand grenades. Seriously, Phee, you know what I'm saying."

"I do. I guess the Paradise Valley police arrested Trevor by now. Do you know if he confessed to killing Sorrel as well as Marc?"

"According to what I heard, Trevor did not confess to the murder of Sorrel Harlan. He had no clue she was outside with that swan petition of hers. He collected the bark scorpions in the middle of the night. Said he never intended to kill Marc Yost either, only to scare him by putting the scorpions in his bed. Marc had a major allergic reaction to the number of stings and died."

"And the police believed Trevor?"

"He passed the lie detector test."

"Oh no. Oh no. That means Sorrel Harlan's killer is still loose, and it's highly doubtful it was Eleanor. It wasn't as if she was helping her brother. Trevor *is* her brother, isn't he?"

"Right on all counts. Rolo got that information to us immediately."

"So now what?"

"Re-evaluate our leads and go from there."

"So essentially, starting over."

Nate let out a quick laugh. "With one exception. We've already eliminated a good number of potential suspects."

"It doesn't matter. My mother and her friends are literally going to have a conniption fit over this. You know how hysterical they can get."

"Please don't remind me."

At that moment, Augusta and Marshall came in the door, with Augusta poking Marshall on the shoulder and pointing to me. "You should be thanking her."

"Um, the person who should be thanking her is Darla Marlinde."

"Your welcome, Darla," I shouted as I walked over to the coffeemaker. Marshall was right behind me and spoke in a low voice. "Mind if I have a word with you?" Then he glanced at Augusta. "In your office?"

I nodded and we immediately walked into my office.

"I think both of us owe each other apologies," Marshall said. "I should go first. I'm sorry if I was rude to you yesterday. I let my anger get the best of me, and it wasn't pretty."

"Well, I should've been open and honest with you. With Nate, too, for that matter. I already apologized to him."

Marshall looked fidgety, almost nervous. "So, are we good?"

"Yeah, we're good. It's not easy having a relationship with someone you work with. I suppose that's why so many businesses don't allow it."

"Businesses can't dictate what the heart wants."

"No, but they can dictate where the paycheck comes from."

"So, feel like grabbing a bite to eat after work?"

"Um, I already made plans. With my mother and her friends. Bagels 'N More. You're more than welcome to join me."

"And what? Get interrogated because we haven't solved Sorrel's murder yet? No thanks. The Salem Witch Trials would've paled in comparison to what I imagine tonight's conversation will be like. I'll take a raincheck. Just you and me, okay?"

"Absolutely."

The tension I felt from what had transpired between Marshall and me yesterday had vanished, only to be replaced by a new tension—the Booked 4 Murder book club's growing fear and hysteria over a cold-blooded, arrow-shooting killer who may or may not be stalking my mother and her friends.

The moment I set foot in Bagels 'N More, the women got right to it.

"Hurry up, Phee, and sit down," Myrna shouted, causing a few heads to turn. "Why was your boss busy with that scorpion killer case when I could've been killed by an arrow during the bocce tournament?"

"Yeah," Lucinda said. "Doesn't he realize the danger all of us are in?"

I tried to tell them that all precautions were taken during that tournament so no one was in eminent danger. After a few grumbles and some minor side conversations involving how old they thought the tuna salad might be, the ladies seemed to settle down.

It was a relatively small gathering—Myrna, Lucinda, Louise, Cecilia, Shirley, Riva, and my mother. The others in the group were either playing cards or mahjong. Our bagel sandwiches arrived in record time, and I was relieved. At least I was guaranteed a few minutes of relative quiet while they ate.

Then, no surprise, the subject of Sorrel Harlan's murder reappeared like one of those dead bodies in a horror movie. Always springing back to life to claim another victim. In this case, me. And who was leading the charge? None other than my mother.

"Herb Garrett thinks it's one of those golf course homeowners. One of the realtors told him prices are already beginning to reflect a change. And why do you suppose those mealy-mouthed board members who supported Sorrel's idea are being so tight-lipped about the vote? Because they don't want to end up face down somewhere with an arrow pierced through them."

"I still think Sorrel must've been fooling around with someone's husband, and that's what got her killed," Cecilia said. "Wedding vows are meant to be taken seriously."

I took another bite of my bagel and let the conversation drift over me. Now it was Lucinda who spoke.

"We've been through that already. How many women do you know who have archery skills like that?"

Eleanor Landrow does. Do I dare open my mouth and unleash that dragon?

Louise reached for the creamer and stared at Cecilia. "Lucinda's right, unless they hired a professional assassin."

Finally, I couldn't take it anymore. My voice got so loud I was afraid other tables would hear me. "Professional assassins, as far as I know, would most likely use a gun or something more conventional. Listen, why don't you all calm down and give the sheriff's department time to solve this? The good news is how wonderful Myrna's team did at the tournament. I never got a chance to really congratulate you, Myrna. Great job!"

Myna beamed and thanked me. "I appreciate that. I really do. It was nerve-wracking. Now we can all look forward to the awards banquet. Tickets are twelve dollars, and I'll be selling them starting next week. The twelve dollars includes nonalcoholic drinks, too."

I smiled and didn't say a word. I'd be stuck. I knew it. I'd have to buy a ticket. Two maybe, if Marshall was also a glutton for punishment. At least the banquet was a month away. I prayed Sorrel's killer would be apprehended by then. I went back to my bagel when Riva decided to open her mouth.

"By the way, that board vote is coming up pretty quick and it's got 'ugly little scene' written all over it. Of course, once it's done, it's done. Sorrel was the real ringleader for that move, and, with her gone, I'm hoping the whole thing will simply fade away. The killer must be thinking the same thing or they would be going after the supporters."

Oh no! How'd we wind up back to the killer again?

I panicked. "Um, when is that vote? What's the date? I'm sure everyone will want to mark it on their calendars."

The women immediately started rummaging through their bags as I closed my eyes and sighed. Lucinda spouted off the date and time while I excused myself to head to the restroom. As I walked past the cash registers, one of the customers caught my eye. If he hadn't been wearing a light blue polo shirt that said GOLFSCAPES, I might not have been able to place him. But I did. He was the maintenance director who'd given the report at the first board meeting. Also, he was the same man who, according to Myrna, was measuring for the new fence when she thought he had other, more nefarious intentions.

I laughed to myself as the guy paid his bill and kept walking. No sooner had I returned to my seat when Myrna stood up suddenly and collided with the waitress who was standing behind her, causing the poor woman to stumble and dump an entire carafe of creamer all over me. Myrna was beside herself, but all I could think of was that Bill was right. Myrna really was clumsy.

"Oh my gosh! I'm so sorry! Here—take a napkin."

The waitress also offered me some napkins, but my shirt was way beyond that.

"I've got a sweatshirt in the back of my car. I'll grab it and do a quick change in the ladies' room. Then, I'd better get going."

I handed my mother some cash and told her to pay my bill and leave the rest for a tip.

"Sure you don't want to come back for a few more minutes?"

"Nah, that's okay. I really do need to get going." Then, I turned to the others. "It was nice seeing all of you again."

I raced to the car and opened the hatchback to grab an old sweatshirt I kept there in case the weather turned cold or the AC in a restaurant was set way too high. As I leaned in, I saw the Golfscapes maintenance guy talking to another man. An older one. They were one car away from me, but their voices carried.

"Are you sure she's the only one we've got to worry about?"

"Yeah, I'm sure. Bloody hell. Had I known they were going to replace me with that Sorrel Harlan, I never would've resigned."

Oh my gosh, it's Edmund Wooster.

"And you're absolutely certain the only obstacle we have is Eloise Frable?"

"Uh-huh. I pulled that bit of info out of Milquist the other day when I went to his house to offer my condolences. He said Eloise is as adamant as Sorrel was regarding the eco-friendly park idea. On the surface, the lady's keeping a low profile, but she's been making lots of phone calls to drum up support."

"I can't afford to let that happen. Actually, *we* can't afford to let it happen."

"What are you saying?"

"We need to get Eloise out of the way."

I didn't know how long I could remain bent over in my car's hatchback, but I didn't have a choice. Worst case scenario, I'd find a good chiropractor. So, I held still and listened. The older guy kept clearing his throat. I was getting impatient.

"I'm not comfortable with this, Brent. You know that."

"Then you'd better get used to living on the poverty line. If those golf courses go down, it'll be a domino effect. First Sun City West, then the other Sun Cities, then Westbrook Village and all the courses we manage from one side of the valley to the other. Golfscapes will go bankrupt, and so will we."

"Another murder? Eloise isn't Sorrel, and she's not going to roam around the golf course like a prime target."

"But she does live alone. Believe me, I've done my homework on those board members. Home invasions aren't that uncommon."

My hands were shaking and my back was starting to seize up. Whoever this Brent guy was, he was Sorrel's killer. And his accomplice was Edmund Wooster. My God! The motive was right in front of us. Only we never matched it up to Golfscapes. All those lucrative jobs would be lost, and Brent wasn't about to let that happen. I was breathing harder now, and I was too scared to make a move.

Please don't let them see me.

The pain in my back shot through me, and I had no choice. I slammed the hatchback closed and jumped into the car, making sure I pushed the lock button before starting the engine and pulling out of the parking lot. As I reached the end of the driveway, I glanced in my rearview mirror. Brent was writing something down and I had the unsettling feeling it was my license number.

Chapter 31

My first instinct was to find Eloise's address and warn her. But the last thing I needed was another uncomfortable encounter with Nate and Marshall about the risks I was taking. And I certainly wasn't about to drive to the sheriff's posse station and tell them. I'd be stuck completing forms while Eloise's life was on the line.

Instead, I headed in the direction of Sun City West and pulled into the nearest convenience store/gas station. My fingers moved automatically as I dialed Marshall's number. Damn it! Voice mail. I left a quick message and dialed Nate next. Same thing. Voice mail. I left him a message, too. Finally, I made one last call (also voice mail) before doing a quick white pages' phonebook search for Eloise's address and typing it into my GPS.

Thanks to Myrna, my shirt was beginning to get that icky sour smell as if a baby had recently "cheesed" on it. I tried to ignore it as I drove to Copperstone Drive, a garden apartment complex with separate courtyard areas, each one named for a different bird. Eloise lived in North Finch, Apt. 14B. I parked my car on the street and charged to her door, pounding on it first until I located her doorbell, disguised as a small frog.

With the door open a crack, and a door chain in place, Eloise peered through. All I could see was short frizzy hair and wire-rimmed glasses.

"If this is something political, I'm not signing. I'm also not buying anything either."

"No. Not any of that. Listen, I think you might be in danger. Real danger. From Sorrel Harlan's killer."

"What? Who are you? I'm calling the posse."

"Yes. Call them. It's a good idea. I'm Sophie Kimball. I work for Williams Investigations. But they didn't send me here. I'm their accountant. Bookkeeper. Well, actually, both."

The words came out of my mouth in spits and spatters. It was a wonder I made sense at all.

"I was at Bagels 'N More and overheard two men talking. In the parking lot. They didn't see me. One was Brent, the maintenance director for Golfscapes, and the other was Edmund Wooster."

"Edmund Wooster is plotting to kill me? I've been sitting across from him for two years at those meetings. Why on earth would he want to kill me?"

"Please, may I come inside?"

I must've looked harmless enough because she unlocked the chain and let me in, closing and locking the door. We stood in her foyer as I continued to talk.

"When Sorrel Harlan came up with that idea to create the eco-friendly neighborhood parks instead of keeping all of the golf courses, it wasn't only the golf course homeowners who had a lot to lose. It was the maintenance company for those golf courses. And that's big bucks. Millions. Edmund Wooster resigned from the board because he took a management position with Golfscapes. A position he will likely lose if the property is converted to parks."

"But murder? People would kill for that?"

"You'd be surprised what people kill for."

"And Brent Haywood was in on this? That's his last name—Haywood. He always seemed like such a nice young man. Very organized. Very capable. Are you sure about all of this? Maybe you misunderstood something."

"I don't think so. I've already notified my boss, since our company has been working on the case. I drove over here to warn you. Keep your door locked. And don't go anywhere until you hear from me or someone from my office. You can make that call to the posse, but I'm on my way over there now."

I handed her my card, and this time, I didn't have to cover up anything with my thumb.

Eloise looked at the card and looked at me. "Murder. Over an eco-friendly park. I hope you're wrong, dear."

The lock clicked behind me as I headed to my car. By now, my shirt really stunk. I couldn't wait to get home, throw it in the wash, and take a shower, but I still had one more stop to make—the posse station. Nate and Marshall hadn't returned my calls. The phone was set on the highest ringtone and nothing. Well, they couldn't blame me if they weren't around to deal with this.

Copperstone Drive was dark and quiet. Unlike the newer parts of town, the streetlights were dimmer, although small coach lights that resembled lanterns were affixed to the outside walls of each courtyard. I reached in my pocket and fished my car key out from under the cell phone, shoving aside the few paperclips I had stashed in there. Since I hated those automatic car door openers, I opted to use the old-fashioned key. The car fob sat in one of my kitchen drawers, along with a screwdriver and a pair of pliers.

I turned the key and reached for the door handle when a crushing pain erupted on the top of my skull.

* * *

The next thing I remembered was severe nausea. I reached out to steady myself on the car door, only I wasn't anywhere near my car. I was on the ground, my back leaning against a wall. I was inside some sort of room, a room where shallow light was seeping through the cracks. Too dizzy to focus, I closed my eyes and concentrated on my breathing.

It was the staple of every Tai Chi class I'd ever attended, not to mention all the other exercise classes I'd tried before quitting. Somehow my breathing soothed me, although I still felt as if I was about to throw up.

What the hell. It's not as if my shirt doesn't stink already thanks to Myrna's creamer.

My eyes felt as if they were glued shut and the more I struggled to open them, the tighter they felt. Finally I was able to blink and eventually I was able to open them. Total darkness. The shallow light was gone. How long was I in here? It seemed to take forever until I could make out my surroundings. Not much to see. I was in a shed. A shed with gardening tools. Or were they golf clubs? Whoever had hit me over the head and locked me in here hadn't bothered to tie me up. It had to be Brent. He must've figured I wouldn't be waking up any time soon. That wasn't good. It meant he wasn't done with me.

My bag and car keys were probably lying on Copperstone Drive, next to the car, but my cell phone was still in my pocket. I moved my hand slowly and pulled it out, thankful I'd remembered to charge it during the day.

The screen looked fuzzy, so I did something I'd never done before. I asked Siri to place a call to Marshall. Again with the stupid voice mail. Same deal for Nate. They both got the same raspy message. "Help! Trapped! Maintenance shed!" I made one more call and left the same message.

Then I decided to try 911 but never got the chance.

Someone was unlocking the door. I shoved the phone back in my pocket and pretended to be unconscious. I didn't have to pretend too hard.

With my body slumped over and my arms hanging loosely at my sides, Sorrel's killer probably assumed I was still out of it. And he was partially right. Still, I was able to figure out exactly where I was the minute he dragged me from the shed and hoisted me over his shoulder into a golf cart. The only thing I didn't know was which golf course I was on.

I played along as the cart rolled through the course, its lights off. The motion was making me sicker by the minute, and I had to fight back the urge to unleash the bile that had come up in my throat. Even on one of my best days, there would've been no way I could've outrun the guy. And now, with a possible concussion (my own diagnosis), it was impossible. I remained bent over trying to strategize my next move.

The golf cart turned onto a narrow path that led directly to one of the streets. Edmund Wooster was standing next to a car, his face partially illuminated by someone's pathway lighting that needed to be adjusted. The beam focused upward and not on the path. Unless the homeowner walked the perimeter of his or her property at night, they wouldn't have noticed the uneven pathway lighting.

"Hurry up and open the door," Brent hissed. "It's like dragging dead weight."

Dead weight. The last words I'll ever hear about myself.

I let him heave me into the backseat and tried to hear what he and Edmund were saying.

"You're going to do what you said, right? Leave her in the desert?"

Brent didn't respond.

"You *said* you're going to leave her in the desert. What do you plan to do? Shoot her?"

"Never owned a gun. There are other ways to get things done. You really don't get it, do you, Wooster? This lady's testimony in court could put us away for life. Let me deal with her and then take care of that Frable lady. You coming along or what?"

"It doesn't look like she's going anywhere. So, no. I'll pass."

"And miss out on seeing the desert at night? All those beautiful moonlit saguaros and chollas."

"If you say so."

I tried to recall the conversation Marshall had had with the range manager for the archery club. Something about people going out in the desert to practice with hay bales or foam archery targets. Brent Haywood had to be one of them. Only this time he didn't need to bring a practice target. He had me. And I was in no condition to make a move. Not yet, anyway.

Saying you're going to take a drive out in the desert is like saying you're going to take a dip in the Atlantic Ocean. The desert is everywhere as soon as you leave city limits, and there are a zillion dirt access roads.

The door next to me slammed shut while another one opened. Brent was getting into the front seat, and I was running out of options. My body felt as if it was made of lead, and every time I moved my head, I got dizzy. I was, however, able to position myself so I could see where he was headed. First, out of the Sun City West complex and onto Route 60, Grand Avenue. He was headed north. We drove under the 303 overpass and were on our way to Wickenburg.

The city lights were gone, but I recognized where we were by the small clusters of house lights—Wittman, the only populated area between Surprise and Wickenburg. Brent made a left-hand turn onto an unmarked road. The car slowed for a minute as he made another turn. Judging by the crunch of stones under the tires, it was a dirt road, probably leading to where the guy did his target practice.

My heart was racing and my head began to clear. I had to think fast. No time for a strategic escape plan. It was minute to minute, if I even had that long. The good news? He didn't have a gun. He'd said as much. I seriously doubted he was going to waste time with a bow and arrow when he could easily dump me from the car and drive over me. I slid my hand in my pocket and felt the phone. Too damn late to make a call and too obvious to send a text. Then, my fingers touched something else—the paperclips. And they were the big ones.

Slowly, I pried one of the clips apart until it was fairly straight. The tip was sharp, but I wasn't sure if it would be sharp enough. It didn't matter. It wasn't as if I had anything else going for me. I kept my head bent down and my body slouched over as Brent continued on the dirt road.

I had one chance to jab that clip into his neck and brace myself for what would happen next. He'd temporarily lose control of the car, giving me enough time to open the door and run. With any luck, I'd be able to call 911. It was better than becoming the next roadkill.

My fingers gripped that paperclip, and, with a sudden burst of adrenaline that I never thought possible, I sat up in my seat, leaned forward, and plunged the paperclip into his neck. It went in easily, followed by a piercing scream—mine.

Brent shoved his hand back and turned away from the wheel, but his foot was still on the gas pedal. The car was moving. Not what I expected. Then, out of nowhere, something heavy crashed through the windshield, and we came to such a fast stop that my body flung forward into the back of the driver's seat before resting against the backseat. At least I didn't have to worry about unbuckling a seatbelt. I shoved the side door open and stumbled out, expecting Brent to do the same. I still had another uncoiled paper-clip left.

The car's headlights were on. The trunk of a small saguaro rested atop the airbag, toward the driver's-side door. Another few feet and the airbag might not have made a difference. Those saguaros weigh a ton. The passenger-side door clicked, and it was as if I'd heard the starter pistol for a race. I grabbed my phone, slid the arrow, and screamed, "Siri, call nine-one-one!" But there was no race. My legs couldn't move.

Brent muttered every four-letter word he knew as he made his way toward me. Then I remembered something Augusta had once told me. "Hells bells with the damn self-defense classes. Kick 'em hard between the legs and poke their eyes out if you have to."

Leg kicking and eye poking weren't my strengths. Unlike Augusta, I wasn't brought up on a Wisconsin farm. My skillset was limited to latte sipping and doing business math.

"Nine-one-one. What's your emergency?"

"Help! He's going to kill me!"

Those were the only words I could scream before Brent grabbed the phone from my hand and threw it as far as he could. In that instant, I became a madwoman.

"Oh hell! That was a new iPhone. Three hundred and thirty hard-earned dollars, you SOB!"

And then I did it. I did what Augusta had told me to do. Almost. I lunged for him, but, instead of kicking, I made a fist and punched him right between the legs. And then I punched again. Brent doubled over as I heard a voice from the car.

"Are you alright, sir?"

At first I wasn't sure where it was coming from or if I was imagining it. The voice from out of nowhere repeated the message, and I suddenly realized what it was—the automatic crash response from ONSTAR. Brent Haywood's vehicle was from General Motors, and it came with ONSTAR. I could've kissed the dealership.

Screaming as loud as I could, my words were still soft and hoarse. "No! Send help now!"

I moved as fast as my sluggish legs would go until I reached the passenger-side door. Leaning in, I tried to yell again, "Help! Car crash! Hurry!"

"We're sending help now," was the response. I wasn't sure if the ONSTAR system could detect my exact location, but what the heck? Neither could I. I did the best I could, shouting, "Wittman, dirt road, desert."

The voice at the other end tried to be reassuring, but whoever was sitting in some dispatch office didn't have a crazed killer a few feet away. I wasn't about to take any chances. I gripped the remaining paperclip as if it was a spear.

"Make one move toward me and, I swear, this time I'll rip out your arteries."

My threat certainly sounded good, although I didn't know an artery from a vein. Brent Haywood stood absolutely still by the driver's-side door, while I kept a wary distance on the other side of the car. A voice in my head kept telling me he wasn't going to stay still for long. Maybe I'd seen too many late-night zombie horror movies, but I knew the paperclip wasn't going to be enough if the guy decided to make a move.

Slowly, I reached my hand to the shattered windshield and with a fist, gave it enough of a push to loosen a piece of the glass. With my other hand, I felt around the seat to see if there was anything I could use to prevent my fingers from getting cut. *Come on. Every car has old tissues and rags stuffed in the console.* All the while I maintained eye contact with my abductor. Not easy. Then I remembered the side door. In my car it was a catch-all for discarded fast food napkins. I felt around in its cubby and sure enough, found a wad of them. *Hallelujah.* Even so, removing the glass shard was tougher than I thought and my head felt as if it weighed a hundred pounds.

"It's over you know," I said. "Killing me now won't save you." Then, for good measure, I added the most overused, hackneyed phrase in the crime movie handbook, "You won't get away with it."

Brent must not have been a movie buff because, in that second, he stepped back from the car and lunged toward me. Only it wasn't me. I had become some sort of wild crazed woman. With a paperclip in one hand, and a fairly sharp piece of glass in the other, albeit the bottom of it wrapped in old napkins, I stabbed at his arms with all the strength I had.

He tried to grab me but somehow missed. I had no idea how long I could hold him off. It didn't matter. What mattered was I heard sirens in the distance and thanked my lucky stars the ONSTAR response was fast. Only, it wasn't ONSTAR. Someone else had come to my rescue.

Chapter 32

The blue and red flashing lights were getting closer. One car, a sheriff's car. No ambulance, no fire truck. Only someone from the Maricopa County Sheriff's Department. I figured they had to have been in close vicinity, and the other rescue vehicles would be along shortly.

My feet felt as if they were glued to the ground, and I was still queasy. I leaned against the frame of the car as two deputies approached.

"This lunatic woman tried to kill me!" Brent shouted. "Look, she even stabbed me in the neck! I lost control of the car and crashed into that cactus."

"That's not what happened," I said. "I mean, the cactus part is true, but he abducted me. From Sun City West. Hit me over the head. Drove me here to kill me."

"She's lying. She's a lying little lunatic, and I can prove it. I'm bleeding."

"What's your name, miss?" the deputy asked.

"Sophie Kimball. And I work for Williams Investigations. That's Brent Haywood, and he's responsible for killing Sorrel Harlan."

The deputy turned to the other deputy. "Send for an ambulance."

"You've got to believe me. I'm telling you the truth," I said.

"We know," was the response. "Sun City West Posse got a call from an Eloise Frable. They sent someone over to her house to speak with her and found a car parked on Copperstone Drive with its keys on the ground by the driver's-side door and a ladies' purse next to it. Your identification was in the purse. They checked the registration and insurance from your glove compartment and it matched up."

Just then, more sirens and more flashing lights. This time it was another sheriff's car, an ambulance, and a firetruck from the city of Surprise.

"What the heck?" one of the deputies said. "They can't be getting here that fast."

"ONSTAR," I replied. "But how did *you* know I was here? How did you find me?"

"Our office got another call. Someone named Augusta Hatch. And she was quite persistent. Said you were kidnapped and gave us your cell phone number to track your whereabouts. Unfortunately, we're not *Hawaii Five-O*. It took a while. Good thing they put up a cell tower in Wittman not too long ago."

"She's lying, and I'm going to bleed to death," Brent shouted.

The deputy closest to me turned to his partner. "Arrest him under suspicion of kidnapping. We'll check into the rest. Have the EMTs look him over and get him to the hospital. Same with Miss Kimball. I'll call for another ambulance."

"I don't need to go to the hospital. I'll be okay."

"You're going to the hospital!" came a voice I didn't expect. Marshall's. He was running toward me.

In all the excitement, I hadn't noticed his car pulling up.

"None of this is my fault. I tried to call you. Nate, too."

"I know. I know." He put his arms around my shoulders and pulled me closer to him.

I inhaled that crisp apple scent from his aftershave and didn't budge.

"It's okay, Phee. Let them take you to the hospital and check you out. I'll follow the ambulance once it gets here."

"How did you . . . I mean, when did you . . . ?"

"I was in the shower when you called. And I didn't check the phone for voice mail. It was only when Augusta called that I saw your message. By then she had already notified the sheriff."

"What about Nate? Does he know what happened?"

"He's on his way, but I'm going to call him and have him meet us at the hospital. He was in Glendale on another case when Augusta finally reached him."

The EMTs were escorting Brent to the first ambulance, and I heard more sirens heading our way.

Marshall put his arm around my waist and pulled me off the car frame. "I'm opening the back door of this car so you can sit down. Come on."

"I'll be all right. But my head is killing me." I touched the base of my skull and the bump scared the daylights out of me. "My God! What did he hit me with?"

"You didn't say anything about being hit. I thought maybe you had some trauma from the car accident. Oh, Phee, I'm so sorry."

"I'll be all right. Honest."

In that instant, another vehicle pulled up. A van this time, and as soon as I read the four letters on its side door, I knew I was in trouble. KPHO—CBS's Channel Five News. The station my mother always watched before she went to bed.

"My God! How did they get here so fast? Oh no! There's more of them. I see the ABC 15 van. And NBC 12. Oh crap. There's Fox 10. What time is it?"

"Five minutes past ten."

The nausea came back, and this time it wasn't from my head injury. "Five after ten? They'll be live with 'Breaking News.' Any way we can stop them?"

Marshall shook his head as four reporters, dragging long cables and mics from their vans, approached us. One by one they started with a similar statement "And we're live from the outskirts of Wittman, where authorities say one woman is lucky to be alive following a foiled abduction."

I tugged at Marshall's sleeve and whispered, "Please call my mother and keep her on the line."

Sure enough, I *was* lucky to be alive. I'd suffered a moderate concussion, and, because my nausea wouldn't quit, I had to remain at the hospital overnight for observation. It turned out Brent Haywood had hit me over the head with a golf club. No wonder I was sick to my stomach.

The sheriff's department was able to get a full confession out of him once they brought in Edmund Wooster for questioning. And while Brent and Edmund were getting interrogated by the authorities, I had my own version sitting across from me in the hospital. At two-thirty in the morning!

"What did Marshall think? That I couldn't see the TV screen while I was on the phone? You're all lucky I didn't have a heart attack. Imagine seeing your own daughter looking dazed and pale in the backseat of some strange car. You should've walked back into Bagels 'N More the minute you were done listening to those men. We all would've followed you to Eloise's house."

"If Eloise Frable had looked out her front door and saw the entire entourage from Booked 4 Murder standing there, I doubt she would've opened the door. Besides, Brent was following me. If he didn't nab me in front of her house, it would've been somewhere else. But it's over, Mom. I'll be fine. And the good news is that Sorrel's killer has been apprehended."

"Remind me to email your aunt Ina and let her know it's safe to return from Belize."

"Uh-huh."

"You know, if it wasn't for the sheriff's department being able to track your cell phone and that ONSTAR system, you'd probably still be in the desert. Which got me thinking. What if something happens to Streetman? What if he gets loose? I know he has a tag and a microchip, but still . . ."

Dear Lord! Is she really obsessing over the dog?

"So, I've made a decision. I'm buying him one of those GPS trackers for dogs. It goes on his collar and sends the information right to my smartphone."

"You have a smartphone?"

"I'll get one."

I closed my eyes and leaned back on the pillow.

My mother took the hint. "I know you must be tired, sweetheart. If you want me to stay here with you, I will. Otherwise, I'll be back in the morning."

"That's okay. They'll be releasing me tomorrow. Marshall's going to pick me up and drive me home. He and Nate have already taken care of driving my car home, and he'll be bringing me my bag tomorrow when he comes to get me."

"Well, at least you'll have a nice weekend to recuperate.

I'll stop by with Streetman so you'll have some company. We can even stay the weekend with you if you'd like."

He better not pee on the carpeting, or I'll lose my security deposit.

Sometime before four, my mother left the room and I fell asleep. I don't even remember the nurses coming in to check my blood pressure or to make sure I was still breathing. At seven fifteen I made one phone call. To thank Augusta.

"Didn't think you needed a circus sideshow, so I didn't go to the hospital last night," she said.

"Augusta, you saved my life. You absolutely saved my life. I don't even know how to thank you."

"You already did. Get some rest. Milk it while you can. I'll see you on Monday. No, make it Tuesday. Milk it. Understand?"

The hospital released me a little before noon, and Marshall drove me home. The deputies had found my cell phone a few yards away from the crash site by calling the number Marshall had given them. Other than a few scratches on the case, it didn't appear to have suffered any damage. Unlike Brent's car, which, according to Marshall, had the whole front end smashed in from that saguaro.

Marshall insisted on staying with me the entire weekend, and I wasn't about to object. Otherwise, it would've been my mother and Streetman. And knowing how she doted on that dog, I might've been forced to relinquish my bed to him.

Lyndy dropped by that evening and brought two casseroles. Nate showed up a little while later with submarine sandwiches and chips.

Adhering to my discharge instructions from the hospital, I ate the tiniest of portions while watching everyone else devour the meal. Thanks to some pain meds, my headache was dissipating. And thanks to my decision to join the

Booked 4 Murder ladies at Bagels 'N More that Thursday night, the bigger headache, Sorrel's murder, was solved. Not the way I wanted it to be solved, but solved nevertheless.

As things turned out, Rolo Barnes uncovered some startling information on one Brent Haywood, and if I'd only waited a day, I wouldn't have wound up with a concussion.

Chapter 33

Marshall was waiting on me hand and foot, and I was beginning to feel guilty. Especially when he had to field the phone calls. I wasn't sure which ones were worse—the book club ladies, Herb's pinochle crew, or the news stations requesting interviews.

Meanwhile, Nate and Augusta were at the office dealing with reporters. Once again, Williams Investigations was credited for solving another murder, making it the second one in less than a week. Good news for business.

It was noon, and I was finishing a BLT that Marshall had prepared, when the phone rang. With his hand over the speaker, he whispered, "It's Shirley Johnson. Do you want to take it?"

"Might as well," I whispered back, before taking the phone and saying hi to Shirley.

"Lordy, Phee! You had us all scared. I'm so glad you're alive. The news keeps playing that clip of you being led to the ambulance."

I'd seen the clip she was talking about on the early news and almost wished I had another concussion so I wouldn't have to deal with *that* reality. I looked like one of those washed-up movie stars on her way to rehab for the tenth time. Only my hair looked worse.

"Um, yeah. It was pretty bad, but I'm doing fine."

"That's wonderful. I called to tell you Lucinda and I got in touch with all the women, and we coordinated meal service for you. I can stop by today with my sweet potato casserole and beans."

"That's very sweet of you and the ladies, Shirley, but—"

"Say no more. I'll be by around four. I got your address from your mother."

"Um, I—"

"Till then, hon."

"Don't tell me," Marshall said. "They're bringing food."

"Oh yeah. Sweet potato casserole and beans. And we still have Lyndy's tuna casserole and most of her noodle and raisin one."

"Hey, what can I say? You're a popular lady."

I smiled and finished the last bite of my BLT as Marshall pulled up a chair.

"I've got to say, you've got some knack for being in the right place at the right time. Well, maybe the wrong place, considering the circumstances, but even with the information Rolo gave us, we would've been hard-pressed to get a confession out of Brent Haywood."

"What exactly did Rolo find out? And when?"

"Believe it or not, he called just as I was getting into the shower Thursday. Talk about timing. Anyway, it turns out Brent Haywood honed his archery skills as a competitive archer in high school. From there, he earned extra money on weekend jobs working the Renaissance Festival in Irwindale, California. He was so good they gave him top billing at shows. With that money, he was able to put himself through college. He majored in recreation with a concentration in golf course management. Need I say more?"

"Wow. And all this time we hadn't a clue. In fact, we all dismissed Myrna's ramblings about the golf course manager poking around the perimeter of the course."

"Let's not beat ourselves up too much. As I recall, Myrna was pretty hysterical about almost anything. Listen, before I forget, the sheriff's department called while you were asleep this morning. They need to take an official statement."

"I thought I did that already."

"You gave them a statement, but it was while you were still sitting in the back of Brent's car, before getting into the ambulance. They need to have you complete and sign one at the posse station, but I told them you were home recuperating. So, they'll be sending a deputy by today. If we're lucky, it'll be at the same time Shirley arrives with the casserole. That should speed things up."

Unfortunately, the timing was off for that, too. The deputy arrived about an hour later. Deputy Bowman, to be precise. The one Herb said had the personality of a tomato. But I liked Deputy Bowman, even though he was all business. From the minute he arrived at my house, the only thing he talked about was Brent's arrest.

"Looks like everything adds up. Brent Haywood finally confessed to the kidnapping but insisted all he wanted to do was scare you."

"Tell him it worked."

"Don't worry. He's been booked on numerous charges ranging from premeditated murder to kidnapping. Oh, and reckless driving resulting in the damage of a protected species. Destroying a saguaro carries a fine in the thousands."

"Gee," I said. "Did he feel the least bit bad about killing Sorrel Harlan?"

"I doubt it. It was all about money. The guy had such a

lucrative position managing a number of prestigious golf courses, he wasn't about to let it go. Getting rid of Sorrel was the most expeditious thing he could do."

"My God! Murder?"

"It was business, as far as he was concerned, and he handled it efficiently and smoothly. Until he got caught. That's when he panicked and you wound up in the desert. Well, looks like I've got everything I need. Try to keep out of trouble, okay?"

I raised an eyebrow and laughed. "You've met my mother, haven't you? I don't know how you can possibly say that."

This time Deputy Bowman laughed as he shook my hand and Marshall's before heading out.

"One down, one to go," Marshall said, looking at his watch.

"Shirley?"

"Unless your mother decides to stop by."

"Bite your tongue. Did she say she was coming? Did you talk to her while I was sleeping?"

"No, but she mentioned something while you were in the hospital."

I rolled my eyes. "Are there any other calls or anything else I should know?"

"The CEO of Golfscapes issued a statement to the media. It was on the local stations early in the morning. The usual stuff. The company was shocked and dismayed at Brent Haywood's actions, which they insist had nothing to do with their corporation. They offered condolences to Sorrel Harlan's family and wished a speedy recovery to Sophie Kimball, who remains in their thoughts."

"I'll bet. They're probably scrambling right now to meet with their legal counsel."

"I'm sure. And Milquist Harlan should be doing the same. Poor guy. To think he was on our top ten suspect list.

With the right amount of finagling, a good attorney might be able to secure some sort of settlement for the guy. Although nothing will bring his wife back."

In spite of her quirks, I imagined Sorrel was a kind and decent human being who didn't deserve to be killed out of greed. As for Brent? It was up to the justice system, and that would take time.

Marshall stayed at my house until Monday morning and insisted on returning once he got out of work. I wasn't going back into the office until Tuesday. Doctor's orders. I had to admit, having Marshall around all weekend was something I could get used to on a permanent basis. I knew he felt the same way. It was only a matter of time, but I wasn't going to be the one to rush it. No surprise, I felt his absence once he returned to his own place. And he wasn't the only one who'd returned to the proverbial nest. My aunt Ina and uncle Louis came back a few days later from Belize.

I wasn't sure what my mother told her sister, but not only did I receive a frantic phone call from Aunt Ina, it was followed by an onslaught of deliveries. Fruit baskets. Muffin baskets. Homemade soup (the restaurant kind) and a fabulous gift certificate for a day spa. Being a celebrity, of sorts, had its perks. At least for a while.

In the week that followed, things were getting back to normal in Sun City West. Well, normal for my mother, the book club ladies, and Herb's pinochle cronies. No alien sightings. No rumors of serial killers, and, most of all, no mention of the eco-friendly parks. Unfortunately, all of that changed ten days later. On a Wednesday night. With a phone call from my mother.

"The board meeting is this coming Monday. At seven. Will you be going?"

"What? No. Why? Why should I go?"

"They'll be voting on that cockamamie eco-friendly park idea. Just because Sorrel has been laid to rest, it doesn't mean her plan was. And now that her killer has been caught, those pro-park board members won't be afraid to open their mouths."

"Didn't you say it was a split vote?"

"A few weeks ago it was. But rumor has it, Mildred Saperstein has been spending a lot of time with Barry Wong."

"Rumor has it? Rumor? Come on, since when does that count for anything?"

"It always counts for something."

"I thought you told me Barry was adamantly against that proposal."

"One look at a fancy skirt passing by, and a man can change his mind in a second."

"Oh for goodness' sake! Mildred may have the fancy skirt, but I doubt she's convincing Barry of anything. For all you know, they're probably in the same club or something. And wasn't the board going to appoint another member?"

"After the vote. Plus, new appointees can't vote for thirty days. Ugh! That imbecilic proposal *has* to be voted down. If it goes into a tie, they can bring it up again."

"And what good will it do if I go?"

"You may get the sympathy vote."

"Huh? The what?"

"You risked your life to find Sorrel's killer. Maybe say a few words when they have open comments. Tell them you're speaking on my behalf since you're not a resident."

"I'm not doing anything of the sort. Seriously, I can't fight this battle."

"Then the least you can do is show up and watch the carnage. I'm afraid even Herb Garrett is giving up. He called this afternoon to tell me if it all goes down, he has a cousin in real estate who lives in The Villages, and it wouldn't take much for the guy to get us all deals on property there."

"Property where?"

"The Villages! That's Florida, for crying out loud. Home of cockroaches the size of most small mammals and worse humidity than the rain forest. Are you listening, Phee?"

"I'm listening, but I'm not agreeing to attend the meeting, let alone speak."

"Fine. Fine. You don't have to say anything. Just sit there and look despondent. No, not despondent. Angry. Look angry. Last thing a governing board wants to see is a room full of hostile people. You can look hostile, can't you?"

"I'm looking hostile right now. I'll catch you later, Mom."

Chapter 34

In the four days that followed, not only was I plagued by my mother's insistence that I attend the board meeting, but some of the book club ladies called as well. Cecilia told me it was the Godly thing to do. Shirley told me it would break my mother's heart if I didn't attend. Myrna told me she couldn't afford to have her property value go down, or she'd never be able to sell the place and move to The Lillian, a prestigious retirement resort, when "the time was right."

If that wasn't bad enough, Bill left a message for me at work. Something about World War II, fighting for his country, and the rights that belonged to him. I wasn't sure where golf courses fit in the Constitution, but I think he mentioned that as well. Finally, when Wayne called to tell me "life will be over as we know it," I charged into Marshall's office and threw my hands in the air.

"I can't take it anymore. These people are relentless. Relentless and crazy. I give up. I acquiesce. I surrender. I'll be attending tonight's board meeting."

"I figured as much so I left my calendar clear. No

client appointments, no nothing. So . . . a quick dinner and indigestion?"

"Seriously? You want to go through that again? I have to be tortured. It's my mother. But you're a free citizen."

He crinkled his nose and laughed. "In theory. I can't believe I'm saying this, but . . . I'd really like to see the outcome. It's kind of like part two of a TV show. We're at the cliffhanger ending. Let's see where it goes."

Fast-food was our only real option in order to arrive on time for the meeting, so the Taco Bell across the road from Sun City West had to suffice. We were in and out of there in less than twenty minutes, but it still didn't give us enough time to get a decent parking space by the social hall, forcing us to once again seek out a spot by the dog park.

"I hate to say it," I said, "but I think there's a bigger crowd this time. Look around. Not many free spots here either."

"It's from all that publicity. Sorrel's murder. Brent's kidnapping attempt. Much better than watching winter reruns on TV."

"Marshall, what happens if the board passes that proposal? Sun City West is never going to be the same."

"Ultimately, they have to make a decision that's right for the entire community, not a handful of people. That's what they were elected to do. Personally, I hope the proposal falls flat on its face. Considering the demographics, I don't think it's the way to go for *this* city. But retirement places are changing. Golf's not as popular as it used to be. Baby boomers and Gen Xers are looking for something different."

"Speaking of something different, take a look on your left."

"My God. Where'd they all come from? I didn't see them when we pulled in."

It was a crowd of at least fifty or sixty people. People with signs. I could only make out one word, but it was enough. No!

As we got closer to the entrance, more and more people were showing up with signs, but not all of them read No! Some signs said YES FOR PARKS.

A number of posse volunteers were ushering people into the social hall, making it clear that the large signs could only be displayed outdoors.

"It's a matter of safety," I overheard one volunteer posse member explain as Marshall and I maneuvered through the crowd and into the packed room.

We were able to find seats toward the back, near one of the exits.

"Good," I said. "If the villagers start lighting torches, we're out of here."

Just then, a familiar figure made her way down the aisle toward us. Louise Munson.

"Phee! Marshall! Save me a seat! Is there a seat?"

There were three seats a few spaces over from us so I ushered her toward us. "Hurry up, looks like it's filling up fast."

We stood up as Louise sidestepped her way to a seat. "I wanted to get here sooner, but my beauty parlor appointment ran late. Your mother and some of the ladies are near the front. Also Herb and Wayne. I imagine the others are scattered all around the room."

With so many people standing or making their way to seats, it was impossible to see where anyone was. It didn't matter. If my mother or her friends were going to speak, we'd hear them.

A long rectangular table with eight chairs took up most of the small stage. A microphone was positioned in front of the table, presumably to allow the audience to hear any discussion. Off to the table's right was a podium and another microphone. A few board members started to trickle in and seat themselves at the table. I immediately recognized

Jeannine Simone. Like Sophia Loren, it was hard not to. She was followed by Barry Wong, Mildred Saperstein, and Clarence McAdams.

Bethany Gillmore and Eloise Frable walked on stage next. Finally, Burton Barre and Harold Stevens made their way to the seats. By now, the social hall was standing room only, and posse members were guarding the doors. From what I had been told, if the room reached capacity, the meeting would be on closed circuit TV in the adjacent rooms.

"From the looks of things, they should've rented Phoenix Stadium." It was the man seated next to me, two chairs away from Louise.

Up front, Harold Stevens was trying to get the meeting started. Unfortunately, the only audible sound was static as he and another man fiddled with the microphone.

"Can everyone hear me?" Harold shouted. "Can all of you in back hear me?"

"Speak louder!" someone shouted.

"Now can you hear me?"

Since no one complained, Harold started the meeting. He began by thanking everyone for their attendance and interest in the community. Then he paused for a minute to reflect on the events that had transpired in the past month.

"We haven't been living under a rock," a woman yelled. "Get on with the meeting. I have a pot roast in my slow cooker. I don't want it to turn to mush."

Ignoring the commentary, Harold expressed the board's condolences for Sorrel Harlan and read a letter that the CEO of Golfscapes had sent to the board. It was similar, if not verbatim, to the media statement that had been issued prior.

"They're just covering their butts," another person shouted.

Again, Harold ignored the interruption and went on. He

explained that the meeting would proceed as planned and a new appointee to the board would be made at the conclusion of the meeting.

"Since our new appointee hasn't had the benefit of background information on our proposals, it's not fair to have said appointee cast a vote tonight."

No one on the board objected and there were no signs of disapproval coming from the audience. Again, we sat through mind-numbing reports from the secretary, the treasurer, and the board committees. The food service director gave a report as well, and a young, female representative from Golfscapes, who spent more time wringing her hands than looking over her notes, presented their report.

"I'm only the temporary replacement for Mr. Haywood until my company and the Recreation Centers of Sun City West can reach an agreement on a permanent manager."

Harold Stevens thanked her, and she rushed off the stage before anyone could ask any questions. Leaning over the podium, Harold took a deep breath. "This is the portion of our meeting devoted to old business. We have one item up for final discussion and vote. The proposal to convert some of our golf courses to eco-friendly parks. Let me now turn over the discussion to our board. When they've finished, we'll allot a few minutes for audience comments as well. No more than three minutes per person."

Mildred Saperstein clasped her hands together and spoke. "Sorrel Harlan gave her life for eco-friendly neighborhood parks that she felt we could all enjoy. What more is there to say?"

"That it was an ill-conceived, altruistic idea that has no place in this community? Let me be the first one to say that." It was Clarence McAdams, and he seemed downright annoyed.

Jeannine glanced at Mildred and spoke softly. "I know Sorrel envisioned a gentle and loving world, and creating eco-friendly parks was high on her list of priorities. However, creating those parks would result in more harm than good. Not to mention the disharmony it would cause for our community. Home values dropping. Privacy issues with park usage. The list goes on. My vote is a no vote, and I intend to stick with it."

"She's good," Marshall whispered. "Especially that bit of Jungian psychology she used on Mildred."

"I'm not sure I'm following you. It's been a long time since I was in a psychology class."

"Carl Jung. It's a technique they taught us in the police academy. Always validate what the other guy says and then twist it around. Something like that."

I was wondering if it might work on my mother when Bethany Gillmore's voice interrupted my thoughts.

"I tend to agree with Jeannine. This is a golf community. People bought their homes knowing full well it was a golf community. They can't suddenly up and change their minds. It would be like eating in an Italian restaurant and complaining because they don't have chow mein."

"Give it up, Bethany," Harold said. "Communities change. Otherwise, we'd be decaying old relics. If we can't support our own golf courses, then it's time to support something else. Good grief. If everyone had that philosophy, we'd still be using slide rules!"

"At least slide rules work, and you don't have to power them up with solar or batteries," Barry Wong said.

Harold made a slight grumbling sound that was magnified by the microphone. "And what's that supposed to mean? We're not talking about buying a math calculator."

I poked Marshall and looked straight ahead. "Is it my imagination, or is it about to get ugly?"

Eloise Frable joined the conversation before Marshall could reply. "Don't you people care about your grandchildren and their enjoyment? Think of all the wonderful time you'd be able to spend with them in a nice park close to home."

Clarence's voice got loud as he turned to Eloise. "If I wanted to spend time with them in a nice park close to home I would've moved into their neighborhood!"

Suddenly, everyone got quiet, but the tension in the room was palpable. Harold Stevens walked to the podium. "Is there any further discussion from the board?"

The shaking of heads indicated they had said all they intended to say. Harold stood for another few seconds and waited before clearing his throat. "The bylaws allow for additional comments from the community. We will do this in an orderly fashion. Raise your hands and wait to be recognized."

Hawaiian shirt guy, Russell (Spuds) Baxter, stood up and waved his arms frantically. Harold had no choice but to acknowledge him first.

"Said it before. I'll say it again. Over my dead body!"

"I don't think Harold is going to be able to apply Jungian psychology to that remark," I muttered.

A woman in her late seventies or early eighties stood up next. "I walk around in my nightgown at night and never worry. Only the coyotes can see me. Now what? Late night picnics under the stars? What if someone snaps a photo and I wind up on that Facebook or Instant thing? I say the golf courses should stay golf courses."

Harold Stevens allotted a few more minutes for the

continued shouting, whining, and complaining before calling for a vote.

"This better not wind up in a tie, or I'll commit hari-kari," I said to Marshall. "I don't think I can take many more of these meetings."

I didn't expect a yay or nay. I figured Harold would ask for a show of hands, and we'd be done with it. Instead, he clasped his palms together and took a step toward the audience. "We beg your understanding during this vote. Under normal circumstances, a simple raising of hands would suffice. However, we don't want any board member to feel intimidated by his or her decision. Remember, these are unpaid positions and a few of our board members have received not-so-subtle threats this past month. Imagine how that must feel in the light of Sorrel Harlan's murder."

Louise Munson leaned forward to get my attention. "Psst! It was only Mildred Saperstein. She said someone put a dead toad by her doorstep, but I think the thing just died there."

I nodded and leaned back as Harold continued to speak.

"Therefore, this will be a write-in vote. Yes or no. 'Yes' means support for the eco-friendly park conversion, and 'No' means the golf courses remain intact. Is everyone clear?"

The board members nodded and muttered to themselves while Harold handed out small white sheets of paper.

"Before you write your response, I would like to request three volunteers from our community audience to count the votes. Do I see a show of hands?"

Herb Garrett was the first one out of his seat, followed by two women I didn't recognize. Harold asked them to wait near the podium until everyone had cast a vote.

"My God, Marshall," I whispered. "What's taking them so long? How hard can it be to write Yes or No?"

"Look at them. You'd think they were taking the bar exam."

"I don't know about you, but I haven't been this concerned about a voter outcome since the 2016 Presidential Election."

When all the votes were cast, Harold Stevens counted and collected the slips of paper before handing them over to Herb and the two ladies. I watched as the three of them approached the podium and tallied the results. They did it three times to be sure.

"There are only eight votes!" someone yelled. "My five-year-old grandson could count them up quicker!"

I didn't think it was possible for time to move any slower but, by golly, it did. At long last, Harold Stevens read the results out loud. "In favor of the eco-friendly park proposal, three votes. Against it, five votes. The motion is denied."

"Wahoo! Wahoo!" Bill Sanders jumped from his seat, waved his hands in the air, and charged to the front of the room. "All in favor of celebrating at Curley's, let's go!"

A number of men in the audience all but fell over each other in a rush to leave the room. It was so frantic that Harold had to call for a five-minute recess before they could resume.

"This is a short break. I repeat, we are taking a short break. We have important new business to discuss— placing holiday lights on the palm trees by our entrances. Holiday lights."

More people left the room as Harold made one final plea. "Doesn't anyone care about entrance beautification?"

Marshall nudged my elbow. "Apparently not."

Chapter 35

"Let's try to get out of here while we have a fighting chance." Marshall reached for my hand.

"Too late! My mother's elbowing everyone in sight in order to reach us. Might as well stay where we are for a few more minutes."

"Ouch!" It was the man sitting next to me. Louise had stepped on his feet in her effort to vacate the room before the meeting resumed.

"Sorry. So sorry, Phee."

I tried to move my feet out of her path.

"Oh, look. There's Harriet. Tell your mother I'll catch up with her later. I've got to get out of here."

Louise made it to the aisle and into the crowd before my mother got to our row. I imagined the other ladies were ducking out of the place as well. Not to mention Herb and his crew. Meanwhile, my mother was gaining ground like a quarterback making his first down.

"Mom!" I shouted as she approached, "Meet us at the entrance, or we'll be stuck in here."

She immediately went for the exit. Once we were outside,

we moved away from the entrance, toward the administration building. It was the only place that didn't seem to have a throng of people.

"Hallelujah! It's over!" my mother shouted. "The voice of reason has returned to Sun City West."

I gave Marshall a slight kick on his ankle, and he had all he could do to hold back a laugh. "Yeah," he said, "I'm sure most of the residents are glad that's over with. Too bad it cost someone her life."

"You know what I feel bad about?" I didn't give anyone a chance to answer. "Poor Milquist. Losing his wife and having everyone suspect him. According to Deputy Bowman, there was never anything going on between Milquist and Edmund Wooster. It was a condolence call after all. And Marlene Krone was a friend, like Milquist said all along. Well, at least the guy has his writing." I lowered my voice as a few people walked past us. "Oh, and Eleanor. Don't let me forget what I was going to say about her. I was almost certain she was the killer. She had the background and the motive—jealousy."

Marshall nodded. "Ironic, huh? Her brother turned out to be the killer in the valley's highest profile case, and his motive was completely different."

"Enough already with the murders," my mother said. "I've got to go and call your aunt Ina. She couldn't make it tonight because Louis signed them up for tango lessons in Glendale. Tango? Can you picture it? Your aunt has as much grace and agility as a sumo wrestler. And don't you dare tell her I said so!"

"Um, of course not. But why don't you just call her from your cell phone?"

"She complains about static on the line. Anyway, I don't want to leave Streetman home alone any longer than I have to. It makes him nervous, and he sometimes has indiscretions. I'll catch up with you this week. Oh look, there's Gloria Wong. I want to say a quick hello to her before she gets to her car."

"Have a good evening," Marshall said as my mother raced to the parking lot. Then he turned to me, "I wonder how many indiscretions Streetman will have."

Midway into the week, I realized two headaches were gone—the one that lingered from my concussion and the one that came with all the drama from my mother's senior living community. On Thursday night, I gave my mom a call. I needed to return the casserole dishes to her friends and figured it would be easier to simply drop them off at her house.

"Why don't you just meet us at Bagels 'N More on Saturday?" she said as soon as I mentioned returning the pans.

"I've got to work for a few hours at the office. Our client list all but exploded after those two cases. Nate and Marshall are going nonstop."

"What about you and Marshall? Are you going nonstop? You're not getting any younger. Mid-forties is not mid-thirties."

"Thank you for the mathematical update, but we're doing fine. We enjoy each other's company, and we enjoy doing things together."

"Good, because Myrna saved two tickets for you and Marshall to attend the bocce tournament awards dinner. You can pick them up whenever you drop off the casserole dishes."

"I, er, we, um . . ."

"I know. It was very considerate of Myrna. The book club ladies all like you. Just think, in ten years you'll be eligible to live in Sun City West."

I hung up the phone and realized something—a new headache had started.

Don't miss the next Sophie Kimball Mystery!

MOLDED 4 MURDER

by J.C. Eaton
is coming to your favorite bookstores and e-retailers
in September 2019.

And don't miss

A RIESLING TO DIE

by J.C. Eaton,
the first of the Wine Trail Mysteries,
available from Lyrical Press
and your favorite e-retailers.

Turn the page for a sneak peek
of this delightful mystery!

Upstate New York

The sign off to my right read Welcome to the Seneca Lake Wine Trail, and I knew in that instant I had lost my mind. What the hell was I thinking? I slowed the car for a split second and then picked up speed. It wasn't that I minded doing favors for people, but they were always on the easy side. Picking up someone's mail while they were gone, feeding a friend's cat or taking a colleague to an appointment because their car broke down. But this? This bordered on insanity.

My older, by one and a half years, sister, Francine, pleaded with me to "oversee" our family winery in Penn Yan, New York, for a year so she and her husband, Jason, who worked for Cornell University's Experiment Station in nearby Geneva, could spend that time researching some godforsaken bug in Costa Rica.

I wished I had never said yes, but Francine could be downright persuasive. Annoying, really. She called me three months ago as I was headed out the door of my tiny Manhattan apartment wedged between Nolita and Little Italy. An apartment I inherited from a great aunt because no one in our family wanted to live in "the city." They equated it with drugs, sex, robberies and lunatics. Unfortunately, they were sort of right. But the advantages to living in a place that didn't shut down at eight o'clock could be mind-blowing. Too bad my sister didn't share my opinion. Her life revolved around that winery and now she wanted mine to do the same.

"Come on, Norrie, you're the only one I trust. It's not as if you have to live in New York City. You're a screenwriter. All you need is a laptop and a phone line. We've got those. Besides, it's only for a year. One year."

"A year? A full year? That's the life span for some species. Can't Mom and Dad do it?"

"You have *got* to be kidding me. The last thing Jason and I want is for them to come back from Myrtle Beach and undo everything we've done in the past five years. I thought Dad would never retire."

"The winery has staff. The winemaker, the vineyard manager, the tasting room manager, the bistro chef, the—"

"Norrie, you don't have to tell me who works for us. That's just the point. They're staff. You're family. And, you're part owner of the winery."

"A silent partner. I like it that way. You know as well as I do I've never been interested in the winery business. Not like you. You have a degree in hospitality and hotel management. Big surprise. Even as a kid you were the one who would go out in the winter to help prune the vines, or badger the winemakers to figure out how they made wine out of grapes. I'm the one who sat in my room writing. Remember?"

"Of course I do."

"For your information, I've made a great career out of it."

"You can still do that. Only from Two Witches Winery instead of Great Aunt Tessie's apartment."

That was another thing. The name. Two Witches Winery. It was located on Two Witches Hill in Penn Yan overlooking Seneca Lake. The hill was named after, you guessed it, two women in the eighteenth century who were thought to be witches. Unfortunately, Francine and I had to go through school with that moniker. Boys teased us relentlessly. "Which witch are you?" "Are you the good witch or the bad witch?" We begged our parents to change the winery name, but they refused. My dad said it reflected the history of the hill.

As far as Francine and I were concerned, it reflected the prior owner's refusal to think up something original and when my parents bought the place when Francine was born, the name stayed. But that didn't mean I had to.

"I'm sorry," I said. "I really can't do this."

"Can't or won't? If it's because you think you're not qualified, don't worry. I'll walk you through everything. Come on, you'll still be able to write those screenplays and maybe living in the Finger Lakes will give you some new ideas."

"I've had twenty-nine years of Finger Lakes living already."

"Great. You can make it thirty. Please, Norrie? Please?"

"I really, really can't."

"Pleeze . . . pleeze, Norrieee."

The "eez" sounded like the worst whine I'd ever heard and, in a moment of sheer weakness, lunacy, really, I said yes. Now I was less than fifteen miles from Two Witches Winery and it was too late to turn around and go back to the city. I had sublet my apartment for a year and crammed all of my personal belongings into my small Toyota sedan. I took a deep breath and looked off to the right.

Seneca Lake was in its glory. It was early evening in mid-June and its sapphire water, set against the deep green hills, was magnificent. A few sailboats dotted the shore. Time for happy hour at the lake's numerous bars. It was idyllic all right, if a Norman Rockwell painting was what someone had in mind. For me, it was simply the place where I grew up. I picked up speed and continued to drive north, chastising myself for ever agreeing to do such a lamebrain thing.

I was so deep in thought I was halfway up the lake before I knew it and almost missed the turnoff to our winery. A giant sign on the road read "Grey Egret Winery and Two Witches Winery to the right."

Grey Egret sat at the bottom of the hill. It was a small winery owned by the Martinelli family. I wondered which one of their kids got stuck continuing the legacy. Their parking lot was emptying and I glanced at the clock. Five fifteen. Most wineries closed at five. That meant I was spared making an entrance at Two Witches. I'd just head to the house.

The vineyards on either side of the road seemed to stretch on for miles. Some belonged to us, others to Grey Egret. Other than the cars coming down the hill, it was one of those quintessential postcard scenes. I pressed on. Then, out of the corner of my eye, I saw what looked like a llama. Nope. Too fat. What the heck? It was on our property, too. Fenced in with the winery behind it.

I don't care what it is, I'm not taking care of it.

The house was about a half mile past the winery, set back near the woods. I pulled into the long driveway and looked at the vineyards again. I had to admit, based on eyesight alone, Francine and Jason were doing a great job. Last thing they needed was for me to muck it up.

A quick slam of the car door and I walked to the house. Francine must've glanced out the window or, worse yet, had sat there waiting. She hurried toward me. Tall, slender, with ash-colored hair, she had the look of a professional model without all the effort.

"Norrie! Thank goodness. I was beginning to think you had second thoughts."

"I had third and fourth thoughts. Give me a day and the number will exceed ten."

She looked at me doubtfully.

I gave her a hug and smiled. "I sublet the apartment. Even if I wanted to escape out of here, I'd have to wait out the year."

"Good. You won't be sorry. Think of it as an adventure. Something new every day."

"Uh, yeah. Speaking of new, what's that animal in front of the winery? Please don't tell me it belongs to us."

"That's Alvin. He's a Nigerian Dwarf Goat."

"My God! He's a dwarf goat? What do the regular ones look like? Camels?"

"Don't be silly. He's really quite small for his breed. We got him two years ago. Jason thought it might be entertaining for the visitors, and he was right. When word gets out that a winery has great wine and is also a fun place for kids, people are more likely to visit."

"You'd better not tell me I have to feed him and clean out his . . . his what? A stall? A barn?"

"He has a small house, but the vineyard guys take care of him. You can cross that off your list."

"Whew."

"Come on, you must be hungry. Jason threw a few steaks on the grill and I made some rice and ratatouille. He's got an evening meeting with his colleagues at the station, so we'll have lots of time to chat. Hold on. Let me get him. He can help you with your bags." Francine took one look at my car and winced. "Pioneers crossing the plains didn't take as much stuff. We have blankets and . . . what's that? Don't tell me you packed a coffeemaker?"

"It's a Keurig. I don't know how to use a real coffeemaker."

"You can relax. We own a Keurig, too. And we have a microwave and Wi-Fi and all sorts of twenty-first century stuff. It's not like when Mom and Dad lived here. We even have satellite TV. No more antenna and three stations."

"Francine Ellington Keane, that's blasphemous."

We both laughed and, for the first time, I didn't feel as if I had made the mistake of a lifetime. Francine shouted for Jason and, after more hugs, the three of us carted my stuff into the house.

"Hope you don't mind," Jason said, "we sort of took down the dorky daisy wallpaper from your old bedroom, removed the furniture, well, sold it, actually, and set up a new, modern guest room. Hey, there's a queen-size bed in there now. That's got to be a plus."

"Uh, sure. I haven't slept in that room in what? Seven? Eight years? It'll be fine."

It wasn't as if I hadn't seen my sister or brother-in-law in all that time. It was just I'd seen them at other locations. Or, to be precise, other events. Our cousin Marianne's wedding in Pennsylvania, our nephew Shane's wedding on Long Island and our uncle Phil's funeral in Ohio.

The one thing that stayed the same was the view from my bedroom window. Since the room was upstairs and at the front of the house, I could see clear across the lake. When I was little and we'd had a blizzard, I used to pretend I was living in the ice house from *Doctor Zhivago*.

Francine and Jason did more than modernize my old bedroom. They totally remodeled the old farm kitchen and re-did the downstairs bathroom. They also added a small en suite to their room but left the old claw tub and turn-of-the- (gasp) twentieth-century bathroom; the one I was to use, as is. At least there was hot and cold running water.

My sister tossed my goose-down pillow on the bed and shrugged. "We've got these, too, but I understand people like to sleep with their own. You can unpack later. Dinner's been ready. What do you say?"

I scarfed down a perfectly grilled steak and dove into the fixings she had prepared. It was still warm outside, so we ate on the small deck behind the house. Nothing but woods and the edge of the vineyard. Jason had to rush off to a meeting so that left my sister and me alone to get caught up.

Francine brushed a strand of hair from her forehead and leaned back. "First thing tomorrow, I'll walk you through the winery. I made arrangements with all of the area managers to show you the ropes. Tomorrow you get to work with Cammy in the tasting room."

"Cammy? What happened to Tim McCauley, the prior tasting room manager?"

"He retired over a year ago and moved down south to be near his kids. Cammy Rosinetti's been with us ever since. Her family's from Geneva and she knows the wine business in an indirect way. Her parents used to own Rosinetti's Bar on Exchange Street."

"I thought that name sounded familiar."

"Listen, Norrie, I know things are moving fast and I hope you don't get overwhelmed. Jason and I fly out of Rochester on Friday. That's less than a week."

My voice sounded as if it would crack. "That's three days. Not counting tonight and Friday."

"You're a quick study. You'll have this all under control by the time we head to the airport. Oh, hope you don't mind, but you'll need to drive us. In our car. The Subaru. Four-wheel drive and all. Use it this winter. Walden's Garage will get the snow tires and studs on for you. You remember where that is, don't you?"

"Of course. On Pre-Emption Road. I may have been gone for a while but my memory's still working."

"I'm sorry. I didn't mean to sound—"

"Like Mom?"

"Yeesh. There's more, too, Norrie. I couldn't get into all of it on the phone with you and tonight's not the best time. We'll talk about it tomorrow, okay?"

"Is everything all right? Are you and Jason all right?"

"We're fine. Nothing like that. It's business stuff. The winery. I'll clean up and you should unpack. We've got the whole day tomorrow to talk."

I helped bring the dishes to the kitchen and wiped off the picnic table. "You can tell me anything, you know."

"That's why I needed you to be the one to look after the place."

Connect with Us

Visit us online at
KensingtonBooks.com
to read more from your favorite authors, see books
by series, view reading group guides, and more.

for sneak peeks, chances to win books and prize packs,
and to share your thoughts with other readers.

facebook.com/kensingtonpublishing
twitter.com/kensingtonbooks

Tell us what you think!

To share your thoughts, submit a review,
or sign up for our eNewsletters, please visit:
KensingtonBooks.com/TellUs.

Grab These Cozy Mysteries
from
Kensington Books